BREEANA PU

GW00632958

ROOTS OF INSIGHT

BOOK TWO OF THE DUSK GATE CHRONICLES

Roots of Insight is a work of fiction. Names, characters, places and incidents either are the product of the author's imagination or are used fictitiously.

Copyright ©2012 Breeana Puttroff
Musefish Independent Press

Cover Image by Mallory Rock
Editing by Tonya Christensen
Interior Design/Formatting by Mallory Rock

Breeana Puttroff
Roots of Insight, Book Two of the Dusk Gate Chronicles
        ISBN (Paperback Edition) 978-0-9839930-7-0
        ISBN (eBook Edition) 978-0-9839930-2-5

For information or questions, please contact the author at breeanap@gmail.com

For my grandmother, Virginia Rose Cornelius
Who gave me the writing bug.
Until we meet again…

ZANDER

Quinn Robbins sighed as she crossed out the third paragraph in her essay for the second time. Homework was the last thing she wanted to be spending this Sunday afternoon doing, but she had been falling behind on her homework during the last couple of weeks, and now she was attempting to tackle the massive pile. Right now, though she couldn't concentrate. Her thoughts kept wandering to faraway places. She finally managed to complete the paragraph in a way she could live with just as the doorbell rang.

Ugh. Who could that be? Her mom had gone to Denver for the weekend with Quinn's little brother and sister. She wasn't expecting them to be home for another couple of hours. She put down her pen and ran downstairs. When she looked through the peephole, her breath caught in her throat.

It was Zander.

Zander Cunningham was … well, she wasn't sure exactly what he was right now, aside from being the seventeen-year-old son of her mother's best friend, Maggie. She and Zander had been close friends since they both were in diapers. Lately, though, things had been changing.

She took a deep breath and opened the door. "Hey, Zander."

"Hey," he said, his smile reaching all the way to his light brown eyes. "Can I come in?"

She stepped back into the entryway and pulled the front door wide. The blast of cold air made her shiver. The tiny, mountain town of Bristlecone, Colorado had finally gotten its first big snowstorm of the year during the night. Zander pounded snow from his boots and brushed more from the hood of his blue-and-white ski jacket as he stepped inside. He set a large shopping bag down just past the entryway.

"What are you doing here?" she asked, as she watched him take off his boots and line them up with the collection of others on the side of the tile floor.

He grinned, "I told you I would help you with your trigonometry homework, didn't I? Last night you said you'd been falling behind."

She blushed. The night before, Maggie had insisted on her going over to their house for dinner since her own mom was out of town. Quinn had been so exhausted and distracted, though, that she couldn't remember what she might have said during the meal. She could vaguely remember mentioning something about trig as she tried desperately to maintain a normal conversation. "I didn't know you were actually going to come over here," she stammered.

Worry flashed in Zander's eyes. "It's okay, isn't it?"

"Yeah," she smiled, in what she hoped was a reassuring way. "I'm glad you came. I haven't even started on it."

"Want to go grab your stuff?" he asked, as he hung his coat on the rack behind the door. "We can work on it in the dining room. I brought a book that helped me." He held up his backpack.

"Sure," she answered. Her mom would probably appreciate it if they stayed in the main part of the house. Her heart fluttered a little at the idea of her and Zander here alone. She swallowed. "What's in the big bag?"

"My mom sent over some of her beef and vegetable stew and a bunch of rolls so you guys wouldn't have to cook tonight."

"That was nice of her," she said, peeking in the bag. It smelled amazing.

"You know my mom. She likes to feed people."

"True," she agreed. Eating dinner with the Cunninghams had been a big part of her childhood, and Maggie was forever sending side dishes and desserts home at the end of the day when Quinn picked up her little sister, Annie, from their house.

"When will your mom and the little kids be home?"

"Probably around five or six," she carried the bag into the kitchen and put the enormous bowl of stew into the refrigerator.

"Sweet. We have time to get you all caught up in trig." he was already piling books onto the dining room table.

She hurried back up the stairs to retrieve her trigonometry book, trying to get her thoughts in order at the same time. Her head was still spinning from the strange experience she had just come home from the night before, and she hadn't really been able to process what had happened. She had appreciated being home alone today. Zander was almost an awkward interruption, though she wasn't going to turn him away.

She checked herself in the mirror, running a brush through her auburn hair. She briefly considered changing into a nicer shirt, but then thought that might be too noticeable. She settled for a quick coat of clear lip-gloss and headed back to the dining room. Zander smiled widely when she sat down in the chair he'd pulled out for her.

Almost as soon as she began trying to solve the first problem, Quinn suddenly became extremely grateful for Zander's presence. After her ordinary weekend had unexpectedly been extended by ten days, she found herself unable to remember how to do the assignment.

"Why does this look like it's written in a foreign language?" she complained after a few trying moments.

Zander chuckled, "Have you been paying attention in class at all?" She shot him a dark look, and he held his hands in front of his face. "Sorry, sorry! I've just never seen you actually have trouble with something."

She sighed and buried her head in her arms as red colored her cheeks.

"Hey, welcome to how I feel around you all the time," he said, tucking a strand of her hair behind her ear. "I'm just glad I'm here to be your knight in shining armor."

If his words hadn't been setting a blaze in her chest, she thought she might have needed to bite back hysterical laughter as she imagined what Zander would think if he knew she'd spent the last ten days in an actual castle. She breathed deeply a few times to compose herself, and looked up. "I'm glad you're here, too."

His answering smile melted everything else away.

Even with Zander helping, the assignment took nearly two hours. Math had never been Quinn's strongest subject, but this was bordering on ridiculous. How could she have forgotten so much? He never seemed to lose patience with her, though, and as they got closer to the last problems, she realized that it was the first time she had ever really understood a trigonometry assignment, rather than just struggling through.

His smile grew wider as he watched her complete those last problems; she did the final one without any help.

"You're not bad at this teaching thing," she said.

Unless she was mistaken, his cheeks took on the tiniest hint of pink. He shrugged, "It's easy to teach when there's a cute girl involved."

Now it was her turn to blush. Her heart pounded as Zander, smiling shyly, reached over and ran a single finger down her cheek, all the way to her jawline, where he paused, turning her face up so she was looking into his eyes.

At that moment, they heard the garage door opening. Quinn jumped, and he dropped his hand. Both of their faces were suddenly bright red, and they started giggling.

I think my mom's home," she said.

By the time the door between the kitchen and the garage opened, they were both bent over papers on the table, pretending to write furiously, though uncontrolled snickers kept threatening to break through. Zander had scooted his chair conspicuously far from Quinn's.

"Hello Zander." Quinn's mother called from the kitchen, carrying her purse and suitcase in one arm, a sleeping Annie in the other. Owen appeared behind her, diligently toting his own bag.

"Hi, Megan." He stood and walked over to her, taking the suitcase. "Do you want me to take this upstairs for you?"

"Sure. Can you come set it on my bed? I'll carry Annie up to her room."

Quinn was left sitting alone at the dining room table, surrounded by books and papers.

Owen took the seat that Zander had vacated, his eyes scanning over the work that she had finished. "Number six should be 47.2," he told her quietly.

She stared at him. "How do you even know that?"

"I read your trigonometry book," he said, shrugging.

She sighed. She should have guessed. "I should have been asking you for help with it, instead of Zander."

Owen shook his head, "Zander can explain things better than I can. Anyway, Zander helping you makes your eyes look all shiny, and your cheeks are pink." He studied her face

5

intently for several moments, his eyebrows furrowing. "Where did you go this weekend?"

Her heart skipped a beat. "What do you mean? I stayed here."

"Your face and neck are tan."

Crap. She hadn't even thought about that. "I, uh, tried some kind of new fake tanning stuff I read about in a magazine."

"Oh," he was silent again. "Well, this one works better than the last kind."

Heat flooded her face. She had never tried any kind of fake tanning stuff, and she knew Owen knew that.

"I'm going to go read until dinner," he said, "but I'm always here if you need me." He stood and walked up the stairs, leaving Quinn staring after him in disbelief. Owen's mild autism often meant he had difficulty understanding things about people, but sometimes the things he did understand were shocking.

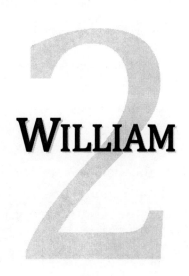

WILLIAM

Quinn arrived at school early on Monday morning. She hadn't slept well the night before, which she hoped wasn't going to turn into a habit again now that she was home. She had left the house earlier than usual, worried about the slick layer of snow on the road. Fortunately, the roads had been better than she'd expected, but now she was wandering the empty halls at school, feeling strangely out of place.

It was like the feeling she sometimes had coming back to school after being out sick for a few days. Anxious, disconnected, wondering what things had changed in her absence. Except that nothing had. She hadn't actually missed anything. She had been here on Friday; now it was Monday. Everything would be the same.

A few people had started trickling into the halls when she spotted him. He was wearing the same long overcoat she had so often seen him in, a hint of purple wool showing at the collar. She now recognized his purple sweater for what it was: a reminder of his home. Knitted in purple for the royal color of his kingdom. The tiny, silver-embroidered design that she would be able to see on his chest once he removed his coat was a symbol that he was a prince.

"William!" she called down the hall.

She thought William Rose looked a bit startled when he first glanced up. Of course, it was possible that no one had ever called to him in the hallway at school before. He had always kept to himself at school, and he had never had any friends. The confused expression turned into a smile, though, when he saw her.

"Hello, Quinn," his gray eyes were friendly behind his wire-rimmed glasses, so different from the last time she'd seen him here at school, when his expression had always been distant or annoyed. "It's good to see you."

"It's good to see you, too." She was surprised at how happy she was to see him, the one person who wouldn't think her feelings about today were crazy, who knew the enormous secret she was keeping. She almost felt like hugging him.

"I have something for you."

"What?" She couldn't imagine William giving her something.

"Hang on, it's in my bag. How are you?" He asked, as she followed him to his locker.

"Um, good, I suppose." She looked around to make sure no one in the hallway could hear them. "It feels a little weird to be back."

His eyes were sympathetic as he dialed the combination, "I know the feeling. Did closing your eyes help?"

"Yes … with the gate part. It's everything since then that's a bit overwhelming."

He nodded. "It can be."

"How are you? How is … everything?"

He knew what she was asking. Although Quinn had come back from Eirentheos, the world that was his true home, on Saturday, William hadn't come back until last night, which had

8

given him another ten days there. "Things are better. We think that all of the contaminated books have been found, and all of the children who were exposed have been treated properly. We've identified the teacher who was responsible for distributing the books."

She wanted more details about that, but there were more pressing concerns on her mind at the moment. "And Thomas?"

"Is fine, just as he promised he would be," he smiled, unzipping his backpack. "In fact, he sent me a letter to give to you."

"He did?"

"Yes. As did Linnea." He withdrew two heavy envelopes from his bag, and handed them to her. "And I brought you these."

She gasped when she saw the three small, colorful stones in his hand. She had found them near the river on one of her first days in Eirentheos, the first time she had gone horseback riding with William and his brother and sister. She had put them in her pocket, intending to bring them home to give to Owen, who collected unusual rocks. But they had been forgotten when she'd packed to leave the castle in a rush.

"Mia found them when she was cleaning your room. I thought you would probably still like to have them."

She nodded, a sudden lump in her throat as she thought about "her" room in the castle, and Mia, the kind servant who had taken such diligent care of her. She picked up the stones and rubbed her thumb against them. They were smooth, like marble.

"And this is from me," he said, holding out another small object. "I figured you might like to have a little something to give to your little sister, as well."

Quinn was stunned. The object was a small horse, expertly carved out of soft, Eirenthean wood. She examined the tiny details carefully. "It's Dusk," she said in surprise. Dusk was the horse that William's mother, Queen Charlotte, had given to her to ride during her time in their world.

"Yes, do you like it?"

"You carved this?"

He nodded, "Nathaniel says carving is good practice for surgery and stitches." His eyes followed hers down to the inside of her right leg, where he had stitched a cut after she had fallen on the night she had followed him through the gate.

She swallowed hard. "It's beautiful, thank you."

"You're welcome." He looked up at something over her shoulder. She turned and followed his gaze.

She hadn't noticed how many people had come into the hallway during her conversation with William. Watching them, from a few feet away, was Zander. Though his eyebrows had been knitted together as he watched them, his eyes lit up when they met hers.

"You'd better go," William said quietly.

She nodded, "Thank you so much."

"You're very welcome." His eyes were soft as he closed his locker and headed down the hallway.

"Hey, Quinn," Zander's smile was infectious.

"Hi, Zander."

"Were the roads okay this morning?" he brushed snowflakes out of his damp hair. A big drop of water landed on her left wrist, and he reached to wipe it away.

Heat flooded through her at his touch. "Yeah, they were fine. I left early, just in case."

"Good," he smiled. "What's all this?"

Quinn's right arm was curled around the two envelopes, and the carved horse and the stones were clasped in her hand.

"Oh, just some stuff for a class…" she trailed off, pulling her backpack off her shoulder so she could tuck them inside the first folder she touched, out of sight. She didn't like lying to Zander, but it wasn't as if she could explain it to him, either, though the idea of how *that* conversation would go made her grin a little.

"Since when do you talk to William Rose?"

"Um, I ran into him on Saturday, and we talked a little." That wasn't completely untrue.

"Huh. I've never seen him talking to anybody before. He's kind of strange, isn't he?"

Quinn didn't know why the question irritated her. Up until this weekend, she'd felt exactly the same way about William. And, really, by the standards of Bristlecone High School, he was strange – more so than Zander could possibly guess. It still rankled, now that she considered William her friend. "He's just quiet," she said. "He's actually a nice guy."

"Okay," Zander shrugged. She could see from his expression that he hadn't meant to offend her. "Maybe I'll have to get to know him."

School was a disorienting experience the entire day. Quinn hadn't been thinking about her classes at all for almost two weeks. She wondered again how William managed to do this all the time. Knowing William, he probably usually spent his last couple of days in Eirentheos completing schoolwork and trying to get his mind back to Bristlecone. Actually, she thought, knowing William, he was just used to it and could make the transition without thinking about it.

Several times, she actually had to check the schedule on the inside of her notebook to remember which class she had next. The discussions in some of the classes felt foreign, the way trig had felt last night. She supposed that the lack of sleep wasn't helping, either. She was grateful that her best friend, Abigail, was too preoccupied with the return of her new crush, Adam, from a football retreat, to notice Quinn's abstraction today.

Then there was lunch. The cafeteria was like an entirely different world today, and it didn't have anything to do with the fact that Quinn had spent her weekend actually away from this one.

The football players were all back from their week-long ski trip, but very few of them were sitting at the group of tables on the side of the room that Quinn was used to seeing them occupy.

She saw Adam right away, sitting at a table slightly to the side, an empty seat next to him, clearly waiting for Abigail to arrive. A second later, she saw Zander approach the same table, pulling another empty chair closer to his. Then he turned and scanned the cafeteria until his eyes met hers. He waved her over. Quinn gulped. When had this happened? Around the room, she could see several couples, newly eating lunch together.

Abigail looked at her in wonder as they crossed the room. "You and Cunningham are getting serious now, too?"

Quinn's face felt red-hot, "I don't know. Is sitting together at lunch serious?" she asked pointedly, tipping her head toward Adam.

Abigail was unfazed, "Serious enough to go public."

Quinn saw the appraising look in her friend's eyes as Zander held out the chair for her, and tucked the perpetually disobedient strand of hair back behind her ear. Abigail smiled in obvious satisfaction as pink spread from Quinn's neck to her forehead.

They hadn't been sitting for long when Quinn caught sight of William, sitting a few tables away. He was alone, as always, surrounded by tall stacks of books, getting far more notes written in his notebook than bites taken of his sandwich. It was as if nothing had changed for him. Of course, nothing had changed for him. Only for her.

She wondered what he was researching now. Studying for a test in one of his high-school or college courses? Or trying to figure out to manufacture a medication that was common here in Quinn's world with the more-limited resources of Eirentheos?

She didn't realize that she was staring until William looked up at her and raised an eyebrow. Just last week, such an occurrence would have turned her face beet-red and she would have wanted to hide. Now, she grinned sheepishly at him. He smiled back, and then his eyes wandered to the side of her. She followed his gaze. Zander was watching the exchange between William and Quinn with interest.

She looked quickly away from William. "You totally saved my life in trig today, Zander. I actually understood what Mr. Bradley was talking about."

Zander's smile reached up past his eyes, and Quinn saw Abigail shoot her an approving look from across the table. By the time she had a chance to glance back over at William, he was absorbed in a thick book.

It wasn't until Quinn was at home that evening, pulling her English folder out of her backpack, that she remembered the letters and the small gifts from William. Re-adjusting to her surroundings and acclimating for the first time to the attentions of Zander had preoccupied her for most of the day. Zander had even followed her all the way to his house after school, where she was picking up Annie, keeping an eye on her on the slippery roads as it had continued to snow for the rest of the day.

She had ended up staying at the Cunninghams' for far longer than usual on a pick-up run, making small talk with Maggie and

Zander. He had helped her with her trig homework again, before carrying Annie to the car. Quinn was glad there were plenty of leftovers from the meal Maggie had sent over the night before so she didn't have to feel guilty about not starting dinner.

Now, alone in her room, she curled up against her pillows and pulled out the two envelopes. They were both made of the same thick, heavy paper that felt almost like cloth. Quinn was glad to discover that neither one was sealed; she would have hated to rip the Eirenthean paper. She started with Linnea's, written in clear, elegant script.

Dearest Quinn,

Your absence has placed me back in the lone company of my brothers, who, wonderful siblings though they are, have absolutely no appreciation for anything other than crumple, their sword training and the intrigues of kingdom politics. I'm surrounded by boys again! Rebecca is usually away with Howard or droning on about his latest gesture of romance (it's enough to turn your stomach, really), and the only one I can discuss clothes and makeup with is Emma while we are dressing her dolls. How could you leave me to endure such boredom without you?

I can't believe that you discovered what was really going on with the children, or that Thomas would be so stupid as to try to hide his symptoms. Thank you for saving them, especially my idiot twin. I don't know what would have happened if you hadn't been there. Mother says to let you know that she is grateful as well. Mostly, I miss your fun company and hope that things are going well for you in your own world. William has agreed to carry a letter back to me, if you'd ever like to write one (hint, hint).

Love Always,
Linnea Rose

Quinn's heart ached to spend time with Linnea. She had said good-bye to William's sweet, energetic sister back at the castle, over a week before she had actually left Eirentheos. Although she had only had a few days to get to know Linnea, their connection had been almost instant – already she regarded William's sister as one of her closest friends, and it felt strange to know that she might never see her again. She sighed, and reached for Thomas' letter.

To the lovely Quinn,

It is my sincerest wish that this letter reaches you well and that William manages not to fall in the river trying to deliver it. I am sure that he won't convey the hug that I asked him to bring you for me, but then again, I think I'll reserve that for giving to you myself. My hands are no longer red and splotchy, thanks to Nathaniel's magic medicine. Little Miss Alyia was quite right when she told me I wouldn't like it, but she was a very sweet companion while I was sick. I followed all of my doctors' orders, and I am completely well, just as I promised I would be, so please don't let me hear of you worrying about anything.

I truly do feel much better and am wanting for the company of the fairest of maidens (I do mean you). I have to thank you for saving me from my own stubborn-headedness, and I am truly sorry if I ever made you feel badly. I hope you are enjoying yourself at home; none of us are the same without you. I miss you Quinn.

Your Own Prince Charming,
(There's a story about that in your world, isn't there?)
Thomas

Quinn had to giggle at Thomas' closing. Children of the royal bloodline in his world were given certain gifts at birth. Thomas' gift translated to charm, which he used to his every advantage. It was difficult for her to wrap her mind around the fact that in Thomas' view, he hadn't seen her for nearly three weeks. On Quinn's end, she had only been separated from him for two days. She found herself longing for them, these people who had become such dear friends in such a short time.

A strange temptation gripped her right then, made her want to call William, but she wasn't sure exactly what she would say. Instead, she put the stones and the little horse carving into her pocket, and went to find Owen.

He was in his room, as usual, curled up on his bed with a book, some kind of non-fiction with a fortress on the front. She sighed, that theme seemed to be coming up a lot lately.

"Hey, buddy."

Owen didn't look up right away. Used to this, she waited patiently while he finished the section he was reading, and carefully marked his page before he closed the book and looked up at her. "Hi."

"I have something for you."

"What is it?" He sat up straight and looked at her expectantly.

Quinn reached into her pocket and withdrew the three small stones. She dropped them into her brother's hand, and he stared at them for several minutes before he looked back up at her.

"Did you get these wherever you went this weekend?" His voice was so quiet that she almost wondered if she'd heard him right. *Almost.*

"Yes."

"They're very pretty. I've never seen rocks like these before. Do you know what they are?"

She shook her head.

She was afraid he might ask more questions as he rolled the stones around in his hands, rubbing his fingers over the smooth surfaces, but he didn't. After a moment, he lined them up carefully along the edge of his nightstand.

"Thank you, Quinn."

"You're welcome."

"Did you give Annie whatever you brought for her yet?"

She frowned, and studied her brother's face. "How do you know so much, Owen?"

Owen looked straight at her, something he sometimes had trouble with. "You wouldn't go somewhere and bring me something and not her." In the next breath, Owen called out across the hall to Annie, telling her that Quinn had something for her.

Annie was enchanted by the little carving. She didn't ask where Quinn had gotten it; at not-quite four, she just accepted gifts as they came. Within minutes, the horse was being ridden by a teddy bear several times its size, while Annie provided the sound effects.

Quinn was on her way back to her pile of homework when her mom stopped her in the hallway.

"Come here a minute, sweetie. I have something for you."

She followed her mom into the master bedroom. "Ooh! What is it?"

Megan smiled, and pointed to the bed. A garment bag stretched across the quilt.

"Mom! What did you do?"

"Oh, just open it."

She slowly unzipped the bag. The dress inside was beautiful, a deep green, cut simply from a heavy fabric, with long sleeves and flowers embroidered on the skirt. It was beautiful – and perfect for a winter evening in Bristlecone. "Wow! Thanks, mom. I love it!"

"I figured even if you didn't come to Denver and go shopping with me, that you still needed a dress for the dance."

The dance. Quinn hadn't given any thought to what she would wear to the Valentine Dance with Zander on Saturday.

"I guess I do. Thanks." She was grateful for her mom's thoughtfulness, and hugged her tightly.

"Want to try it on? I might have had a little too much fun shopping – I bought you some shoes and a necklace, too."

"Mom! You didn't have to do all of that!"

"Of course I did. It's your first real dance with a boy – and it's with Zander."

Suddenly, she felt a little nervous, just thinking about going to the dance with Zander.

ADJUSTING

By Tuesday, Quinn was finally feeling a little more like herself again. She had been so exhausted on Monday night that she'd actually slept, and she was mostly caught up on her homework. She even remembered what classes she was supposed to go to and when.

On Tuesdays, she worked after school at Bristlecone Public Library. She loved her job, and it felt good to be back among the stacks of books. The library was small, and usually not very busy. She started to work right away re-shelving several carts of books that had accrued during her days off.

She was in the middle of her second cart when she heard the main door of the library open, and as she looked up, William walked in. She chuckled to herself as she remembered the last time he had come in while she was working, and she had followed him around, feeling like a stalker as she tried to figure out what he was researching. Tonight, she felt glad to see him and walked right over to the table where he was unloading his backpack.

"William!"

He smiled as she approached. It was going to take her awhile to get used to his being pleased at seeing her, rather than irritated.

"Hey, Quinn. How are you?"

"Good. Working." She smiled.

"Do you always work here on Tuesday nights?"

She nodded. "Tuesdays and Thursdays. Every so often, I pick up an extra shift on a Saturday, if it's been really busy, but there isn't a budget to have me come in all the time."

He nodded, looking around. "It seems like a pleasant place to work, especially if you like being surrounded by books."

"Who can complain about being surrounded by books?"

"Thomas." William grinned. "He would probably be thrilled to spend as much time as I do in a world with video game systems."

She laughed. "Somehow, I can see that. Hey, speaking of siblings, I wanted to thank you again for bringing those stones, and that horse. Annie loved it. She hasn't stopped playing with it since I gave it to her."

"You're very welcome. I like to find little things here sometimes to take back to my family, too. Linnea, as you know, is quite fond of makeup, and Emma enjoys plastic dolls with 'real hair' as she calls it."

Underneath William's grin, she could see the longing in his eyes as he talked about his sisters. For the thousandth time, she wondered how he did it – come to her world for five days at a time while he missed close to two months of his life at home.

"That reminds me, I'm going to send a couple of things back with you on Friday. Linnea thinks you could have better taste in my world's makeup department."

He narrowed his eyes, though the twinkle in them belied his expression. "She's an ungrateful little thing, isn't she?"

Quinn giggled.

William shrugged, "What does she expect? I'm a guy. She'd be lucky if I noticed whether her hair was brushed or not."

"She says she should send Thomas."

He let out a guffaw, "She probably should."

"So what is all this?" Quinn asked, surveying the thick binder and several books that William had pulled out of his backpack.

"Um, Calculus II – though most of that's finished, and Organic Chemistry. And I was going to do some more research to see how I might be able to improve the treatment for shadeweed poisoning."

"Organic Chemistry? Is that even an option at Bristlecone High School?"

"No. I'm taking it as an independent study through Mountain State. Bristlecone doesn't technically offer Calculus II, either. It's just me, sitting in the library with my own book, completing assignments. They used to make me actually sit in a lower-level class, but Nathaniel finally convinced Mr. Bradley to let me do it this way."

"Ugh. Calculus II? I don't think I'll be making it that far. Trig is giving me enough of a headache."

William smiled, "It's okay. You're not a doctor in your other life."

"No, definitely not."

Behind her, Quinn heard the whoosh of the door opening, and she turned automatically. William's eyes followed hers. "Your boyfriend seems to have great timing," he told her.

Quinn flushed scarlet. "He's not my boyfriend."

"Maybe not yet."

William sat down at the table and tried to look like he was already engrossed in his work, but Zander reached them before he had the chance.

"Hey!" Zander placed his hand on her shoulder, brushing her hair back slightly. Quinn saw William raise his eyebrows in an "I-told-you-so" gesture.

"Hi. What are you doing here?" Quinn asked.

"I knew you were working tonight, and I thought I'd just drop by to see how you were doing."

"I'm fine. Surprised, but fine."

"Is it a good surprise?"

Butterflies hit with a vengeance, "Yes, it's good."

Zander's shy smile turned into an ecstatic grin, and Quinn's heart rate accelerated further.

"Hey, you're William, right?" Zander asked, looking behind Quinn.

William turned slightly, not looking all the way up from his notes, "Yes. And you're Zander Cunningham?"

"That's me. What are you working on?"

"Homework."

Zander's eyes widened. "That's a lot of homework."

William shrugged. "I suppose it is. And if you'll excuse me, I need to get working on it or I'll never finish tonight."

"Sure. See you around."

"Yes." William didn't even look back up to answer; he was already scribbling furiously in the binder.

Zander followed Quinn back to her cart of books. "He's not exactly friendly, is he?"

She shrugged, "No, not at first." Not in this world anyway. For just a moment, her thoughts drifted to the William she had seen at Mistle Village Medical Clinic in his own world. She had watched as he had treated a little girl with the most gentle compassion she had ever seen. Then there had been the day she went swimming in a river with William and Thomas… a day filled with horseback riding and water fights and basking in the sunshine. No, William definitely wasn't always distant and unfriendly, not once you got to know him.

"Is it snowing again?" she asked Zander, noting the

dusting of flakes starting to melt into his light brown hair.

"A little, but it isn't sticking to the roads yet. You should be okay getting home tonight."

"Ick. I'm ready for summer."

Zander laughed, "You never have been a fan of winter, have you?"

"It's not my favorite."

"Good thing you live in the Rocky Mountains, then."

She stuck her tongue out at him.

Zander stayed at the library with her for the rest of her shift. Her boss, a kind, older librarian named Sylvia Williams, didn't mind, as long as Quinn got her work done. Zander tried to help her with re-shelving some of the books, but he didn't understand the system she had for getting it done quickly. He was more help in the back room, though, making small repairs to damaged books, and putting the new magazines into their protective binders. He was good company, too. She had forgotten how easy it was to talk to him. The evening ended long before she expected it to.

A few minutes before her shift ended, Zander asked her for her keys, and then went outside, promising to warm the car and scrape the windshield for her. She glanced back at the table where William had been sitting, but it was empty.

THE VALENTINE DANCE

Quinn felt like the anticipation might turn her stomach inside out as Zander walked around to the passenger side of the truck to open the door for her. She closed her eyes and took one deep breath while she had the time. She rubbed her hands against the green material of her Valentine dress to make sure they were dry, and then the door opened.

Zander was smiling widely, she wondered if he was really this calm, or if his was a show, too. She smiled back as she took his hand and stepped down.

The curb near the main entrance of Bristlecone High School was still snow-packed and slushy; Zander was careful to lift her all the way to the mostly-shoveled sidewalk. Ice-melt crunched under her heels, and she wished again for summer. Zander drove away to park the car, leaving Quinn to join a cluster of girls in the school's foyer.

Abigail spotted her immediately, and rushed over. "Quinn! You look gorgeous!"

"Thanks, Abbie. That dress is amazing on you." Abigail was wearing a dark-blue strapless gown with a billowing skirt that reached only to her knees. She had dyed several strands of her short, black hair to match, and pinned the rest of her hair back with a silver headband. She looked spunky and beautiful, as usual. Quinn wondered if her own style was too conservative.

"Thanks. It's awesome, isn't it? Did Zander get that for you?" Abigail pointed to the small arrangement of red roses and baby's breath pinned to the front of Quinn's dress.

"Yes, isn't it pretty?" Quinn felt a tiny burst of heat in her cheeks as she played back the memory of Zander pinning it on her, with her mother and Owen and Annie watching. It had taken him two tries, his large fingers fumbling over the tiny pin.

"Ooh, so pretty! Adam got me this." She held up her wrist so Quinn could see the bright pink tiger lily corsage.

Quinn smiled. It looked like Adam was already getting to know Abigail rather well.

"It suits her, don't you think?" Quinn was startled by Adam's voice. He had suddenly appeared beside Abigail.

Quinn nodded, "Definitely. I was just thinking that."

"Zander was parking right next to me; he should be here in just a second." Adam leaned into Abigail and kissed her cheek. Abbie giggled, but didn't blush the way Quinn was certain she would have.

And then Zander was there. He was smiling, happiness twinkling in his brown eyes the way it had been all evening. She swallowed hard. Despite all of Zander's advances over the last couple of weeks, she hadn't realized until she'd seen the look on his face as she came down the stairs tonight, just how serious he was. *He really liked her.*

"Shall we?" he asked, extending his hand toward her.

Quinn accepted it. "That sounds so formal," she stifled a nervous giggle.

He smiled and shrugged. "It's a semi-formal dance, right?" He led her through the double doors into the gym. Red and white streamers zig-zagged across the ceiling, anchored everywhere by matching balloons. Soft lamps around the room had replaced the glaring overhead lights she was used to, and a disco ball dangled in the middle of the gym.

She had never been to a dance before, but the whole thing reminded her of every high-school movie she had ever seen.

Pop music blared from the speakers, and people were dancing mostly in groups, not as couples. Several of the groups were doing more standing and talking than dancing, and Zander and Quinn quickly joined one of those, along with Abigail and Adam.

The evening went just as she had always expected it would. Zander didn't know how to dance, and until her time in Eirentheos, Quinn hadn't either. They stayed with their small circle of friends, chatting, and occasionally swaying to the beat of a song they liked. Quinn found herself trying to imitate Abigail, who was in her element here, carefree and having fun.

When Zander had first asked her to the dance, Quinn had felt relieved that he wasn't a dancer, and that he wouldn't expect her to be, either. Although she was still giddy at the sensation of being here on Zander's arm, her mind kept flashing back to the dance in the castle, where she had somehow glided effortlessly across the floor on the arms of both William and Thomas.

The dance was nearly over when the DJ finally began playing a slower tune. The change of mood in the gymnasium was instant. The large, fluid groups spread out and paired off. Three bars into the song, Quinn glanced over at Abigail and saw that she was wrapped tightly around Adam, their lips locked.

She glanced up at Zander. He'd seen where she was looking, and now he was smiling shyly down at her. He held out his hand, a questioning look in his eyes. Quinn accepted the offer and followed him to a spot near the edge of the dance floor.

Her heart hammered in her chest as he put his arms around her waist. Now *this* was different than dancing with Thomas or William had been. The way Zander stared into her eyes with his brown ones, so familiar, and yet so entirely different than she had ever seen them before, let her know that his intentions ran much deeper than this dance. Hesitantly, Quinn placed her hands on his shoulders, and he smiled. Suddenly, her shy awkwardness melted away, and she smiled back.

They swayed to the music together there in the dim room, Zander studying her face intently. "You are so beautiful, Quinn."

Heat flowed into her cheeks, and his smile grew wider. He traced the pink stain on her cheek with the side of his finger. "You always do that to me," she said.

"I try." He brought his hand up to her chin, and rested his forefinger underneath, stroking her cheek with his thumb.

She was suddenly having trouble remembering how to breathe. "You're very good at it."

And then, he kissed her. Just the lightest brush of his lips against hers, but it was enough. The swarm of butterflies that had occupied her stomach felt as if they'd exploded into a million tiny, fluttering fragments that rushed everywhere, up to the top of her forehead, and down to the bottom of her toes.

The rest of the evening passed in a blur. Zander held her wrapped in his arms as they swayed on the dance floor to the rest of the songs – even the ones that weren't slow. He drove her back home, and then walked her all the way to the porch, where he stopped to gently kiss her again, first on the lips, and then on her forehead before whispering "Goodnight," and walking back to his car.

Roots of Insight

Inside the house, her mother was sitting in the big, brown armchair in the living room, a book open on her lap, though she looked slightly out of breath, and Quinn noticed the curtains on the front window still quivered slightly.

THOMAS

Quinn arrived at school early on Monday morning. It had snowed again during the night, and she'd long since decided that if she was going to have trouble sleeping, she might as well get up if her insomnia struck at any hour close to when she'd have to get up anyway.

Last night's dream had been particularly vivid. It had been a perfect replay of the dance in Eirentheos that she had shared with the mysterious Alvin at the naming ceremony for Hannah, William's newborn sister. Well, an *almost* perfect replay. There had been something different about the end, something significant, darker somehow, but she couldn't recall that part of her dream. Once it ended, though, she had been unable to fall back to sleep. Part of it had to do with the dream, but an even larger factor was the fluttering feeling in her stomach at the thought of seeing Zander today at school. She hadn't seen him since he'd walked her up to her porch on Saturday night, after the dance.

The hallways were empty and quiet, as they always were when she arrived at such an early hour. After re-organizing her already-immaculate locker, she was bored, and started wandering. She found herself walking toward the hall that led to William's locker – she had learned that he was *always* here before her, regardless of when she arrived. She was feeling too jittery to be alone anymore, and she thought that maybe he would have something to share from his weekend in Eirentheos.

She was startled when she turned the corner and heard two voices. One was William's, but there was another voice she thought she recognized. *It couldn't be ... it couldn't possibly be ...*

"Thomas?"

"Quinn!"

William's younger brother practically ran the rest of the way up the hall to meet her. He wrapped her in an enormous hug, spinning her around in the process.

"What are you doing here?"

"I couldn't go another three months without seeing you. I had to come and visit."

William was noticeably glaring at his brother. She guessed that he probably wasn't too pleased with Thomas' loud demeanor.

"Did you miss me?" Thomas' gray eyes twinkled. He paid no attention to William.

"How could I not?" She smiled back. "How are you doing?"

Thomas rolled his eyes. "I'm fine. I've always *been* fine, and I'll always *be* fine. The real question is how are *you?* Adjusting to being back here after your grand adventure?"

Quinn shrugged. "Sure. I live here, don't I?"

He chuckled. "I've certainly missed you. I was just on my way out of here, so I don't disrupt William's day," he shot a glance at his brother, who still looked irritated – and worried. William worked hard to keep a low profile and avoid questions about his background here in school. "But what do you say to meeting up later when you're both done with school? Dinner at our place?"

"Your place?" Quinn raised her eyebrows.

"Nathaniel's house, on Bray Street," William corrected his brother. "Do you know how to get there?" His look was wry.

"Sure, I'll come," Quinn answered, ignoring William's reference to the weeks she'd spent following him, trying to uncover his secret.

"Great! See you after school." Thomas hugged her again, tightly. "It's really, really wonderful to see you again, Quinn." He turned and walked away down the hall, pulling his hood up over his head against the bitter mountain cold outside.

Quinn turned the other way, intending to ask several questions of William, but she stopped cold when she saw Zander walking toward her. Her heart skipped several beats.

She glanced at William. He was busy in his locker, paying no attention to her whatsoever. She sighed, confused at this sudden change in the direction of her thoughts, and hurried up the hall to Zander.

"Hi." She felt a little shy, now that he was in front of her again.

"Hey, I was looking for you." Zander smiled brightly, though he looked maybe a bit nervous, too. His nose and cheeks were still pink from being outside.

"Good. I got here early, and was just walking around, waiting for you, and trying to get warm."

Zander's eyes lit up. "You're cold?" He asked, starting to pull at the sleeve of his jacket.

"No, I'm okay, now that I've been inside for awhile."

"Okay. So, who was that you were talking to?" Zander nodded toward William, who had closed his locker and had now turned toward them.

"Uh … that was Thomas. He's William's … um …"

"Cousin. He's my cousin. He came to visit for the weekend. He drove me to school this morning so he could use

33

the car today," William answered for her, stopping only long enough to finish his sentence before he turned the corner into another hallway.

Quinn stared after him wide-eyed. She had never actually heard William lie before. Conceal information, yes, but not actually lie. As far as she knew, William didn't even have a car that Thomas could be borrowing. And, in any case, Thomas was still too young to drive, even if there was any chance of his having had an opportunity to learn how.

She cleared her throat, trying to pull herself together before turning back to Zander.

"Yeah, he's William's cousin."

"William has a cousin? I thought he was some kind of an orphan or something, living here with his uncle."

She shrugged.

Zander's eyes were still full of questions. "How do you know his cousin, anyway?"

She was used to feeling flustered and embarrassed, especially around Zander, so she was surprised at how quickly she was able to come up with an answer. "Remember, I told you I ran into William a couple of weekends ago? Thomas was with him then." *Dang, Thomas.* She was beginning to understand why William just avoided talking to people here as much as possible, and she was quickly gaining sympathy for his annoyance at his brother who seemed to disregard the careful work he had done to establish privacy.

"And he's already hugging you?"

Oops. Though it was innocent, Zander probably hadn't appreciated seeing that. Quinn shrugged. "Thomas is very friendly."

"I guess. Does he visit William very often?" She could see in his eyes that he hoped the answer was a resounding 'no.'

"I really don't know. I don't know them *that* well."

34

Zander frowned, and stared at her face. She looked back at him calmly, silently willing him not to ask her any more questions that she didn't know how to answer. Finally, his expression smoothed, "Can I carry this for you?" He had his hand on the strap to Quinn's backpack.

"Um, I'm not going to say no." She smiled, shrugging off the straps. Zander put one strap over his own shoulder, and then reached to take Quinn's hand in his own.

"What's your first class?"

As the day progressed, it became very apparent that everything had changed between her and Zander. He walked her to the door of every class she had, and was waiting to pick her up when she was done. She thought it was kind of silly at first, but she quickly started enjoying their little five-minute breaks together.

By the end of fourth period, she was anticipating seeing him standing there. When she stepped into the hallway, and he wasn't there, she was surprised at the sudden, heavy feeling of disappointment in her chest. When she turned around the corner toward the cafeteria and he was there, heading towards her, she knew her elated smile matched his.

When the final bell rang, Quinn wasn't quite sure what she should do. Thomas had said "after school," but he hadn't exactly specified a time. She had texted her mom just before her first period class that morning, letting her know that she had plans and wouldn't be able to pick up Annie. She had been going to ask William, but the only time she had seen him for long enough to actually ask him something had been at lunch, and Zander had been by her side the whole time. She hadn't wanted to get that conversation going again.

Although, it had been a little sad to know he wouldn't be there waiting for her after her last class, she was feeling a little grateful that Zander left school early on Mondays, excused from study hall so that he could make it to his job on time.

35

Now the day was over, though, and she regretted not having more details about what was going on. Should she just head straight over to the Roses' house? That seemed a little awkward. And of course, neither William nor Thomas had a cell phone.

As soon as she got outside, she discovered that her worries had been for nothing. Thomas was there, leaning against her car like he belonged there, an impatient look on his face.

"So I guess you meant right after school, huh?"

"Of course I did. It's not like we have a lot of time to waste before sunset."

"Before … You're going back tonight?"

He nodded. "It's already a long time to be away from home. Mother tends to get a little worried having two of us completely out of reach."

"Right." It would have already been ten days in Thomas' world. The thought of him leaving so soon after he had gotten here made Quinn sad. She was glad she had freed up her afternoon.

"So, what shall we do today, Princess Quinn?"

She rolled her eyes. "I don't think I'm the royal one here, Prince Thomas."

Thomas shrugged. "You're a princess in *my* mind. Where is that brother of mine, anyway?"

She turned around to watch the stream of students exiting the school. The flow was growing thinner and thinner. She was beginning to think that they had missed him when she finally saw his familiar coat, the purple collar of his sweater peeking out at the top.

"You don't spend enough time in that place? You have to be the first one there and the last one out?" Thomas chided.

"It's less noticeable. The less attention I draw to myself …"

"… The fewer questions you have to answer. I know."

William gave Quinn a chagrined look. "There's a reason they send me. I'm surprised my parents even allow Thomas to visit."

Quinn giggled. "Thomas is Thomas." She looked back and forth between the brothers. They looked incredibly alike, though Thomas' dark, nearly black hair clung close to his scalp in tight waves, and William's was straight. Although Thomas was almost two years younger than William, he was more muscular than his brother, and nearly as tall. They had the same deep gray eyes ringed with dark lashes. Thomas' were nearly always twinkling with laughter; William's were usually serious, though kind. Quinn knew, though, that when he was home and surrounded by the people he loved, that his eyes could sparkle, too.

"Yes," William sighed, "Thomas will be Thomas."

Thomas ruffled his brother's hair, "You know you wouldn't have it any other way."

William rolled his eyes, but Quinn knew how important his little brother was to him. During her time in their world, the two had been nearly inseparable.

"So, am I meeting you guys at your place, or … "

"You're driving us." Thomas answered.

"Me?"

"You have a car, and you know how to drive."

"How did you get here?"

"I walked. But it's cold, and besides, how often do I get to ride in a car? Please?"

William and Nathaniel lived in a small, white bungalow in an older section of Bristlecone. The wraparound porch

37

immediately reminded her of the medical clinics she had spent time in during her stay in Eirentheos. She wondered which one had inspired the other.

Dr. Nathaniel Rose had been Quinn's doctor for as long as she could remember, probably since she was born, but until her recent visit to Eirentheos, she had never seen him outside of his office, except possibly in passing. Certainly, she had never been to his home. She felt strange as she followed William's directions and pulled the Honda Pilot up next to the house on the narrow, brick driveway.

Nathaniel was waiting for them at the door. He helped Quinn remove her heavy coat in the entryway. "It's lovely to see you again, Quinn." His smile was wide and sincere. Dr. Rose had always been a rather quiet and reserved man. She had always liked him, but she had only really just begun to get to know him.

"It's nice to see you, too, Dr. Rose."

"You can call me that if you're ever in my office again, Quinn. When you come to dinner, please call me Nathaniel."

"All, right … Nathaniel."

"Good. And, welcome, please make yourself at home. Do you like burritos?"

Quinn smiled, "Yes. They're one of my favorites, actually."

"When Thomas visits, he likes to eat food that he can't get at home," William said.

"He's not the only one," Nathaniel answered, somewhat facetiously.

"Indeed not," William retorted, returning the look.

Quinn giggled. "*I* would miss Mexican food too, if I was away for a long time."

For the next two hours, Quinn felt as if she was back in Eirentheos. Although Nathaniel's home was small and modest, there was a distinctly Eirenthean quality to her surroundings. It might have been the way it was decorated – everything was simple and comfortable, but somehow elegant at the same time -- but more likely it was the atmosphere and the company.

There was no television; the living room was lined with built-in bookshelves, filled with books of every description. Quinn was certain that not all of the titles had come from Earth, though a large number of them had. According to William, the main reason he and Nathaniel were here was to take advantage of knowledge in her world that was unavailable in theirs. The only nod to modern, American life in the house was the long desk along one wall, which held two laptop computers, and the blinking lights of a wireless router.

Quinn, William, and Thomas sat in comfortable armchairs in front of a crackling fire, while Nathaniel worked in the kitchen, refusing all offers of help. Thomas and William filled her in on stories about their family, and shared special greetings from their mother and from Linnea.

When dinner was ready, they gathered around the table in the dining room, and Nathaniel asked the Maker for blessings over the meal. She enjoyed the casual banter between the brothers and their uncle. This was a side of William she never got to see at school. He was so relaxed and cheerful, even laughing several times. She felt an ache in her throat when she thought, again, how hard it must be for him to be away from his family all of the time. She couldn't imagine spending that much time apart from her mom, and Owen and Annie, from the whole life that she knew and loved.

Actually, as she sat there, she realized how much she missed *their* family, and wondered how much things had changed in the time she had already been gone. She hadn't known any of these people for long, but they were so instantly familiar, and comforting, that she loved them as if she'd known them forever.

All too soon, the afternoon ended. The sky outside was turning brilliant shades of orange and pink. Thomas looked outside rather dejectedly. "I guess it's time for me to go, if I'm going to make it to the gate before the sun sets."

Quinn's heart felt as heavy as his face looked. "Do you want a ride?"

"No, but thank you; it's actually faster to walk from here, and it's less conspicuous to go alone." He cast a meaningful glance at William and Nathaniel. "It was lovely to see you, though Quinn. Please try and keep my brother out of trouble until the next time I see you."

William rolled his eyes.

"If there is a next time," she said.

"Of course there will be a next time! You didn't think you were getting rid of me that easily did you, lovely Quinn?"

A DATE

"Where is Zander taking you tonight?" Quinn's mom asked, as Quinn entered the kitchen.

"I don't know. He wouldn't tell me." she grabbed one of the freshly-peeled potatoes from the pile next to the sink and began chopping it into small pieces, then throwing the pieces into the big pot of water on the stove. Megan continued peeling. "He just said it was something special, so I dressed up a bit."

"Well, you look beautiful, sweetheart. I'm sure you will have fun." Her mother scooped up a pile of the peelings and carried them over to the trashcan, planting a kiss on Quinn's forehead as she passed.

Owen sat at the long counter stirring cake batter with a wooden spoon in a big, glass bowl. "That's a pretty skirt, is it new?"

"Yes." She twirled so that Owen and Annie could get the full effect of the long, flowing skirt. Last weekend, she and Abigail had gotten permission to drive up to Grand Junction, over an hour away, to go shopping at the mall there.

"Can I go with you, Quinn?" Annie asked. "I have a pretty skirt, too."

Quinn laughed. "That's for your birthday party next week." She had picked up a sparkly purple tutu for Annie on her shopping trip. It had been intended as a surprise birthday present, but Annie had spied the bag as Quinn had tried to sneak it into the house. She'd worn it for part of every day since.

"It's mine. I can wear it whenever I want."

"That's true, pumpkin," Megan interrupted. "But you still can't go with Quinn and Zander tonight."

"But I want to! I want to go with Zander!"

"Maybe you can sometime soon," Quinn said. "How about tomorrow we go out for hot chocolate, just you and me?"

"Mmm … I like hot chocolate."

"So is it a deal?"

"Can Zander come too?"

Quinn shot an exasperated look at her mom, who smiled. "I'll ask him."

At that moment, the doorbell rang.

"I'll get it! I'll get it!" Annie screeched, running toward the front door.

Quinn followed her. She waited patiently as Annie struggled, first with the dead bolt, which opened successfully, and then with the small, rotating lock on the doorknob, which she still couldn't manage by herself. Finally, she allowed Quinn to help.

"Did you get it this time, Annie?" Zander asked, stepping into the entryway.

"Almost," she answered proudly.

"All right! Give me five." Zander held out his hand, and she promptly smacked it, as hard as she could. "That was a good one, kiddo." Annie held up her arms, and Zander scooped her up.

"Hey gorgeous," he said, kissing the top of Quinn's head. "Are you ready?"

Quinn nodded. He still made her blush every time he did that. "I just have to grab my coat." The familiar butterflies filled her stomach again as she appraised him. He was dressed more nicely than usual, too, wearing gray slacks and a blue sweater over a white-collared shirt. She could tell he had shaved just before coming.

Zander smiled as he carried Annie into the kitchen and set her in one of the tall chairs that flanked the island where Megan was now peeling carrots into the sink. "That smells fantastic."

"Thanks, Zander," she answered, smacking his hand away from the pile of carrots as he snatched one. "Aren't you going to miss eating it? Your parents will be here in about an hour." Lately, since Quinn and Zander had been together so much, their families had been spending more time together, too. They shared dinner at one house or the other at least twice a week now.

"Nah, it will be nice to be with Quinn without all of the munchkins hanging off of us the whole time," he ruffled Annie's hair as he spoke. Zander had three younger siblings. His brother, Ian was thirteen, and his sisters, Ashley and Sophia, were seven and four.

Megan chuckled. "I suppose that's true. So where are you two off to tonight, anyway?"

"Café d'Italia."

"Nice." Megan raised her eyebrows. "What's the occasion?"

"It's our one-month anniversary."

"Is it now?" Megan looked over at Quinn, who had turned a fierce shade of red. Had it already been a month? She hadn't realized. She wondered when he had started counting. She counted weeks backward in her mind. It had been almost exactly a month since the Valentine Dance.

A whole month. Was she supposed to do something special for Zander? Should she have gotten him something? What was the protocol for a one-month anniversary in high school? Abigail would have known what she should do. Quinn mentally kicked herself for not thinking to discuss something like this with her. Of course, apart from the shopping trip, lately she hadn't been spending much time with Abigail who was always with Adam, and Quinn was usually with Zander

"Young love," Megan said, smiling again. "What fun. You two have a good time tonight. Curfew still stands, though, even if it is your 'one-month anniversary.'" She directed a firm look at Zander.

"Yes, ma'am. I'll have her home before eleven."

In the end, Quinn's worry was unnecessary, as it usually was with Zander. She had never been to Café d'Italia, which was a cute little restaurant in Powder Mountain, a ski town not too far from Bristlecone. It was the most romantic date that Zander had arranged so far, although he always seemed to be working to find ways to please her. Tonight, he held her hand as the host led them to a small table draped with a red-and-white checked cloth. He even pulled out the chair for her, helped her out of her coat, and asked the waiter to bring a cherry Coke, Quinn's favorite, before he seated himself.

In the last month, her relationship with Zander had blossomed. She couldn't imagine having a nicer boyfriend. She enjoyed his company, and regretted the first two years of high school when the two of them had somehow drifted away from the friendship that they had shared since they were toddlers.

They had become inseparable again during the last few weeks, spending most of their time together when neither of them was at work. They did their homework together most evenings, and Quinn had actually been getting the hang of trigonometry. Zander's English grades had improved, as well.

44

Although she still wasn't sure exactly how significant it was to celebrate a month-long relationship, it had certainly been a wonderful month. She had even managed to mostly push her memories of her trip to Eirentheos out of her mind.

She still saw William at school every day, of course, but over the last weeks they had talked to each other less and less. Most days now, they'd exchange a wave at some point during the day and that would be it. It wasn't exactly the same level of non-contact they'd had before her time in his world – she didn't feel like a stalker when she caught herself watching him study in the cafeteria, but it wasn't much more.

AN INVITATION

Quinn glanced up, out of habit, when she heard the whoosh of the library door while she was working on Thursday night. When she saw the William's familiar outline against the glass she paused briefly to wave. She had almost turned her attention back to the books she was checking in at the desk when she realized that William was not alone. Her head snapped back up.

Thomas had seen her before she saw him, and he was headed purposefully toward her, a huge grin on his face. "Hey, beautiful."

Quinn's smile was nearly as wide as his. "Thomas! What in the ..."

"I told you I wouldn't be away for too long. Face it; you're stuck with me now."

She rolled her eyes; she caught William's gaze in time to see him doing the same. William shrugged. "He just showed up here about an hour ago, now I can't get rid of him."

She giggled as Thomas punched his brother playfully on the shoulder. "You'll die of boredom if I don't start coming

47

more often, Will. I keep trying to convince Mother and Father that you need me here once a week."

William ignored him, looking around the library. "Where's Zander?"

Quinn was surprised at the sudden rush of irritation that filled her chest. "He works on Thursday nights." He didn't on Tuesdays, though, and it was true that William had seen him here with her often. Zander usually volunteered his services for most of Quinn's shift on Tuesday evenings, just so he could spend more time with her.

Even here in the library, she and William hadn't talked much in the last weeks. On Tuesdays, Zander usually occupied her attention, and on Thursdays, they had drifted back to their old habits of Quinn working, and William being absorbed in his research. There had been a few times she'd almost gone over and talked to him, but she was never sure exactly what to say, and anyway, he always looked so engrossed in what he was doing that she didn't think he'd notice anyway.

"So Zander isn't coming tonight?" Thomas asked. "How unfortunate. I was hoping to meet the man who could capture the attention of the lovely Quinn."

"So, why are you here again, Thomas?"

"You're going to hurt my feelings if you don't start believing the truth – that I really would come all the way here just because I've missed you."

Quinn raised her eyebrows.

"But it does so happen that I have come this time for a particular reason."

"And that is?"

"To see you."

Quinn sighed, exasperated with Thomas, but also thoroughly delighted, as she always was, by his irreverence. He was too charming for his own good.

48

"What's the real reason?" She directed this question at William.

"That is the real reason." Thomas intercepted her gaze. "But more specifically, I am here to extend an invitation for you to come back with us to Eirentheos this weekend. You can come with us tomorrow night, and then be back on Saturday evening."

Quinn's jaw nearly hit the counter. She glanced across the library at Sylvia, her boss, hoping that she hadn't overheard any of her conversation. Fortunately, she seemed to be deeply engrossed in a distribution catalog, and didn't appear to be paying attention to Quinn at all.

"What? Why?"

"Simon is getting married, and you are officially invited to the wedding."

"I am?"

"Of course you are. William was supposed to give you your invitation ages ago, but he keeps not doing it. So I came."

She glanced over at William, who had turned several shades of purplish red. She didn't understand why a hot lump suddenly rose in her throat. "You didn't want me to come?"

A panicked expression took over William's face. "It wasn't that, Quinn. I just ... didn't think you would want to go."

"Why wouldn't I want to go?"

"I can think of a number of reasons why a person might not want to leave their life for almost two weeks so they can go stay in a strange world. A world, I might add, where they were nearly attacked, and then nearly poisoned the last time they were there, just so they could go to the wedding of someone they barely know."

Quinn's eyes were wide.

"What William means," Thomas said, "is that he is too much of a coward to ask a pretty girl to go to his brother's wedding with him."

49

The look that William gave his brother just then almost made Quinn giggle. Almost. Her brain was too overrun with conflicting thoughts and feelings to be actually amused. She had been invited back to Eirentheos, to attend Simon's wedding. This weekend. How could she get away this weekend – tomorrow – without anyone noticing? Did she *want* to go back to Eirentheos, knowing that once she decided to go, she would be there for ten days?

And why had William not asked him herself? His explanation hadn't made any sense. Even if she didn't *want* to go, he still could have asked. She had thought he had forgiven her for the last time, for the following him, and discovering his secret. She had even thought that they might have been becoming friends, at least a little. Tears stung the corners of her eyes as she thought about how she had been mistaken.

"Quinn? What's wrong?" Thomas' words pulled her out of her reverie. She looked up to see him looking at her intently, concern in his gray eyes. William had already disappeared; she could see him beginning to unload the contents of his backpack onto his usual table at the back of the library.

"Nothing's wrong. I'm fine."

"Liar. Did I say something that upset you?"

"No."

"Not that you'd make it easy on me and just tell me if I had, would you? I'd have to do something to really make you mad, and then you'd just explode and tell me everything."

Quinn laughed. "How do you know me so well?"

"I'm good with people. It's part of my gift, you know. Besides, you're not *that* difficult to read." He studied her face for a long moment. "It's Will, isn't it? You're upset that he didn't invite you himself."

She opened her mouth to deny it, but the sincere expression on Thomas' face stopped her. He wasn't teasing her. Instead, she shrugged.

"Look, Quinn, I know my brother can seem pretty serious a lot of the time, but that doesn't mean you should always take him seriously."

She raised an eyebrow.

"You don't really think he doesn't want you to come, do you?"

"He didn't ask me to, and he could have."

Thomas shook his head. "He was afraid you would say no."

"That doesn't make any sense, Thomas. He still could have asked."

"You would have hurt his feelings if you had said no."

"Right, Thomas."

Now Thomas rolled his eyes at her. "You don't understand how people respond to you, Quinn."

Quinn didn't acknowledge this statement. "Besides, I probably wouldn't have said no."

"Great! So you're coming!"

SNEAKY

Quinn hated feeling like she was sneaking around, but it was exactly what she was doing. Last night, when she'd gotten home from work, after Thomas had talked her in to coming with them to the wedding, she had taken a deep breath and called Abigail.

"Abbie, I need your help."

"Sure, Quinn. What's up?"

"I need an alibi for tomorrow night and all day Saturday."

She could almost hear Abigail's eyes pop open wide. "Why? Where is Zander taking you? What are you guys *doing?*"

"Um ... it's not that. Actually ... I need you to cover for me with Zander, too."

"*What?* Quinn Rose Robbins! You're not cheating on Zander, are you?"

"No, no! Abbie, it's nothing like that! It's not another guy. I'm not sneaking off with a guy. It's just ... I need to go somewhere, just overnight. And I need it to be quiet, just for now."

There was a long pause on the other end of the line. "Is everything okay, Quinn? Are you okay?"

"I'm fine, there's nothing wrong, or anything like that. I just need to do something. It's ... going to be a surprise."

"Ooh ... a surprise for who? Do I get to hear details?"

"Not yet."

"Why?"

"I just can't tell you right now, Abbie. If I could, I would. But for right now, I need you to help me out with this. Please?" Quinn took a deep breath and waited, hoping that this would not backfire terribly. She felt a surge of irritation with William for not asking her to go back when he was supposed to, when she might have had time to come up with a less conspicuous way of disappearing overnight.

"Are you sure that everything is okay?"

"Everything is fine, I promise."

"When will you be back?"

"Saturday evening, before it gets all the way dark."

"You'd better be."

"I will."

"If it gets dark on Saturday, and I haven't heard from you, I'm going straight to your mom and telling her everything."

Quinn swallowed hard, suddenly a bit worried. What if something *did* happen to her in Eirentheos? Nathaniel would come and talk to her mom, wouldn't he? "That's fine, Abbie. Tell you what. I'll write down everything, all of the details about exactly where I am, and how to find me, and I'll seal it in an envelope and put it under my mattress. That way you have a back up."

"I don't know, Quinn ..."

"Please, Abbie?"

Abigail was quiet again. "Does this have anything to do with William Rose?"

A thrill of fear ran down Quinn's spine. "Why would you think that?"

"I don't know. It's just … a while back you were acting all weird, and then you got normal again, except you'd started talking to him, acting like you know him or something. And Zander said he saw you hugging his cousin or something? And now you're being all weird and secretive again. So what is going on between you and William?"

Quinn thought quickly, her heart racing. "Nothing is going on between us. We've just gotten to know each other a little – he hangs out at the library a lot." She swallowed hard, wavering between lying, and giving as much of the truth as she could. "You're right, he does know about this. He's been helping me with something – kind of a project."

"He knows about this?"

"Yes." An idea clicked suddenly in Quinn's head. "And so does his uncle – Dr. Rose. He's helping me out with this too, Abbie. I'm totally safe, I promise." Would the promise of adult supervision be the key?

"All right." Quinn was relieved at the calmer tone in her friend's voice. "I'll cover for you. But you'd better make it up to me."

Although Abigail had agreed to help, she watched Quinn suspiciously all day at school. Quinn had made sure to make a point of stopping by William's table at lunch to say hi, just to make her claims appear legitimate, although her short conversation with him had made Zander raise his eyebrows.

Through a stroke of luck, Zander had to work that night, so he wasn't disappointed to hear that Quinn was going to be spending the night at Abigail's. On Saturday morning, Abbie was going to get up and leave the house early to drive back to Grand Junction "with Quinn." They had both told their moms that Abbie had discovered that a sweater she had admired at the mall there last time had now gone on sale.

After school, Zander walked her to her car. He took her hands in his as she leaned against the driver's side door. "Have fun with Abigail."

She swallowed hard. She *hated* lying to Zander. The truth, the whole story, almost poured out of her right then and there, though she knew she couldn't tell him. "I'm sure I will."

"Call me as soon as you get back from Grand Junction tomorrow?"

"I will, I promise."

"We can get together in the evening. Maybe watch a movie at my house?"

"Sure." She reached up and wrapped her arms around Zander's neck, and he leaned down, pressing his lips tenderly against hers. The kiss lasted a little longer than it usually did, as if Zander could somehow feel that there was something more going on here than he knew.

He opened the car door for her, and helped her inside. "See you tomorrow."

"Yes, tomorrow evening."

He leaned inside the car, to plant one more kiss on the top of her head before he closed the door. Quinn watched him waving in the rearview mirror as she pulled out of the parking lot. She saw him heading to his truck as she drove up the street.

Although she was aware that nobody was paying any attention at all, she still took a convoluted path through town before making her way to the little house on Bray Street. William and Thomas were waiting there, on the side of the house, to direct her to pull all the way up the driveway to the tiny two-car garage behind the house.

Nathaniel's car wasn't there. He was working at the hospital tonight. Thomas had already told her that Nathaniel couldn't get away from his duties here in Bristlecone to make it to the wedding. Just the three of them were headed to Eirentheos this evening.

Two hours later, Quinn and William stood together, hidden in a small stand of pine trees near the river, peering between the branches as Thomas nonchalantly walked up to the broken bridge. He glanced around quickly, to double check that nobody was around to see him, and then he climbed up the steps and disappeared. Quinn gasped in spite of herself. Though she had known it was coming, she had never witnessed the phenomenon for herself. One second Thomas was there, and then his right leg had disappeared into thin air. In the next instant, he was gone.

"Your turn, Quinn," William said behind her. "The eyes-closed trick is even more useful on this side."

Quinn let out a nervous giggle. "I'm not sure I could step over the edge of a broken bridge with my eyes open."

"I know I can't. I tried it once when I was about twelve. Not a good plan."

She looked at him in surprise. "I'll bet Thomas keeps his eyes open."

"Not everyone is Thomas. Now go, before we get stuck here until tomorrow and miss the wedding. I'll keep watch."

She took a deep breath, and walked toward the bridge. She paused for a second at the base, gathering her courage, and then climbed the stone steps to the broken landing. Resisting the temptation to look down over the edge at the swirling mountain stream below, she closed her eyes and took a step forward.

The ground beneath her foot felt solid. Keeping her eyes closed, she took another step. The bridge was still solid underneath her. Suddenly, there was a pair of hands holding on to her upper arms. Quinn opened her eyes, and Thomas grinned widely at her.

"Thought I'd make sure you didn't fall again."

She narrowed her eyes. "I wouldn't have."

Thomas only laughed. Hands still on her shoulders, he guided her to the end of the bridge. "William will be coming soon." He took her by the elbow and led her down the stone steps onto the wide, dirt path that led up to the bridge.

"I can walk, you know."

"Who said you couldn't? But you're in Eirentheos now, Quinn, and princes treat ladies like ladies."

Quinn rolled her eyes, though she could never actually be irritated with Thomas – he was too fun, and always sincere.

While they waited for William to appear, she took in her surroundings. The crisp, clean smell in the air was wonderful and familiar. A calm feeling washed over her. She walked through the lush, green foliage to the edge of the river. Thomas followed close behind her. The water flowed lazily over the smooth rocks buried in its bed. It was so clear that even in the dusk she could see the details of every stone, and every leaf of the green grasses that tried to grow up from between them. She knew that if she wanted to, she could put her head in the water and take a long, deep drink.

Quinn knelt down at the edge of the water, and rested her hands in the shallow water there. It was cool, though not cold. It felt good against her skin in the surprisingly warm air. It was warmer than she remembered it being. She sat down and stripped off the heavy coat she had been wearing against the late-winter chill of Bristlecone, and then removed the sweater underneath. She was much more comfortable in just her light, short-sleeved shirt. Thomas, such a natural at taking care of people that he probably didn't even notice what he was doing, scooped up the articles of clothing, folded them neatly, and tucked them into the large backpack he'd been wearing before he sat down next to her on the bank.

She closed her eyes for a long moment, absorbing the utterly clean smell of the air and the sounds of the summer evening. Suddenly, her eyes popped open; something wasn't quite right.

"Where are the birds?" she asked?

"Hmm?"

"Aelwyn and Sirian. Aren't they usually right nearby when you come through the gate?"

Thomas grinned, a knowing glint in his eye. "Remember when we told you we suspected they had become a mating pair?"

Quinn nodded.

"We're certain about it now. They're nesting, taking turns sitting on the eggs. Neither of them will go further from the nest than is necessary to find enough food."

Quinn's eyes were wide. "I thought they always stayed with their person."

"Always – unless there are eggs in the nest."

"What will happen when the eggs hatch?"

"They'll both stay with the chicks until they can fly. At that point, they'll allow us to choose one of the babies to raise as a companion bird, and the rest will fly away, wild."

"And then Aelwyn and Sirian will return to us." William's voice startled her; she hadn't heard him appear behind them.

"Wow."

"Yes. Absolutely nothing like it in your world."

Suddenly, she remembered something about the birds that made her curious, but she'd never asked. "What *do* the birds do when you're gone – in my world, when they're not nesting? How do they handle when you're away for so long?

"I'm sure it's strange for them," William said, "watching us disappear. But they are wild creatures, not fully pets. They have their own lives, too. I can't speak for the whole species, since it doesn't exactly apply to many people outside of us – but Aelwyn and Sirian seem to be fine with it. They have each other when we're gone. Somehow, though, they always seem to be waiting near the gate when we return. Nathaniel's bird, Aidel finds him here, as well."

"Does she have a mate, too?"

"She may, but I've never seen any other seeker around her long enough to be sure."

"Neither have I," said Thomas. "But Nathaniel has said a few times that she's disappeared for awhile, and then has a different sort of attitude when she returns."

Quinn smiled. "Definitely nothing like that in my world."

The three of them stood there for a moment, watching as the last of the sun's rays reflected off the river and the sky turned deep blue. Then they turned and started down the path together.

9
RETURN TO THE CASTLE

The castle seemed bigger than Quinn remembered it. As they grew closer, its massive shape took over the western skyline. Twinkling lights from the many windows lit the now-dark evening. Of course the last time she had approached it from this direction, she had been unconscious. William led them around the southern end of the castle, toward an inconspicuous entrance. The southern side of the castle was coming into view when Quinn saw a figure about one hundred yards up the path.

She instantly recognized the petite silhouette. "Linnea!"

Linnea took off at a run toward the trio, wrapping her arms around Quinn's neck as soon as she reached her. "It's about time! What took you three so long?"

"Impatient today are we, dear sister?" Thomas grinned slyly.

"Says the one who's already had to take two trips to Earth to see her. How would you feel if you were stuck here in the castle while I was off visiting William and Quinn?"

"Touché. Next time, I'll sneak you into my backpack."

"I'll hold you to that." Linnea turned to Quinn. "How are you? You look fabulous!"

"I'm good. Happy to see you." And she was. Until this moment, she had forgotten just how much she liked Linnea, how quickly they had fallen into a close, unbreakable friendship.

Once inside the castle, they went straight to the large dining room. Stepping inside the double doors, she felt as if she had never left Eirentheos. People – adults and children – were scattered everywhere around the room. At one end of the table, three adolescent boys sat, playing some kind of card game, while several women conversed at the other end. Small children were all over the place, running back and forth, chasing one another, jumping from one colored tile to the next, and dragging toys across the floor.

She couldn't name everyone in the room, but she was surprised at how many of the faces were familiar. Over by the fireplace, she could see William's little sister Emma, who was always full of spunk, trying to re-tie a ribbon in the hair of Sarah, the second-youngest Rose child.

Across the room, a young boy and girl were throwing a ball back and forth, getting dangerously close to knocking over a tall vase of flowers. Although Quinn hadn't seen him walk over there, she saw Thomas suddenly step in front of the boy and intercept the ball.

"Will, catch!" He yelled, tossing the ball neatly across the room into William's waiting hand. Instantly, the conversation and chaos in the room stopped. Everyone's attention was now on William and Quinn.

One of the women from the end of the table rose and started toward them. A tall, muscular man joined her only a second later. Quinn recognized them as William's parents, King Stephen and Queen Charlotte.

She always felt uncomfortable in the moment before she greeted the king and queen, always fighting an odd urge to curtsy, or kneel, or whatever else it was people in movies did when they were approached by royalty, but any of those actions would have made her feel even more awkward than she already did, and so she just stood there.

Charlotte walked straight up to her, taking Quinn's hands in her own soft, warm ones. "Hello, sweetheart, we're so glad to see you again, so happy you were able to come."

At Charlotte's words, Quinn's shy insecurity inexplicably melted away. Though she never could have explained it, somehow, she was at home here.

"Thank you, Charlotte. I'm quite happy to be back here. I've missed everyone."

Charlotte's eyes held the same glimmer that Quinn had grown so accustomed to seeing in Thomas' as she hugged Quinn tightly.

Behind them, Thomas cleared his throat. "Don't I rate a greeting around here anymore?"

Quinn looked around. Stephen was hugging William, speaking to him in low tones.

"When you're gone for as long as William and Quinn have been, we'll greet you first." Charlotte chided him gently before she wrapped her arms around his neck.

Stephen now turned his attention to Quinn. "Welcome back. We're so pleased to have you. You've been missed – by Linnea and Thomas in particular."

She smiled widely. "It's wonderful to be here, Your Majesty ... Stephen," she amended, when he cast a disapproving look at her.

Quinn was exhausted by the end of the dinner, wonderful though it had been. It was such fun to see all of William and

Thomas' younger siblings, who were sweet and funny as always. Emma had wanted to chat with her endlessly, and little Sarah had climbed into her lap as she was finishing her dessert. She even managed to snag a few moments of cuddling with tiny baby Hannah.

She had been impressed with herself when she'd managed to remember everyone's names, and the order of the siblings. Simon was the oldest, and he was there with his fiancée, Evelyn, whom Quinn was meeting for the first time. Next came Maxwell, then Rebecca, who was married to Howard – they were warm and welcoming as always. William, Thomas, and Linnea were next, followed by Joshua and Daniel. Alex and Emma were another set of twins, then quiet little Alice, the toddler, Sarah, and finally Hannah.

Dinner had run long, with lots of conversation and laughter, and Quinn had enjoyed herself thoroughly.

She was glad for the quiet, though, as she followed William, Thomas, and Linnea upstairs to the wing of the castle that contained the family's private apartments. Near the end of the hallway, Quinn could see light spilling out of the open doorway of the room that had been designated as "hers". She paused just before she reached the door.

"Are you okay?" Thomas turned to her with a concerned look in his eyes.

"Yeah, I'm fine. I just need a second."

"Are you sure?" Linnea chimed in.

Quinn nodded, and glanced over at William, who hadn't said anything. She was surprised at the expression in his eyes. His look held no questions, no concern, only understanding, as if he expected the reaction she was having and he appreciated it. A strange, new emotion welled up in her throat before she looked away and walked into her bedroom.

Once inside the room, she felt like she had last been there only this morning. Everything was the same: the soft, white bedding on the four-poster bed, the sofa, the little table and two chairs under the window, and the young woman who stepped out of the bathroom at the sound of their approach.

"Miss Quinn! I was just finishing the preparations for your stay."

"Thank you, Mia." Quinn walked over to her, and took the small bucket of cleaning supplies from her hands, setting it on the floor before turning to face her again. "It's so wonderful to see you. I've missed you."

Mia's round cheeks became just a little rosier. "It's lovely to see you, too, Miss Quinn. It hasn't been the same around here without you."

It was Quinn's turn to blush. "I'm sure that's not true, Mia. I only stayed here for a few days."

"That was enough to make us miss you once you left," Thomas interrupted.

"Yes, Miss. I don't think a day has gone by when Master Thomas hasn't mentioned you, or I haven't caught him here in your room, looking for something." Mia's expression was teasing, which surprised Quinn, who had only ever seen her behave in a way that was both kind and subservient.

"You've caught me," he said, turning to her. "It's true that I've been pining away for your company. But don't think for a moment that I'm the only one."

"No, he isn't. Did you bring any of those magazines from your world that you were telling me about last time?" she turned around to see Linnea already camped out on her sofa, one hand on Quinn's small backpack. She didn't know when the backpack had been brought up here for her.

"Do you need help unpacking, Miss Quinn?" Mia asked.

"Thank you, Mia, but no, there's nothing in there worth troubling yourself over." Knowing that most of her own clothing would be out of place here, and mollified by Thomas' assurances that his parents enjoyed providing for her needs while she stayed, Quinn had packed very lightly, bringing only a few small things to give as gifts. William had actually taken advantage of her mostly-empty backpack to cram in more medical supplies.

She did notice, as she sat down next to Linnea, that the packages of bandages, tape, medical tubing, and syringes had disappeared. William and Nathaniel worked hard to share their medical knowledge and healing technologies with their world, but William had explained to her that certain things, especially plastic and adhesives, were either difficult or impossible to manufacture here.

"Is there anything at all I can do for you?" Mia was still fretting over her comfort.

"Actually, Mia, could you bring bedding in for me? I'm going to sleep in Quinn's room tonight – if that's all right with you, Quinn?"

Quinn smiled at Linnea. "Of course it's fine. We'll have a sleepover."

AN EMERGENCY

"It's warmer here than I remember."

"It's much later in the summer," Thomas told her.

"Not that I'm complaining. I hate cold weather."

"I like warm weather better too," William said. "Although I do think there's such a thing as too hot."

Quinn, William, Thomas, and Linnea were walking out through the back gardens of the castle, headed toward the stables. The late morning sun was beating down on them; they were all dressed in shorts and short-sleeved shirts. After spending her first full day back in Eirentheos with the family in the castle, Quinn was excited about the chance to spend a day on a horseback ride with the siblings out in the sunshine.

Thomas led the group as they walked into a large, airy stable, passing a number of stalls before he paused in front of one.

Quinn would have recognized Dusk anywhere. Her glossy gray coat seemed to shimmer, even here inside the stable. She held out the apple she had been carrying. Dusk turned her nose at the offering, eyeing Quinn with a look that was almost reproving.

Thomas snickered, standing in front of his own horse, Storm, whose gray-black coat was even darker than Dusk's. "I didn't mean to disappear on you for so long," Quinn said, returning Dusk's gaze.

In response, Dusk reached down and snatched the apple. She still looked aloof as she chewed.

"See, I told you I wasn't the only one who missed you," Thomas said.

After two more apples, Dusk seemed to be through punishing her and a short while later, the four of them were riding down a path away from the castle. Quinn was surprised to find that some of her surroundings were already familiar.

"So the wedding is in six more days?" she asked.

"Yes. So we have plenty of time to just visit and have fun while you're here." Linnea smiled widely from atop her mare, Snow, a beautiful horse who was almost white, but her flanks were flecked with gray.

"Linnea is quite pleased that she's been assigned to keep you entertained, rather than working on wedding preparations," Thomas said.

"A job that Thomas is *so* disappointed to be helping with."

Quinn chuckled, and looked over at William. "What about you? Are you being forced to spend time with me as well?"

"Nah," Thomas answered, before William had a chance to respond, "Will's pretty much off the hook whenever he's here. Nobody requires him to do anything. Of course," he added, watching William's expression turn into a glower, "he never leaves off from working, even when he is home. You should feel privileged that he even came with us today, instead of cooking up potions in his lab."

"That's not fair. I do fun things with you, too." Quinn thought William looked abashed – something she had never seen on him before. "Some people just have more responsibilities than others," he added pointedly.

They rode for nearly an hour, giving themselves – and the horses – a chance to stretch out. Quinn soaked up the sunshine, enjoying the weather, even though sweat was dripping down her back after the first twenty minutes. Although they rode in silence, it was companionable, and she felt happy and at peace.

Finally, the path they were on wound back down near the river, and they led the horses into a shady grove near the bank. The river here was wide and full. The horses waded in immediately. Of the group of four horses, William's horse, Skittles, loved the water the most. She had stomped her feet impatiently until William had released her, and she was first into the water, heading almost to the center of the river, where the water reached all the way to her underside. She was the most unique of the horses, a chocolate-brown color with perfect, white circles of color scattered in random locations on her body. These patches did, in a way, look like handfuls of candy.

Quinn, Thomas, Linnea, and William sat down at the edge of the water in the shade.

"Are you glad you came back to visit, Quinn?" Linnea asked her.

She rested her chin on her knees, looking out over the water, noticing the sunshine sparkling off the currents. "Yes, I am."

"You weren't scared off after the last time?" William asked.

"No. Why would I be?"

"I don't know. That whole almost-getting-poisoned thing?"

She raised her eyebrows. "I would hardly call that 'almost'. I could accidentally touch a dangerous plant at home, you know. I wasn't hurt."

"And you were nearly attacked the last time you were here."

Quinn paused for a second. "Tolliver isn't coming to the wedding, is he?"

"Definitely not." Thomas answered before William could. "Even if that hadn't happened, things are not exactly going well between Eirentheos and Philotheum these days."

"Because of what happened with me?" Quinn remembered Tolliver's threats at the Naming Ceremony when Thomas had stood up for her to protect her from him.

"No. That, um, incident didn't help the situation any, but there are much bigger problems between our kingdoms than that."

"Like what?" Quinn wondered, intrigued. "Just that whole thing with Tolliver claiming to be the heir when he shouldn't be?"

"There's that," William said. "And then there's the fact that we were able to trace the source of the shadeweed poisoning back to Philotheum."

"*What?* You never told me that." She glared at William.

"You never asked about it again. It's not like there's ever much of a chance to talk to you in Bristlecone. You're always with Zander."

"And you're always off by yourself in a corner somewhere with your nose in a book."

Linnea's eyes were wide. "Who is Zander?"

"Quinn's boyfriend." William answered.

"Quinn, you have a boyfriend, and you didn't tell me? I'm spending the night in your room again tonight. I need details!"

Quinn pretended not to hear her. Although she had shared nearly everything about her life at home with Linnea, she'd sort of left out the part about Zander. She wasn't entirely sure why she hadn't told Linnea about him. "I want to hear about this shadeweed thing."

"Well, you knew that we had traced the poisoned books back to one particular teacher."

"Right, I remember that."

"There are still a number of things we're not sure about. The teacher has been arrested and imprisoned. He was from Philotheum, and had come to live here in Eirentheos about a cycle ago. We've been able to trace the first reports of poisonings back to a short while after he began teaching."

"How could someone from Philotheum just come here and be a teacher?"

"Up until now, Quinn, our kingdoms have been at peace for generations. We were originally one big kingdom – remember the story from the History book? Our ruling families descend from the same ancestors. People have always been free to come and go between the kingdoms, and to live or work in either one. Nathaniel and I have helped friends and relatives of ours establish a few medical clinics in Philotheum. We've never stopped people coming here and working any kind of job they choose."

"Until now." Thomas said darkly.

"So, what? Why? Why would a teacher be poisoning children's books, even if he was from Philotheum?"

"We really don't know," Thomas said. "It's one of the strangest things that have ever happened here. An attack on children is just … unthinkable. There is obviously more to it than just that. I've no doubt that Tolliver is involved, but we don't really know. All we really know is that the teacher was from Philotheum, and he was poisoning the books."

"Well, that's all Thomas and I personally know, or all we've been told, anyway," William amended. "Our father doesn't share every detail of kingdom politics with us, only with his political advisors and with Simon."

"It's an awfully beautiful day to waste talking politics." Linnea said, directing a rather dark look at her brothers. Quinn had the distinct feeling, though, that Linnea wasn't actually uninterested – it seemed more like she was changing the subject for Quinn's benefit. Linnea stood, taking off her shoes and wading into the river.

William and Thomas rolled their eyes at each other, which made Quinn laugh, but Thomas quickly joined his twin. Quinn wasn't quite as ready to let the topic drop, but it really didn't seem the time. When William headed for the water, too, she followed him.

The cool, clear water felt incredible in the hot sun. Quinn was tempted to submerge herself completely, but she didn't want all of her clothes to be soaked on the hour-long ride back. She contented herself by engaging in the water fight William started – a much more subdued one than she knew the brothers were capable of, because Linnea didn't want her hair messed up when she went back to the castle.

Of course, they were all still dripping when they climbed back out of the water and found a sunny spot to stretch out in. Quinn was lying there, soaking up the sunshine, and watching an occasional bird fly overhead, when she realized that she had been hearing a sound that she didn't expect.

"Are there children nearby?"

"Yes," Thomas replied, without opening his eyes. "We are very close to a village here. It sounds like there are children playing near the riverfront not too far away."

"Oh." Her curiosity satisfied, she laid back, enjoying listening to the distant shouts and giggles.

Less than five minutes passed before the four of them sat up simultaneously.

"That doesn't sound good," Linnea said.

They all listened for a minute, straining to see if they could decipher the noises. A few moments earlier, the shouting and shrieking had sounded lighthearted and fun, but there was a different tone to it now. William had nearly mounted Skittles before the rest of them had even stood.

"Quinn and Linnea, you stay here. We'll go check on them and see if everything is okay."

"Are you kidding, Thomas?" Linnea asked, clicking her tongue to call Snow. Quinn had already reached Dusk; it wasn't in her to be able to ignore the panicked shouting of children. She hit the trail right behind William, with Thomas and Linnea following.

It wasn't hard to locate the children; the sense of alarm in their voices only increased as they grew closer. Quinn followed William through a deep thicket into a tiny clearing about fifty feet from the edge of the river. Two young boys stood at the base of an enormous tree, shouting and pointing upward. Tears streamed down both of their faces. One of the boys had an abrasion on his right cheek; small drops of blood were running down to his chin.

"What's going on?" William asked, dismounting and running up to them.

But Quinn could already see.

Perched about ten feet up in the tree's massive branches was a wooden structure. It was probably a treehouse, or some kind of child's hideout. It had been there long enough that the wooden boards were beginning to fade and splinter at the edges. And now, it had slipped. The entire platform had tilted, and then slid down, probably about four feet from where it should have been. It had landed against another limb of the tree, which had stopped it from falling all the way to the ground. For now.

Sticking out of the window of the treehouse, now tilted toward the ground at a precarious angle, was the face of a third child, younger than the other two. She thought he was maybe six or seven. His face was as white as a sheet, and he was silent, staring out the window.

Thomas and Linnea arrived in the clearing a few seconds after Quinn had dismounted. William had reached the boys and was trying to get them to explain to him what had happened, but they were too upset to be helpful. He was worried about the injury he could see, and was asking the children where else they were hurt. He still hadn't seen the child in the treehouse above him.

"William!" she shouted. "Get those boys away from here. Thomas, I need you to climb up onto that branch and hold the bottom of the treehouse."

William's head snapped around, his eyes quickly assessing the condition of the structure before they widened in alarm. "It's going to fall. We all have to get out of here."

Quinn shook her head. "There's another little boy up there. That's what these boys are trying to tell you. Thomas, now! I need you up there now!"

William looked aghast when he finally saw the third little face in the window. He seemed to freeze in panic. The two boys on the ground were both sobbing hysterically. Thomas was climbing into the tree.

"Linnea," Quinn said, "help him get those boys away in case it falls." She looked over at the boys. "What is his name?" she asked, as calmly as she could manage.

"Elliott," one of the boys choked out. "Help him please … we didn't mean to …"

"William, come help Thomas hold it so it doesn't fall," she said, as Linnea began to lead the other boys away.

"Elliott," she called into the treehouse as she walked around the perimeter, trying to assess the situation. "Are you okay up there? Are you hurt?"

The boy didn't answer.

On the other side of the treehouse, she could see the doorway. A rope ladder hung from the threshold, swinging a few feet from the ground, pulled too high by the tilted angle of the structure. She tugged on the bottom rung of the rope, and the entire platform wobbled slightly. She walked back to the window side.

"Elliott! Hey buddy, do you think you could let us help you climb out the window?"

There was still no answer. He looked okay; he was sitting up near the window, alert. William and Thomas had positioned themselves completely underneath the two corners of the house that they could reach, bracing it to keep it from falling further.

"We need to get him out through that window," Quinn said, "but he won't talk to me."

"Elliott!" Thomas called. "We're here to help you! Can you talk to us?"

Nothing.

"*Crap!* He must be freaked out." Quinn was reminded suddenly of Owen, who sometimes reacted to stress by shutting down completely, speaking to no one. She stepped up into the tree between Thomas and William.

"Get out of here, Quinn! This thing is heavy, and it could fall at any second," Thomas hissed at her.

She ignored him, scooting to the large limb that the treehouse was braced against. She wrapped her arms around it and began to climb.

"Quinn, that is too dangerous. We need to get some more help. Thomas and I might not be able to keep this thing up. You can't risk this."

She kept climbing, "It could fall before anyone else could get here. You two are going to have to keep it balanced for long enough for me to get him."

"Quinn! No!"

She paid no attention, shimmying around the limb and climbing along the side of the house until she reached the window. Elliott was still staring out blankly.

"Hey, Elliott," she spoke as quietly and calmly as she could. "My name is Quinn. Can I help you get out of here?" She glanced over him; there was a scrape on one of his knees, and his hands looked a little scratched up, but otherwise he looked okay. She noticed, now, that he was *much* younger than the other boys, maybe only five or six cycles. A single tear was beginning to slide down his cheek.

"All right, buddy, you're going to be okay. I'm going to get you out of here and down to your friends. I just need you to listen to me, okay?"

Relief flooded through her when he silently nodded.

"Can you scoot all the way over here to the window for me?"

The platform creaked loudly when the boy moved. Quinn reached through the window, and grabbed the boy under his arms. As soon as she started transferring his weight from the floor to her arms, though, the entire platform shifted unexpectedly to the left. The frame of the window slammed into the side of her arm, knocking the boy from her grip, and pinning Quinn to the trunk for a second before it shifted again and the corner of the house finally caught on a branch next to her.

"Quinn! Are you all right?" Thomas called from below her.

She couldn't answer for a moment; the weight of the house had knocked the wind out of her. She struggled to re-position herself, pulling her body up and off the window frame, trying to get an angle where she could grab hold of the boy again. "Yeah, I'm okay," she called back once she had caught her breath again. "Are you guys hurt?"

"No, the tree branch caught it. It almost bumped my head, but right this second I'm not even holding it. It looks shaky, though. You need to get down here."

"Now!" William said, his voice harsh and demanding.

Her arm was beginning to sting from where the window frame had scraped it, and she paused, reassessing her plan. She looked down below to the ground, and then up above her into the tree. "Okay, Elliott, I need you to come stand right here by the window, because we're going to have to do this really quickly. I'm going to help you get out the window, and then we're going to climb *up* for a second."

Elliott looked terrified, but he nodded.

"Thomas? William? When I say the word, you need to get down and away from the tree."

"No! It's too dangerous. You need to get out of the tree right now." William's voice now had an extra layer of stress.

"What? Quinn, what are you going to do? This thing could fall on you." Thomas wasn't as forceful, but his worry was also evident.

"Just trust me. Get out of the way."

"Quinn, we're not going to leave you up there. Get down, and we'll go get help."

"No, William. I can do this. I see what to do. You and Thomas just get out of the tree and as far away as you can." She braced herself against the branch again, and reached for Elliott. "Go now!" she yelled.

As soon as she could see William and Thomas below her, moving clear of the tree, she grabbed Elliott and pulled him against her chest. "Hang on tight, buddy." Thankfully, he obeyed and wrapped his arms around her neck. Quinn climbed up, past the roof of the structure. Sweat was draining down her face with the effort of hauling the boy with her, but she managed to make her way to a branch that would support them. She set him in the fork of the branch, and helped him shift his grip from her neck to the tree.

When she was relatively certain that Elliott wouldn't fall, she carefully climbed a few feet back down, clung to the limb, and set her feet against the roof of the building. Hanging on tightly, she pushed hard against the house. It wobbled slightly, and then came to rest again. Her heart was pounding in her ears too loudly for her to understand what Thomas was yelling at her from across the clearing.

She readjusted her grip, and then pushed again, with all her might, and then had to clutch wildly to keep from falling as the structure gave way under her. The treehouse tottered to the side, banged against a branch, and then fell, collapsing into hundreds of pieces in the base of the tree trunk, shaking the tree violently. She almost fell again.

As soon as all of the pieces had landed, William and Thomas came running.

"Quinn! Are you all right?" Thomas yelled, as he climbed over the debris and began scaling the tree.

"I'm okay. We're both okay," she called back, gathering the boy into her arms again. She did notice a streak of blood trailing down her shirt, but she couldn't tell where it had come from; neither of them appeared to be hurt.

Thomas reached them quickly, and supported Quinn as she carefully made her way down and out of the tree with Elliott clinging tightly to her neck. William, wanting to get a better look at the boy, tried coaxing him out of Quinn's arms, but Elliott refused, burying his face in Quinn's shirt. The other two boys ran up to him, with Linnea following closely behind.

"Hey boys, Elliott's okay, all right?" Thomas said. "My brother here is a healer; he just wants to look at him for a minute. Do you live near here?"

One of the boys – the older of the two – nodded.

"Can you go get help? One of your parents?"

Another nod.

"I'll go with them," Linnea said, following them as they turned and headed out of the clearing.

Thomas looked at Quinn, alarm in his eyes. "Quinn, what happened to you?"

"What?" Her heart was still thumping rapidly, and her breathing was accelerated. She didn't know what he was talking about.

"There's blood all over your shirt." He placed his hand under her elbow and lifted. She couldn't see around Elliott's small body, but the side of her woven top felt damp and sticky.

William turned his attention to her. "There's some blood on Elliott's shirt, too. But it doesn't look like any of it is his." He reached over to Quinn's arm and gently pushed her shirtsleeve up to her shoulder. She heard the sharp intake of his breath, and Thomas stood, reflexively going to retrieve William's medical bag. "What did you do?"

"It must have been when the window frame bumped into my arm. I didn't think it was too bad, though. It doesn't hurt that much."

William raised his eyebrows. "It will when the adrenaline wears off, don't worry. I'm going to need to clean it up a bit to see how bad it is. You're definitely going to have some bruising."

Quinn nodded.

Thomas returned with the bag, setting it down near where they were standing. "Elliott," he said softly, "can you come see me for a second, little man? We need to check on your friend here. She hurt her arm."

The little boy didn't respond, but his grip on her tightened. She shook her head.

William sighed, looking over at Thomas.

"It's not far … only a few minutes' walk into Bay Run from here," Thomas said. "We could take them to the clinic."

William nodded. "Do you think you can carry him, Quinn? It's maybe five minutes."

"Yeah, I can."

"Okay. I want to get a bandage on your arm first, though, keep it from bleeding everywhere."

When he lifted her sleeve again, his anger returned.

"What were you thinking climbing up there like that? You could have been killed!"

The anger in William's voice made Quinn feel defensive. "I was keeping this little boy from getting killed."

"That was a crazy, dangerous stunt. You had no business climbing up there like that."

She looked him straight in the eye, unfazed. "What was the alternative, William?" She glanced down at Elliott, who was staring at him with wide eyes, his arms tightening more than she thought possible.

"You weren't the only one here. We could have come up with a plan that didn't risk your life."

"And what would that plan have been, William?"

He didn't answer for a minute; he just dug angrily through his bag. "I don't know."

"You don't know. That thing would have fallen on its own by now with this boy inside, and you 'don't know,' but you want to yell at me for getting him out of there?"

"Both of you could have been crushed."

"But we weren't. We're fine. *Ow! Crap!* Is that really necessary?"

He raised his eyebrows at her. "You're fine, huh?"

She narrowed her eyes at him. "It's just a scratch."

"Try a huge gash, Quinn. You should never have risked yourself like that."

"You said that already."

William was silent for several minutes before he spoke again. "We have to get this taken care of now … even the bandage I'm putting on it is going to bother all of these splinters. You can't be doing that kind of thing here, Quinn. What if something happened to you? How would I explain that to your mother? We're not in …" he stopped himself

80

before he said too much in front of the boy. "… You have to be careful."

Quinn saw, in a sudden flash, right through William's anger. She'd scared him. She looked back at him apologetically. "All right. I'm sorry."

William's shoulders relaxed a tiny fraction. "I'm just glad you're okay," he mumbled.

As soon as William had a bandage wrapped around Quinn's arm as best he could with the child she held, the three of them began walking toward the village.

It appeared through the trees more quickly than Quinn had been expecting, even though they had told her the walk would be less than five minutes. Only a few feet down the little path that led from the clearing, they came to the yard of the first house.

Not for the first time during a stay in Eirentheos, she was reminded of a fairy tale as soon as she saw the little stone house nestled in among the trees. Its roof was made of heavy, well-kept planks. Vines wound their way up the walls, and flowers were everywhere.

They were almost past the house on the small road they had been following, when the other two boys from the clearing ran up to them, Linnea following closely. Behind Linnea, both looking distraught, were a man and a woman.

The way the man's arm curled protectively around the woman's shoulders told Quinn that they were a couple, but they didn't look anywhere near old enough to be Elliott's parents. She was actually fairly certain that both of them were around her own age. Regardless, as soon as they caught sight of Elliott they ran to him, and he finally relinquished his iron grip on Quinn's neck in exchange for the young woman's.

"Thank you so very much, Your Highnesses," the man said.

"Please, it's Thomas and William," Thomas said, "and this is our companion, Quinn. She's the one who helped get your … uh … son out of the tree."

"I'm Colin," the man said, "and Elliott is my brother's child. My wife, Lindsey, and I are caring for him at present."

"Where are his parents?" William asked. "Should we speak with them as well?"

"My brother and his wife live in Philotheum," Colin said. "They both felt that it was … safer for Elliott to stay here with us."

Quinn glanced questioningly at Thomas, but he only shrugged, frowning as if he were as confused as she was.

"Well, Elliott is fine," William told them. "He has some small scrapes, but nothing looks at all serious. The blood on his clothing is from my friend Quinn, here. She took quite a risk saving your nephew today."

Both Colin and Lindsey turned their attention to Quinn, grateful looks in their eyes. "Thank you so much. I don't know what we would have done if something had happened," Lindsey said, kissing the boy on the cheek over and over.

Once Elliott's guardians had finally been sent on their way, William, Thomas, and Linnea continued leading Quinn into the village.

They passed several more of the picturesque houses, and then, almost suddenly, the forest broke, revealing a bustling little town. They walked through two streets of houses, and then the next corner revealed a busy square in what appeared to be the center of the village.

"It's a Market Day," Linnea told her, as they passed a number of little stands where merchants sold a wide variety of goods. Some stands held fruits and vegetables, while the aroma of spices Quinn couldn't recognize drifted from others. One older woman's stand held shelves and shelves of glass jars in every color; one next to hers sold jewelry.

They didn't pause long enough to really look at anything – William seemed determined to get Quinn to the clinic quickly. Fascinated at her surroundings though she was, she didn't argue. Her arm was really beginning to hurt. She found herself holding her elbow, trying to keep their quick pace from jostling her arm. The bandage that he had wrapped around it was becoming saturated, and more red splotches kept appearing on her shirt.

Only one street over from the busy square, William stopped and began climbing the steps of a small house sandwiched between two others. She was confused, until she saw the small wooden sign that read "Bay Run Clinic" hanging from the wooden porch railing. At the door, William knocked, but didn't wait for an answer before walking in. Thomas and Linnea, who were right behind her, escorted her inside.

Though the clinic was smaller than any she had ever been in, it was also distinctly familiar. The main room held two treatment areas, separated by low, wooden walls. Rough, heavy curtains that could be pulled around the beds hung from the ceiling. The room was empty when they entered, but a moment later a man appeared through a doorway that led to the back of the building.

"William!" the man said, walking right up to him. He was probably in his late twenties, with sandy brown hair and kind, green eyes. "And Thomas and Linnea, too. What a surprise." He turned his eyes to Quinn. "And this is?"

"Our friend, Quinn," William said. "Quinn, this is our dear friend, Robert, the doctor here in Bay Run."

"Very nice to … oh! What happened?" Robert asked, suddenly taking in Quinn's bloodied shirt and the way she cradled her right arm.

"She's scraped up her arm pretty badly," William said. "Can I borrow your clinic to take a look at it?"

"Of course," Robert said. "Anything you need."

While William explained what had happened to Robert, Thomas led her over to the first cot, and lifted her on to the crisp, white sheets. Linnea busied herself propping pillows up behind Quinn's back.

Robert stood near the edge of the bed and watched with interest as William began to unwrap the bandage. She winced when the gauze pulled at the gash, and she heard the collective intake of breath from everyone who was watching.

After several long minutes of investigating and cleaning, each touch growing more painful, although she knew he was being as gentle as he could manage, William looked up at her with a serious expression on his face. "You really scraped this up, and it's full of splinters. You're going to need stitches." He glanced over at Robert, who nodded, and walked over into a little room, which she guessed was probably a supply closet.

Quinn turned pale white. "No. I'll be fine. It's just some scratches."

William raised his eyebrows.

"What is it about you and coming here?" Thomas teased. "Can't manage to keep from injuring yourself for ten days? Are you like this at home?"

She shot him a dark look. "No. I scratch and bruise myself all the time, especially in the summer when I'm leading horseback rides at the ranch, but I've never needed stitches until the last time I was here."

"Never *needed* them, or never *gotten* them?" William asked her, eyeing a scar just above her left knee, where Quinn had snagged herself with a fishing hook when a group she had been leading had gone fishing on the ranch last summer. She blushed, wondering when, exactly, he had noticed that. She hadn't worn shorts in front of him very often.

Her eyes narrowed. "Never *needed* them." She glanced down at the scar, though, realizing for the first time how much more pronounced it was than the little line that William had sewn up for her on her last visit, which had nearly disappeared.

She remembered that day, promising the nurse at the ranch that she would have her mom take her to have it looked at that evening if she needed to, but she'd been convinced it was fine, and had just worn pants to hide it for the next few weeks. And it was fine. She hadn't *needed* stitches.

Thomas chuckled. "Maybe you don't spend so much time at home trying to play hero of the day, and that's how you avoid stitches there."

She glared at him, and then looked up at William. "I'm fine."

William's expression was sympathetic, but unwavering. His hands never stopped moving over her arm. She turned to Linnea, a pleading expression in her eyes. Linnea looked back compassionately but said, "I don't argue with William about stuff like this."

Robert returned then, setting down a metal tray of supplies on the little table near the bed. "I have some patients I need to ride out and check on. Are you okay here?"

William nodded, and began organizing the things Robert had brought.

"Okay, then. If I don't see you again today, I'm sure I will soon." He said, looking at each of the three siblings. "Quinn, it was nice meeting you. I know you'll recover quickly with William taking care of you.

"Thank you," she said. "It was very nice meeting you, too."

As Robert walked out the front door, there was a clink of glass against metal on the tray next to her, and Quinn's stomach rolled. "Are you okay?" Linnea asked, looking concerned.

Thomas, who had disappeared to the other side of the room, returned now with a folded washcloth. "Lie back sweetheart," he said, helping her. "She and William have similar feelings when it comes to needles," he explained to Linnea.

"Oh." She watched as Thomas placed the washcloth on Quinn's forehead. "*Oh.*"

"She can climb trees and fearlessly rescue small children, but when it comes to needles …"

Quinn rolled her eyes, though she couldn't argue. Her stomach turned with every noise that came from beside the bed.

"And she can't have valoris seed, either."

"Right." Linnea laid her hand on Quinn's shoulder.

"Either?" Quinn wondered, feeling a little less lightheaded with the cool cloth on her forehead.

"Actually, none of us are supposed take it. It's very rare to react to it at all, but bad reactions run in our family."

Quinn was stunned. "You never told me that before."

Thomas shrugged. "I've never even tried it. Simon reacted when he was little. Maxwell took it once, and he was fine, but then Rebecca had a bad reaction to it when she was about Emma and Alex's age. After that, Nathaniel refused to allow it's use on any of us. He won't take it, either. One of his brothers had a reaction when he was younger and Nathaniel never wanted to risk it.

"That is really weird – wait, one of his brothers? He's your uncle, right? Isn't he the brother of one of your parents?"

"Um, no," Linnea answered. "We've always called him our uncle, because he came to live with our grandparents when he was a young teenager, and our father considers him a brother, but he isn't technically."

"Then who is he really?"

"I don't know all of the details. I know that he is actually distantly related in some way, but the rest of it is one of those, 'we don't discuss it in front of the children' things.

"Maybe it's just something that hasn't come up because it isn't important. Nathaniel is our uncle, 'technically' or no." William's voice carried a hint of irritation. She knew how close William and Nathaniel were, and guessed he didn't much like the discussion.

He softly took hold of her elbow with his left hand, and her stomach wobbled. Her head turned automatically to watch what he was doing.

"Eyes over here, Quinn." Thomas put his finger under her chin, turning her head to the side of the bed where he stood. He stared at her, trying to keep her eyes on his. Linnea sat down next to the pile of pillows, running her fingers through Quinn's hair.

"And relax," Linnea said. She put one hand on her shoulder, steadying it, and shifted her body slightly to obscure Quinn's view of William.

Next to her, William moved, too, turning his back to block her view completely.

"You're fine, Quinn. I've got you." Thomas took her right hand in his, holding it securely while William prodded some more at the wound on her upper arm. His touch was feather-light, but several times she had to bite her lip to keep from crying out.

"I know," she said, trying to sound upbeat, "You guys must think I'm a big coward."

"Yeah, we do," Linnea said, "but we like you anyway."

She managed a giggle.

"That's better," Thomas said. He tightened his grip when she flinched at a sudden, cold swipe of alcohol.

"Sorry, Quinn," William said, and she turned to look at him, despite Thomas' attempts to distract her. Her gray eyes were wide with anxiety. "I don't think any less of you," he said, and he meant it. "These two aren't kidding when they tease me for being the same way." He knew he was just as bad. Really, he was probably worse. The small, badly healed scar on the girl's leg amused him, mostly because he could picture himself doing the exact same thing if he could ever have gotten away with it.

He'd always hated needles, and his heart ached now for the nervous girl in front of him, although part of him was still irritated at her for putting herself in such danger in the first place.

Her arm was a mess. It hurt him to look at it. He was actually glad that most of the injuries were out of her line of sight – if she could see her arm right now, she'd probably be in even more pain. Though he hated that he had to use a needle to do it, he was anxious to get it numbed up for her. The poor girl was already gritting her teeth every time he so much as breathed on it, and he was pretty sure that her earlier rush of adrenaline hadn't quite worn off yet.

Three long, jagged cuts ran most of the length of her upper arm – nails or something must have come loose from the frame near the window as the structure disintegrated. The one in the middle was the worst, but all three needed stitches if she was going to avoid some serious scarring.

There were several smaller cuts, and most of her skin was covered in abrasions. Hot red and purple bruises were already beginning to form underneath many of the scrapes. The worst part though, was the splinters. He'd never seen that many small flecks of wood buried around wounds before. Even if she hadn't needed stitches, he would have had to numb her arm to even begin to work on removing those.

"No, we're not." Linnea chortled. "I heard he fainted the last time."

William rolled his eyes. He had *not* fainted, he'd just … come close. "Just wait, Linnea … if it's ever you …" Bold as his little sister was about most things, she was usually more cautious than he and Thomas were when it came to anything physical. Or else she was just luckier. She'd never needed stitches, or even gotten seriously hurt.

Linnea just smiled, looking kindly at Quinn. "It's true. I've never had them come at me with needles. I might be the same way." She squeezed Quinn's shoulder.

"Thomas has." The girl looked back over at his carefree younger brother. William seized the opportunity of her being distracted again to pick up the first syringe full of anesthetic.

"Sure. But I freaked out pretty good the first five or six times, too. Keep hurting yourself and you'll catch up with me."

"I don't think that's a competition I want to win." She actually grinned.

"There's my smile," Thomas said.

His disappeared along with hers a second later, though, with the first jab of the needle. William felt her arm tense up, and he worked as carefully as he could, injecting as large a radius as possible before he had to remove the needle and stick her again. He silently willed the numbness to spread faster than the stinging sensation he knew she was feeling.

"Just breathe," Thomas told her. William was overcome with an odd emotion as he watched his brother rub the back of Quinn's hand soothingly with his thumb – for a moment he wished he were one comforting her, rather than the one hurting her more. He shook it off, realizing that was ridiculous. He was grateful for Thomas' presence here, which always made these kinds of things easier on everyone.

She nodded, exhaling as William finally pulled out the syringe.

"See, you're already doing better than the last time."

She tried to smile again, but only made it halfway.

"Another pinch," William told her, though it had already happened before he got the words out – he knew that

89

anticipating the shot was often the worst part. He was glad that nobody seemed to notice how he worked to keep his own voice steady.

She took a deep breath, and concentrated on Thomas' eyes. She wasn't quite so tense this time, which made William feel better – the medicine must have been starting to do its job. She lay there, perfectly still and watching Thomas as William worked carefully to numb her entire upper arm.

He was thorough; after all of this, he didn't want her to feel *anything* when he did the stitches, or especially when he started digging in for the splinters. Several of those spots were literally becoming red and inflamed as he watched. She still flinched at each new poke, but she didn't actually lose her patience until he was – fortunately – on the last one. "You didn't give me this many shots the last time."

Thomas smiled at the girl's exasperation, but her eyes were on William now.

"You didn't scrape up half your arm the last time. You've got three separate cuts here that need stitches. Besides, you were unconscious for most of it last time. How would you know?"

Thomas chuckled at her sigh.

"I'm done with those now, though. I'm just going to give it a minute to make sure it's completely numb before I clean and stitch it."

"The bad part is over," Thomas said. "You can just lay here and relax now."

"Almost," William amended, and Quinn looked up at him in surprise.

"What do you mean, almost?" she asked, suspicious.

He sighed, and watched as the expression in her eyes became even more accusing. He was rather glad that the arm closest to him was too numb for her to move, and that Thomas had hold of the other one. He had a feeling it wouldn't take much at this point to upset her enough to throw a punch she'd regret later. "There's a lot of debris in these wounds. I would feel a lot better if I got some antibiotics into you."

The muscles in her face relaxed. "That's not so bad. I've taken antibiotics before. I'm not allergic or anything."

Thomas raised his eyebrows, and William's heart sank. It was true, in her world, that most of the time, "antibiotics" meant taking pills for a week. In Eirentheos – not so much.

"What?" she demanded.

"It's not like there are pharmacies here and it's easy to just write a prescription for some pills, Quinn. Besides, you're going to need some in your system a little faster than that." The way the skin around some of her splinters was beginning to swell, he was actually wishing that he'd given her the antibiotic shot first.

"Oh." Her color drained again. "Does that mean what I think it does?"

"One more shot, that's all," he promised, cleaning a spot on the side of her thigh, before she had a chance to protest. Her pulse started to beat so rapidly that he could actually see the artery in her neck throbbing.

Thomas gripped her hand again. "It's just for a minute, Quinn." She nodded, clearly trying to hold herself together. "Not nearly as bad as shadeweed remedy."

If Robert hadn't left, William would have considered asking him to do this part. Instead, he hid behind his irritation from earlier. "Not nearly as bad as an infected arm, either," he said. "Or, say, falling out of a tree and being crushed by a couple hundred pounds of wood and nails."

She glowered at him, and he used that second of distraction to stick her with the needle. Thomas held her hand tightly.

"Almost done," William said, watching her concentrate on breathing in and out. He knew the medicine stung, but outside of her clenched teeth, she stayed as calm as he had ever seen her. "Sorry, Quinn. I really will stop torturing you after this." If he hadn't been studying her so closely, he would have missed her tiny nod.

"Awesome," Thomas told her, as William taped a piece of cotton in place. "See, you're already getting better at this."

"Probably best if you avoid becoming an expert at it, though." William said, patting her softly on the shoulder.

"I'll keep that in mind," she said.

Linnea chuckled as she helped Quinn sit back into the pillows.

"So, you've had to have stitches before?" Quinn asked him, probably bored and trying to keep her mind occupied as he worked on her arm.

"Oh yes." He'd lost track of how many times now, although, unlike his brother, it never seemed to get easier for him. "It kind of comes with the territory, since I spend so much time riding around the kingdom on horseback, visiting clinics. We are often in rural areas, and there are many times we have to hike … Besides, I'm usually with Thomas. You see where that's gotten you already."

Quinn laughed; her irritation with William had faded now that her arm was numb.

"I am a walking hazard zone," Thomas said. "But I know how to have fun."

"Fun is one word for it," Linnea chided.

"You're just mad that you don't usually get to come."

"It's hardly fair. You two are always getting to have fun adventures without me."

"Here, you can have *my* adventure," Quinn told her, brandishing an empty syringe she'd picked up from the bedside table.

William actually snorted.

When they had finally all recovered from the laughing fit, he looked up at his siblings. "This is going to take awhile," he said. A *long* while, probably. For every splinter he pulled out, he seemed to find three or four he hadn't seen before. "You should go check on the horses – maybe even go take a peek at the market stalls. I'm sure the vendors would be happy to have a prince and princess stop by."

Linnea's eyes lit up at the idea – he knew she'd seen the jewelry stands as they walked by – but she looked down in concern at Quinn. "We aren't going to leave when you need us," she said.

Quinn shook her head. "I'm fine now. I can't feel anything. You should go, this has to be about as exciting as watching paint dry in here."

"Are you sure, Quinn?" Thomas was more reluctant.

"I'm sure. Go."

"We won't be long," he promised.

She shrugged, though only one shoulder actually moved. "From the sounds of it, you have plenty of time."

"Is there anything you'd like?" Linnea asked.

Quinn chuckled. "Do they have books?"

"I'm sure someone does," Thomas said, brushing the girl's hair back from her forehead. "We'll bring you something."

William saw Quinn begin to object, which didn't surprise him, but his brother and sister disappeared, likely intentionally avoiding hearing her.

After Thomas and Linnea were gone, William worked in silence for several minutes before looking up. "So, later, when your arm is feeling better, you can punch me. I know you wanted to."

She chuckled. "You were not my favorite person there for a minute. But I'm over it now … mostly."

He grinned. "You'll be grateful later. The scars on your arm would have been a lot more visible than that one on your leg."

"I didn't even know you'd noticed that." She did surprise him when the base of her neck began to glow a soft red.

He shrugged, catching her gaze -- trying to convey with his expression that he hadn't meant to embarrass her. He actually kind of liked the distinctive little scar on her leg. It was so … *Quinn*. "It's not that bad, I just notice things like that. Nathaniel and I both spend a lot of time practicing doing stitches well. It's not so important on a leg, but for a cut on your face – there are no plastic surgeons here. You can't tell me that Nathaniel ever saw that injury and let it heal like that."

She shook her head.

"What are we going to do with you, Quinn?" He wanted to lighten the mood.

It worked. She smiled.

"So, Nathaniel isn't really your uncle?" she asked, changing the subject just a little too casually. Although she tried to hide it, he could see the burning curiosity in her eyes. He'd become all too familiar with that expression of hers lately.

"Yes, he is my uncle. In every way possible other than that his parents don't happen to be my grandparents."

The understanding in her eyes as she nodded caught him off guard. "Does that make sense to you?"

"Very much. It's kind of like Jeff. I had a dad before him, and I know that he loved me very much, and that I loved him, but he died when I was three and I don't really remember him. Jeff adopted me when I was six, and he is my *real* dad. I don't like when people say he isn't. Even if he wasn't there when I was born, he has chosen to be. I just have two *real* dads."

"Yeah, it's kind of like that with Nathaniel."

He could see that she was still curious, though. "So who are his parents, then?"

"*That* I don't know. He doesn't talk about it, and I've never heard it discussed at all. He came to live with my grandparents when he was a young teenager, and from that point on, he was raised with their children, with my father. I don't know why he came to live with them. I do know he is family, related somehow. He's a fourth-born royal, with the gift of healing, but I've never been able to figure out what line he's from.

"He started living in your world most of the time, though, when he was my age. He was gone for a number of years while he went away from Bristlecone to go to college, and medical school, and complete his residency. Even now, he doesn't come here as often as I do, and when he does, he's usually away at one of the other clinics, training those who have served as his apprentices, stocking and helping at the clinics."

"If he's a fourth-born royal, doesn't that mean he has an older brother who's a king or something?"

William smiled. He often forgot how foreign all of this must be to her. "No. The gifts pass through every royal bloodline. The firstborn child is always given the gift of leadership, but only the first-born of the king becomes king. My own first child will have leadership, but would be far from first in line for the throne, because I'm a fourth-born. Simon's son will be the heir once Simon becomes king."

"I guess that makes sense."

"Very different from your world, I know. Okay, a few more splinters, and I'll be just about done here. I'm going to look in my bag for some ibuprofen."

"I'm okay," she said. "It's not hurting."

He rolled his eyes. "Quinn, I know that you think everything is fine and that you didn't really hurt yourself, but your arm is torn up. It is going to be hurting tonight. If you take some ibuprofen *now,* and keep up with it every six hours, you *might* – and only might – not be asking for something stronger before you go to bed tonight. And," he added, staring her down, "if you do need something stronger, you'd better ask."

She nodded, subdued.

"You're going to need to be really careful with this for a few days. Let Mia or Linnea help you with getting dressed, because this is right where it's going to rub against the sleeve of your shirt all the time." There was a definite downside to the fact that the injuries were on the outside of her arm. "I don't want to be putting these stitches back in anytime soon, okay?"

She nodded again. "William?"

"Yes?"

"I'm already grateful."

11

FRUSTRATED

As William had expected, his mother was beside herself by the time he walked into the dining room with Quinn. Thomas and Linnea had gone in a few minutes before them to explain, and now they were sitting together at the far end of the table, looking guilty. *Good.*

Queen Charlotte flew across the room as soon as William and Quinn entered.

"Quinn! Are you all right sweetheart?" Her forehead creased as she appraised Quinn's bloody shirt and bandaged arm. "Is she all right?" she turned her gaze on William before Quinn even had a chance to answer.

William sighed. "She will be fine. She's banged it up pretty good. She will be pretty sore for a few days, but it will heal. Some of those stitches will still have to be in when she goes home, though."

Quinn's eyes popped wide at that news. *Good,* William thought again. Let her think about that. Choices have consequences. Let her explain that one to Zander Cunningham. He'd had plenty of time on the ride home for his irritation to build again. The danger that girl had put herself in … she just didn't think. She treated his whole world like it was imaginary … she could step in and have fun, and then just go home as if it had never happened. He did wonder exactly what she'd told her boyfriend she was doing this weekend.

"What were you thinking, Quinn? You could have been seriously injured. Or worse!"

William's shoulders sank at the tone in his mother's voice, so he nearly choked when Quinn looked her straight in the eye. "I wasn't thinking about anything except that little boy."

"A fact which we are very proud of." King Stephen had joined them. "From what Thomas and Linnea say, you probably saved that child's life today, and for that I am grateful. Our entire kingdom is grateful." His father paused; emotion had crept into his voice. "But to put yourself at that kind of risk while you are under my care, away from your home, when I think about what could have happened to you today … Your poor mother …"

"I'm sorry I frightened you, Your Majesties. Truly. I did not mean to worry you, or put your family at risk. But if I had just stood there and watched …"

William's jaw dropped – when had the shy and quiet Quinn turned into someone who would talk to a king that way? He watched several emotions flit across his father's face before his expression suddenly softened. Stephen exchanged a wordless argument with Charlotte, which, from the look of acquiescence in his mother's eyes, his father won.

Stephen cleared his throat. "We'll settle on grateful then, Quinn. We're grateful to you for taking such a risk to rescue that boy, and to the Maker, for protecting you both today and returning you to us."

William looked on as his parents simultaneously wrapped Quinn in a hug. There was moisture in his mother's eyes.

"And William," Stephen said after a moment, "we are, as always filled with gratitude and pride for your skills and your willingness to share them. The Maker has blessed us indeed, to have given us you for a son." The tears ran freely down his mother's cheeks as his parents embraced him tightly.

William escaped the dining room quickly, without having eaten. He would ask someone to bring him up something later. Linnea had been sent upstairs with Quinn, to help her get cleaned up and changed. He knew he would have to check on her later but for now he needed some time to himself. Besides, his own clothing hadn't fared too well with all of the tree-climbing and blood, either. A hot shower would clear his head.

What was it with that girl? The whole scene with his parents had renewed his frustration from the afternoon. Why didn't she – or anyone else – see how dangerous this was? First, she came strolling through the gate behind him, and now she was running carelessly about the place. She had nearly poisoned herself the first time, and today … an image of that treehouse crushing her kept playing in his mind. No, it hadn't actually happened, but what if it had? She was running back and forth between the two worlds like it wasn't a big deal, as if there wouldn't be any consequences to the choices she made.

Did she realize that this was real? That something could really happen to her while she was here? And what exactly were her intentions here, anyway? This wasn't her world. She was building all of these relationships here, and she was just going to leave. Soon enough, she would go off to college in her own world, and marry Zander Cunningham, or someone like him. What was the point of her getting involved here? He sighed. Thinking about this was only making him more tense, so he decided to concentrate on clearing his head.

After the hot water had finally unknotted most of the muscles in his shoulders, William put on clean clothes and wandered down the hall. He ended up, as he often did, in the room of his little sister, Alice. Technically, she shared the room with Emma and Sarah, but he could hear them running and screeching in the playroom across the hall. Alice was in here alone, sitting at a little table, contentedly coloring with the colored pencils and sketchbook William had brought back for her from Bristlecone.

He sat down next to her in an undersized chair. "Hey, precious girl, what are you doing?"

She looked up at him, all wide gray eyes behind her wire-rimmed glasses, but she didn't dignify his question with the obvious response.

He smiled. Even at only four, Alice was easily the most serious of his siblings, and he loved her for it. "Can I draw with you?"

She pushed the box so that it sat between them, and pulled a blank page out of the notebook.

They sat there like that for quite awhile. He watched as Alice drew a very detailed picture of the swing set in the play yard. He mindlessly sketched a picture of Skittles; she would like to keep it when he was finished. "What did you do today?"

She didn't look up; she was carefully outlining a red flower, "I played outside with Emma, and then Mama had a tea party for just the little girls."

"That sounds like fun."

She nodded. "We had cookies shaped like flowers."

William smiled.

"How did Quinn hurt her arm?"

"I didn't see exactly how she did it, but she scraped it somehow when she was getting a little boy out of a treehouse that was about to fall."

"Is the little boy okay?"

"Yes, he's fine. He didn't even get hurt."

"Is Quinn okay?" Alice looked up at him now, concern in her wide eyes. He knew all of his little sisters liked the girl.

"Yes, she'll be fine. Her arm will probably hurt for a few days."

"I'll tell Emma not to hang on it then," she blinked before turning back to her paper.

"I'm glad Quinn got the little boy out of the treehouse, aren't you?"

"Yes, I suppose I am."

"And I'm glad that she's okay."

"Me too."

She was silent again, concentrating on her picture. Finally, she looked back up at him; he could see his own eyes reflected in hers. "Were you scared?"

How could such a tiny girl see so much? "Yes, I was."

She nodded, then put down her pencil and climbed into William's lap. Her little arms wrapped tightly around his neck. When she was done, she climbed back down, carefully removed a purple pencil from the box, and began drawing again.

William smiled. "Thanks for drawing with me. Do you want to keep this picture?"

She nodded.

He slid the paper under her sketchpad, and kissed the top of her head as he stood. "I love you, Alice."

"I love you too, Will."

Thomas watched William skulk out of the dining room after Linnea took Quinn upstairs. It was going to be one of *those* nights. Will was never great company when he got himself all worked up like this.

Across the table, Maxwell was watching, too. His eyes met Thomas' and he sighed. "Why does he always take everything so seriously?"

Thomas nodded. "You're his older brother. Can't you do something about him?"

"I thought that was your job. Use your charm to keep him happy."

"You see how well that's going."

Maxwell chuckled. "After dinner, Simon and the boys and I were going to go and play that basket game you and William were teaching us. It looks like Will's out, but what about you."

"Well, you do owe me a rematch after that last time, but …" he glanced uncomfortably toward the dining room doors.

"Let me guess, you're going to go up and check on Quinn, and then we won't see you again until tomorrow."

Thomas shrugged.

"If I didn't know better, Thomas …"

"Since when have you ever known anything 'better' Max?" He stood and winked impishly at his brother. "We'll have that rematch soon, though."

He stopped at the end of the table to kiss his mother before leaving, and then scooped baby Hannah from her cushioned high chair. "I'll get her bathed and changed before I bring her back to you for her bedtime feeding," he promised.

"Are you just trying to charm your way out of trouble?"

"Who's in trouble? Quinn is fine, the boy is safe at home, and everything is as it should be. She made that decision today all on her own, you know. There was no stopping her." He smiled warmly. "Besides, Hannah and I haven't had any quality time together lately, have we?" He cooed this last part to the rosy-cheeked baby.

Charlotte rolled her eyes, but kissed the baby's cheek. "She had a late nap today, so she should be happy for a while yet."

The door to Quinn's bedroom was propped open. "Can we come in?" Thomas called. He didn't wait for an answer before carrying Hannah in. Quinn was sitting on the couch with her back to Linnea, who was gently pulling a comb through her damp hair. They both looked up at him curiously, the word *we* probably having caught them by surprise.

Quinn's eyes lit up when she saw the infant.

"How's your arm?"

She made a face. "The feeling is starting to come back."

He frowned. "Did Will bring you something for it?"

"No, but Mia knew where my bottle was from last time. She just left here a couple of minutes ago to take our dinner dishes down."

Thomas nodded. Of course Mia would have already taken care of it. That girl was amazing. "So are you feeling up to some baby kisses?"

"Always," Quinn answered, holding out her arms for the baby, though her right one didn't make it nearly as far as the left.

Thomas smiled, and set Hannah down right in Quinn's lap.

"Mmm... she smells good." Quinn said, pressing her nose to Hannah's hair.

"She just had her bath; now she has that clean-baby smell to her."

"You gave Hannah a bath, and didn't bother to clean yourself up?" Linnea asked, appraising his shirt and shorts, which were still caked in dust and spattered with drops of blood.

"What? I think it makes me look roguish."

Linnea rolled her eyes. "You'd think you looked roguish if you were wearing a dress."

"Wouldn't I?" he asked, batting his eyelashes. "I'd need lipstick, though."

"You're hopeless."

"True story."

"She's grown," Quinn said, after she had played with the baby for several minutes, "but not as much as I expected she would have." She looked up at Thomas and Linnea questioningly. "Hasn't it been so much longer here than in my world? How does that work, exactly? I mean last time I was here, you told me that people in this world have longer life spans, but …"

Thomas shrugged. "If you ever figure that one out, let Nathaniel know. He has stressed over it for years. Actually, I don't know that it's accurate to say that our life spans are longer, because we really seem to age at the same rate. It's just that more days pass in our world for the same amount of aging."

"What do you mean?"

"Well, look at William and Nathaniel. They both spend significant amounts of time in both worlds, and physically they've aged the same amount they would have in either place. Hannah here is the same size she would be if she had spent this time in your world. It's just that more days have passed here."

"Wow. How is that even possible?"

"Who knows? How is anything possible?" William's voice startled her. She hadn't seen him come into the room. "How can two entirely different worlds exist together in the first place? Maybe the days here are really that much shorter and they just feel like they're about the same length because we can't directly compare. Time is a strange concept in the first place. Why would the rules for time in your world apply to ours?"

Quinn's eyes were wide, but Thomas and Linnea only laughed. "Be careful listening to him for too long, Quinn. You'll find yourself holding on to the floor because he'll have you convinced that there's no way to know that anything is real." Thomas grinned.

She sort of understood him though. "What you mean is, nobody really knows, right? Even though our worlds are so different, in many ways they're the same, or at least the people in them are."

"How is your arm?"

"It's … okay." She was caught off-guard by the question; he had looked like he was going to say something in response to her.

"Is it still numb?"

"A little, but it's kind of starting to hurt. I can't take more ibuprofen yet, though. It hasn't been six hours."

He nodded, gently lifting up the short sleeve of her shirt and scrutinizing the bandage. He touched lightly around the edges of the tape, raising goose bumps down her arm. "You'd be okay taking one more. It's going to hurt more than last time did. It's a lot more stitches. Once you can feel it all the way, you can put ice on it too. I'm sure Mia will bring some up for you."

After Thomas took Hannah back to his mother, he made his way back to his room. William wasn't there, which didn't surprise him. He was probably in the laboratory attached to the castle clinic, working on one of his numerous projects. Depending on how upset Will still was, there was a good chance that Thomas wouldn't see him before he went to bed.

As he walked toward his dresser, he reached into his pocket and retrieved the object he had purchased today from one of the jewelry vendors. Well, perhaps *purchased* wasn't the right word. The man had looked startled when he'd recognized Thomas at his stand. He'd tried, a little too hard, to direct Thomas' attention to a small case of expensive-looking rings, but Thomas had already caught sight of the necklace he now held in his hand.

The man had mumbled something about having recently discovered the item was a fake – a replica, and then he'd told Thomas to go on and take it. By the time Thomas had reached Linnea, across the square, he'd turned back and the man had disappeared, his market stall empty.

He held the chain up in front of him, and the pendant dangled, catching the light from the lamp. That was what had caught his attention earlier, a glint of sunlight reflecting off the silver charm.

It was a gift pendant, given to a child of royal blood at the time of his or her Naming Ceremony. Thomas reached automatically for the silver pendant at his own neck, and rubbed his thumb against the etched surface. Where his pendant bore a heart, the symbol for his gift – grace – this pendant showed the sign of the healer, the ameliorosa flower.

Even tarnished as it was, he could tell it was real. The chain was cheap, and too clean and shiny to have been on the pendant for long, but the actual charm was as genuine as the one around his neck. Now, he took a clean cloth and polished the pendant, so that he could examine it more closely.

When he could finally read the tiny letters engraved near the bottom of the circle, he gasped. Lily Elise Rose was the maiden name of one of his cousins; she was the fourth-born child of one of his father's younger brothers. She had married a fourth-born healer from the Philothean royal line, and moved to a small village in Philotheum quite some time ago, long enough ago that their two young children had both been born there.

Nathaniel had been working with Lily and her husband, Graeme, as they established a medical clinic in their village there.

How would her pendant have ended up in a market stall in Bay Run? They hadn't visited since Sarah's Naming Ceremony. They had sent kind regards and a gift for Hannah's Naming, but Graeme's sister had been full-term in her own pregnancy at the time, and both Lily and Graeme had wanted to be there for the birth of that baby.

He couldn't make it make sense. Perhaps they had already traveled near the capital city and were staying with relatives? Maybe she had dropped it along the way, and some wayward thief had picked it up? It had to be something like that. Certainly, *she* wouldn't have sold it. It still didn't sit right with him, but he decided he would just return it to her and ask about it when she arrived for the wedding.

THE WEDDING

"How are you beautiful ladies doing?" Thomas asked, walking into Linnea's room. "Anyone need any more help?" He looked around at the flurry of activity in the room. Quinn, Linnea, and Rebecca were all here, getting dressed and ready for the wedding. Mia was standing behind Rebecca, doing something to her hair.

With Rebecca sitting down in the form-fitting dress she was wearing, Thomas could see something he had been suspecting: a tiny bump was forming between her hips. He smiled. Rebecca caught his gaze and followed it. Her cheeks flushed slightly pink as she gave him a glare he would dare not disobey today. "Actually, Thomas, since you're just standing around, would you please fetch my wrap for me? I accidentally left it on the bed in my room."

"I can get it, Master Thomas, there is no need for you to ..."

"It's not a problem, Mia," he interrupted her. "You have enough to do, and I have time. I'll be right back."

He hurried down the hallway, still grinning. He wondered if he would soon be meeting his first niece or his first nephew.

Knowing his sister, she hadn't yet shared her news so she wouldn't detract from Simon and Evelyn's big day. Rebecca had been the first of his siblings to marry, and now there would be a grandchild for his parents. He wondered how long it would take Simon and Evelyn to produce an heir.

Thomas found Rebecca's wrap easily, lying on the bed exactly where she had said she'd left it. The bathroom door in the apartment was closed, but even as thick as it was, he could hear Howard's deep voice as he sang to himself in the shower. He chuckled.

He was walking down the hall back to Linnea's room when he heard footsteps behind him. He glanced around, and then quickly wished he hadn't.

"Thomas!"

Gavin was several years older than Thomas was, though he didn't usually behave like it. He was the son of one of Charlotte's older brothers. Like Thomas, he was a fifth-born, but Thomas liked to think that was where the similarities ended.

"Hello, Gavin."

"Letting those girls use you as their servant-boy again?" Gavin asked, eyeing the purple fabric in Thomas' arms.

It wasn't easy, but he managed to restrain himself from sighing out loud. "I try to help where I can." He tried reminding himself that Gavin was the youngest of five boys and didn't have any experience with sisters, but it didn't help much.

"So, after the wedding, are you still going to be tied up doing girly things with your sisters, or will you be up for meeting some real girls?"

"You know me, Gavin. I wouldn't know what to do with a real girl if I found one. Have fun, though."

"I don't know about *that* Thomas. I heard you've got that Quinn girl here with you in the castle again. Surely, you'll be keeping her entertained tonight. Or is she free?"

110

Thomas' blood ran cold for a split second before it began to warm up again – violently. "Watch your words, Gavin."

Gavin chortled. "Or?"

"Or we'll watch them for you." He hadn't heard Maxwell approaching, but his older brother now stood behind him.

"Take it easy now, Max. It was just a little friendly man-talk."

Gavin always had been a coward when he was outnumbered.

"Let's just agree to keep that kind of 'man-talk' outside the castle then."

"Of course."

"Thanks, Max," Thomas said, when Gavin had disappeared down the hall. "Not that I couldn't have handled him, but it's probably better I stay clean for the wedding."

"Probably," Maxwell chuckled. "He's not worth it, anyway."

"No, definitely not."

The late-morning sun was high in the sky as Quinn followed Linnea and climbed into a carriage outside the castle. Thomas lifted Emma, Alice, and Sarah in with them before he latched the door and re-secured the garland of flowers that hung from the outside. They watched as he walked up to the next carriage and climbed inside to sit down next to William. Rebecca and Howard sat across from them.

A long line of identical carriages, all drawn by white horses, stretched out before and behind them. At the very end of the line were two much-larger, enclosed carriages. These were white, with elegant silver trimming, and heavy purple curtains that covered the windows. The first carriage would carry Simon, the groom, and his parents, the King and Queen of Eirentheos.

Inside the very last carriage, already hidden from view, were the bride, Evelyn, and her parents, who would escort her to the wedding dais.

Quinn felt self-conscious, riding amongst the royal children, but Stephen and Charlotte had been insistent that she was welcome among them, that she need not ride further forward in a carriage that carried extended family, mostly people she didn't know.

All at once, the carriages began their procession forward, winding through the front grounds of the castle before passing through the grand stone archway onto the main street of the capital city.

The stone road that stretched between the castle and the church was lined on either side with long garlands of white and purple flowers. Throngs of people stood behind the garlands, waving and cheering. Most of the quaint, stone-and-wood houses had been decorated for the festivities as well. The whole city seemed to have been covered in flowers and purple and silver banners.

Alice sat quietly, her hands folded across the deep purple folds of her dress, but Emma and Sarah both had difficulty staying still. After twice returning the toddler to her seat, and watching her nearly fall as she stood to look over the side of the moving carriage, Linnea gave up and pulled Sarah onto her lap.

Emma, though old enough to know to stay in her seat, was a constant blur of motion. She bounced and kicked her feet, and her head darted from side to side so quickly that it made Quinn laugh. Emma had to see *everything*. After a few minutes, she realized that the bouquet of exquisite purple and white flowers that Emma was holding might not survive until the wedding, so she reached out and took it.

The little girl looked up at Quinn, appropriately abashed, and settled down in her seat.

Linnea raised her eyebrows and chuckled at her little sister. "What do you think? Two minutes?" she asked Quinn.

Quinn snickered. There was entirely too much to see to expect the inquisitive Emma to sit still for a whole two minutes. "Less," she said.

It was much less.

Fortunately for the little girls, the ride through the city to the massive church was short. One by one the carriages wound their way through the crowds of people lining the city streets and stopped at the bottom of stone steps that had been draped with a purple carpet. Quinn accepted help down from a tall guard who was decked out in a full, intricate purple uniform. She recognized the circular royal crest over his heart.

William and Thomas came up to meet Quinn and Linnea. Thomas lifted Sarah into his arms, while Linnea took Emma's hand and William took Alice's. The Rose siblings, plus Howard and Quinn climbed the steps and entered the doors together.

Once inside, the church was nothing like Quinn had been expecting. The sanctuary was an enormous circle with three identical entrances. Each entrance opened onto a wide aisle that led down to the center platform. Most of the curved pews were already filled, save for the first few rows in two of the three sections. She followed Linnea and Thomas down the aisle, her cheeks turning pink when she realized they intended her to sit with them in the second row.

In the section to the right of where she sat with the Rose children, sandwiched between Alice and Emma, she recognized some of Evelyn's siblings, whom she had met two nights before at a formal dinner and dance. She smiled at the sudden sense of familiarity -- the bride's family in one section, the groom's in another. Not everything about this wedding would be different from one on Earth.

She glanced over at the third section, which was packed to overflowing – several more rows of people were packed into the space behind the pews, prepared to stand for the entire ceremony. The tall, wooden doors to that entrance had already been closed.

Suddenly, an enormous purple-and-silver banner dropped over the entrance Quinn had just come through, while at the same time, a curtain of purple and white flowers – there must have been thousands of them strung together to create the effect – closed over the remaining entrance. A hush fell over the crowd.

Though she hadn't seen him sitting there – hadn't it just been empty? – A familiar figure rose from the row in front of Quinn and stepped up onto the platform. It was Alvin. He was cloaked in velvet robes of dark purple, accented with silver trim. On his head was an odd square-shaped purple velvet hat, with three silver tassels dangling from the sides and back.

"Dear Ones," he said, his voice ringing out clearly over the now-silent crowd. "We have gathered here together today to celebrate a momentous occasion. The joining of two who have declared their love for and commitment to one another, and who have chosen to seal that bond in the name of the Maker is a monumental undertaking, one whose importance cannot be overestimated. The future of any people, of any kingdom, lies in the hearts of those who come together and create a family. You are here today to witness the combining of two families through the power of love, and from that, the birth of a new family.

It is from the union of these two souls, so dear to the Maker, that the future of your kingdom will spring forth."

He paused, and smiled at the crowd, "And what a glorious future it looks to be!

His pause was longer this time, and the already-quiet crowd somehow grew quieter, almost as if they'd stopped breathing.

"Every morning, the sun rises in the east, in celebration of the new day and the new chance the Maker has granted us. It is a precious reminder of all he has given to us already, and all of his promises to come. From the east, we usher in a new life!"

At these words, the curtain of flowers parted in the middle, revealing Evelyn, resplendent in a flowing purple gown, a silver tiara atop her dark, rippling curls. A low note rose within the crowd, and soon grew into a beautiful melody as the entire cathedral filled with song, a thousand voices singing in unison while Evelyn's parents led her slowly down the aisle.

The voices, raised in celebration of sunrise, and the one who provides it, tapered off slowly, ending just as the bride reached the platform. Her parents gripped her hands tightly, tears running freely down both of their faces. Evelyn turned and kissed her father, and then it was her mother's turn. Together, they wrapped their daughter in a fierce hug, an unbreakable circle. When they finally parted, the tears had ended. Each parent took one of their daughter's hands, and they walked together up onto the dais.

"In the middle of the day comes a point when the sun is at its zenith. It is the time when the sun's heat is strongest, often the most trying and difficult time, but also the time that the most light and life emanate from it. If we can endure this fire, it will refine us, strengthen our crops and our souls, it will make us who we were meant to be.

We must take this new life, and bring to it the strength to endure, to change, to grow, to become something greater than what it started as."

The great purple curtain opened, and there was Simon. He stood one step ahead of his parents. A long, purple robe trimmed with silver fur hung from his shoulders, the heir's crown was atop his head. His face was solemn at first, but as he looked down at the platform where his bride stood between her parents, he broke into the biggest smile that Quinn had ever seen.

It was with that same feeling of joy that the crowd broke into song again, this time a song of strength, of trial, of triumph. It ended as Simon reached the platform with his parents. King Stephen laid a hand on his oldest son's shoulder, and Simon turned to face him, and then knelt low in front of him. As he knelt, his father pulled a delicate silver circle from within his robes. From where she sat, Quinn could see tiny purple gems embedded in the silver.

King Stephen placed the circle on his son's head; it rested perfectly just inside the heir's crown. When the band was in place, Simon rose, and his father wrapped him in a hug before turning him over to Charlotte.

There were no tears on Charlotte's face. Her gray eyes were alight with joy and pride as she embraced her son. The happiness emanating from Simon and his parents was so obvious and overwhelming that Quinn could feel it rising up in her own chest. She glanced over at the rest of the Rose children. Even tiny baby Hannah seemed to be grinning.

King Stephen and Queen Charlotte took the hands of their first-born son, their heir, and led him up the steps where his bride stood, waiting for him. They paused as Simon knelt before Evelyn and kissed her fingers tenderly. Then they and Evelyn's parents walked to the back of the platform, where four cushioned chairs were waiting for them – four seats of honor where they could witness their two families becoming one.

13

THE RECEPTION

Thomas smiled and waved as the procession of carriages wound its way back from the church to the castle. The streets were swollen with well-wishers and friends. Simon and Evelyn's wedding ceremony had been beautiful, and Thomas could not remember when he had been more proud of his oldest brother. Evelyn was a kind, intelligent woman, and she and Simon appeared to be an excellent match. He couldn't wait for the chance to get to know his new sister better.

He had been looking forward to the wedding and the party afterward for ages. He'd been especially excited since he had known that Quinn was going to be there. Now that it was here, though, he was worried that he was going to be too distracted to enjoy it.

Lily's pendant sat in his pocket, feeling heavier with each moment that passed. She and Graeme had not been among the massive number of out-of-town guests that had been arriving at the castle in the last few days. He had managed to keep it at the back of his mind until they weren't at the dinner party the night before last. All of the excuses he had been making to himself about how the necklace could have ended up in the market stall no longer made any sense. If he didn't see her at the wedding party ...

He hadn't wanted to share his concerns with his parents or older brothers, still holding on to the hope that he would find her at the party today and there would be a reasonable explanation.

He would have talked to William about it, but his brother was being so … *pig-headed* about the whole Quinn thing that he had barely been around. He had been spending most of his days in the main medical clinic in the city, though one morning he had gotten up early and headed all the way to Mistle Village without telling anyone where he was going.

Thomas had tried to reason with him, but William was adamant that they were putting the girl in danger by "encouraging" her to be here. He'd rolled his eyes at that one – Quinn was fine. William said that the girl didn't know what she was getting herself into, straddling the fence between the two worlds and that she was going to regret it.

Thomas had stopped listening to William's litany of reasons for limiting his contact with Quinn after about five minutes. His brother might be fooling himself, but Thomas had seen the look on his face when he realized what Quinn was about to do in that tree. He also heard the tone in William's voice whenever he mentioned Zander Cunningham – which had been often since the first time he had come back from Bristlecone after Quinn's last visit.

No, none of William's behavior had anything to do with protecting *Quinn*. Even now, sitting beside him, Will's eyes were on the girl in the carriage behind theirs, although he probably didn't even realize it.

Quinn had always thought that the back gardens were the most beautiful part of the castle grounds, but today they

118

astounded her. Giant purple and white cloth banners hung over the entire patio area, creating a sort of tent that shaded the party from the sunny day in the places that weren't already protected by the shade from the many large trees. Long garlands of the exquisite white and purple flowers wound their way around the trees.

Small, round tables dotted the patios, draped in purple and topped with bouquets of pretty white roses. The smell in the air was intoxicating. A small orchestra had begun playing light, lively music, and the enormous white gazebo was now a dance floor.

The little girls had run off to join the throng of children as soon as their feet had touched the ground.

"They're not excited," Quinn said, grinning at Linnea.

"They're just glad to be running around after all of that sitting and trying to be still."

"I know the feeling," said Thomas, coming up behind them. "Ready to dance, Quinn?"

"Nobody's dancing yet," she said, looking up into the empty gazebo.

He shrugged. "Somebody has to be first." He took her hand and started walking toward the steps. She didn't object.

Between Thomas and Linnea, the dancing was going strong in no time. At the dinner party the other night, Quinn had been surprised to realize that she still remembered many of the dance steps she had learned on her first visit. Today, she found that not only was she starting to get good at some of them, but that she was truly enjoying herself.

She partnered with Thomas the most, but she danced with nearly everyone else as well – Maxwell, Howard, several cousins she didn't know well, and after dinner, she even took turns with Joshua and Daniel, the next two siblings in line after Linnea. The only person she hadn't danced with was William.

Ever since the day she had gotten hurt, William had been utterly kind and polite to her, but she had felt the distance. He stopped by her room once a day to check on her arm, but always when both Thomas and Linnea were there, and he never stayed for more than a couple of minutes. She hadn't seen him much otherwise. Even the other night at the big dinner party, they had only danced together for a moment during one of the large group dances.

It was getting on her nerves.

She knew he had been upset over the treehouse incident. In the short time she had known him, she'd gotten to know him well enough to understand that he reacted that way to things that scared him and were outside of his control, so she had given him some time to calm down. It had been six days, though, and it was time for him to be over it. Quinn would be going back home the day after tomorrow, and she didn't want things to feel this way between them there.

Her edginess had been exacerbated by Thomas. Something was up with him as well, and she couldn't figure out what it was. She didn't think it had anything to do with her – when he was spending time with her and Linnea; his abstraction would often disappear for awhile. She would see it come back, though, whenever he had time to think. Today, however, the little crease between his eyebrows had grown substantially, and it hadn't faded at all, even as he laughed and danced.

When Thomas finally stepped down from the gazebo and walked over to get a drink, she followed him.

"What's going on?" she asked him.

"What do you mean?" his tone was too innocent.

She shook her head and raised an eyebrow at the same time. Then she waited.

Thomas blinked, surprised for a second before he recovered. "It's nothing, really. I'm just a little distracted."

"By?"

"I've been looking for a cousin of mine, and her family, but they're not here like I expected they would be."

"Oh." She paused, thinking. "You've been distracted all week about your cousin when you didn't know she wouldn't be at the wedding until today?" She frowned, concerned. "I realize it's probably none of my business, and you can tell me if it's not, but are you okay?"

Thomas smiled and put his hand on her shoulder – careful to touch only her left shoulder, since the right one still bothered her – "I'm fine. I'll tell you more about it later, but yes, I have been hoping to see Lily all week."

"Lily?" A young man whom Quinn vaguely recognized interrupted their conversation. He was older than Thomas, probably by a few years -- or cycles -- or however time was measured here. She wasn't sure exactly who he was, but there was a look in his eyes that made her instantly wary. Thomas quickly positioned himself between Quinn and the newcomer.

"Isn't she still off in Philotheum in one of your brother's little clinic projects? Why would she be here?"

"I'm not following you, Gavin. How would Lily's work in Philotheum have anything to do with whether she would attend Simon's wedding?"

"Are you so sheltered, Thomas, that your father and your older brothers share nothing with you? Even I, lowly 'royal cousin' that I am, have heard the rumors about the accusations the king has leveled against the healers of Philotheum. Lily is one of those healers – you really think she would dare to show her face here?"

Thomas stood, unmoving as he processed the words. Quinn remembered Gavin now. The first time she had ever seen him he had been chatting it up with Tolliver at the dinner party she had attended before Hannah's naming ceremony. A shiver ran down her spine at the thought of Tolliver. She had no idea what was going on here, but she was certain of one thing already – she didn't trust Gavin.

"Really, Thomas, you should spend more time acting like a man. Maybe you wouldn't be so clueless about such important matters." Gavin tilted the last of his drink into his mouth before setting the dirty glass on the table next to the full ones and walking away.

Quinn raised her eyebrows at Thomas.

"I don't know," he said, answering her unspoken question. "He's lying, you know."

"Well, it's Gavin. Obviously he's lying; I just don't know how much or about which parts."

She sighed. "What can you do about it tonight?"

He reached over and pulled Gavin's glass from the table, and walked the two feet to a tray full of used ones. Then he held out his hand to Quinn. "Shall we dance?"

14

AN ARGUMENT

Quinn awoke the next morning before the sun was even up. The strange dreams that frequently plagued her hadn't been a problem when she had first come back to Eirentheos, but they had returned with a vengeance a couple of nights ago. She couldn't remember what had happened in the dream, but she couldn't shake the odd, heavy feeling of it when she woke. It felt like she was forgetting to do something important, or that she was late for something, but she didn't know what.

She lay in bed for awhile, trying to fall back asleep, but the harder she tried, the more awake she became. Besides, her arm was starting to ache and itch again, and she was hungry, so she got up and headed into her bathroom to get ready for the day.

This second visit to Eirentheos had turned out very differently than her first. She had spent most of her time here in the castle with the family. She was much more comfortable here than she had ever imagined she could be. Stephen and Charlotte were so welcoming and accommodating; they treated her as if she belonged. Everyone did, except perhaps William.

Once she was dressed, she opened her door and quietly walked down the hall, which was still dark except for the nightlights every few feet along the floor. Next to one of the children's playrooms here in the family's quarters, there was a large common room where members of the family often gathered to spend time together, to chat and play games. This was Quinn's destination, for this room also contained a small kitchen area.

Aside from her own bedroom, the common room was her favorite room in the castle. It was filled with comfortable chairs and couches. Enormous bookshelves held games and hundreds of books. It felt homey in there, and casual, a place where everyone just hung out and laughed a lot.

The dark and silent corridors had indicated to her that she was the only one awake in this part of the castle, so she was surprised to see lights on when she opened the door to the common room. William was there, setting a kettle of water on the small, wood-burning stove, which was already bright and hot.

As soon as she saw him she had to fight an overwhelming urge to turn around and head back to her bedroom, but he heard her enter and turned around. "Good morning."

"Morning."

"Would you like some tea?"

"Um, sure. Thank you." She had never felt this awkward around him before; this was the first time she'd been alone with him since she had gotten hurt and he'd started acting so weird.

"Why are you up so early?"

"I couldn't sleep."

"No?" A look of concern flitted across his face. "Is everything okay?"

The bubble of irritation that filled her then chest startled her; he always spoke to her in a polite and caring manner, despite the increasing distance she could feel between them. "Yes, everything is fine. Why are you up already?"

He frowned; her voice must have betrayed her. "I'm usually up this early. I was going to head out to Cloud Valley in a little while."

She raised her eyebrows. "That's a long trip for one day." Cloud Valley was several hours away on horseback; it would take him much of the day just to get there.

"Yes. I was planning to stop in Mistle Village for a couple of hours, and then make it to Cloud Valley by evening. I'm actually glad to see you; I was going to check on you again before I left, since I won't see you again until Monday at school."

So, he was just going to be gone for the rest of her visit? He wasn't even planning on going back to the gate with her tomorrow? The bubble grew, threatening to explode ...

"What is going on with you, William?"

"What do you mean?"

"I *mean*, ever since I got hurt you've been treating me like I barely exist. You haven't even been spending time with Thomas or Linnea, and I *know* you usually spend all of your time with them, so clearly it's because they've been with me. You never even danced with me yesterday at the wedding – I barely even saw you the entire day. Now, you're taking off and I won't see you again while I'm here. It feels intentional. So what is it? What did I do to make you mad or whatever your issue is?"

His eyebrows furrowed. He studied her face, looking like he was trying to decide something. Then he sighed. "You're right. I have kind of been avoiding you."

"Kind of?"

"Okay, I have been. But it isn't because I'm mad at you or that I think you did something wrong."

"Then what is it?"

"It's just … I don't think this is a good idea, Quinn."

"You don't think what is a good idea?"

"You coming here, going back and forth between my world and yours."

The bubble suddenly burst, turning into a heavy, sticky glob in her ribcage. She was shocked at how much his words hurt, at the sudden lump in her throat, and at the faint stinging in the corners of her eyes.

"Oh." She turned away, hiding her face.

She heard a sudden intake of breath. His voice changed instantly. "That's not what I meant, Quinn. I don't mean that I don't want you here, or that I don't enjoy your company. I actually do."

Still reeling, she sank into one of the big, comfortable chairs as she pondered this. "Then what do you mean?"

"I mean that this is serious stuff you're playing around with here, Quinn, having one foot in each world. It's real, and it will affect your life. You already lied to your mom to come here. And where exactly does Zander think you are this weekend?"

Quinn was silent.

"That's what I thought. And there are real people on this end, too, Quinn. Thomas and Linnea. My little sisters are becoming quite attached to you. How do you think this is going to end? A year from now, in your world, you're going to graduate from high school, go to college, and maybe get married not long after that." He carried over a large mug of tea and set it down on the table next to her before sitting down in a chair across from her. "What's going to happen then?"

She picked up the mug and sipped at the hot, sweet liquid, contemplating his words.

"I don't know," she said, finally.

"Exactly."

"Exactly what, William? Because I don't know how every single thing is going to work out in the future means I shouldn't make friends and enjoy spending time with people now?"

"But what is the point, Quinn? You're building up all of these relationships and friendships that you can't keep. You're going back through the gate tomorrow. What are you going to do? Keep risking yourself by lying to your family and your friends to come back here? And why come back at all? Just to prolong the inevitable farewell?"

She sat back deep in her chair, pulling her knees up in front of her and resting her cup on them. "So, are you asking me what the point is of caring about people if I'm not going to get to see them every day for the rest of my life?"

"Try ever again, Quinn. When you walk through that gate tomorrow, there's a good chance that you will never see any of these people ever again. Why put yourself through that? Why make them care about you and then put them through that?"

"Maybe it's worth it to me, William. If tomorrow is the last time I ever see Thomas, I'm not going to regret having known him. For the rest of my life there is going to be this part of me that is different because of him. And you. I've seen you at school every day for the past how many years, and I'm only just now getting to know what an amazing person you are. I don't feel like I'm losing out on something just because I might not get to see you all of the time once you leave Bristlecone. What I really feel like is that I've lost all of these years we could have had that connection."

William looked taken aback.

"And what is the point of *that*? What is the point of spending all of these years in Bristlecone completely locked up inside of yourself? You spend so much energy keeping yourself from everyone, sharing nothing. What does it accomplish? You don't have to miss them when you leave? Is that really worth all the time you've had to spend alone? You're right. When I leave Eirentheos tomorrow, I may never come back, but I still don't think I've wasted my time. For all the *years* you've spent in Bristlecone, what are you going to take with you when you leave? A few hundred books worth of knowledge that Nathaniel could have carted back with him through the gate?"

"That isn't fair, Quinn. You don't understand the sacrifices I've made – the sacrifices you would have to make if you keep going back and forth, trying to be part of two worlds. It isn't easy trying to live a secret life. These people you claim to care about, Quinn? You're lying to them. You've lied to your mother. What kind of relationship are you thinking you're going to have with a boyfriend you're already lying to? Are you going to run off and marry someone that you can never share some big part of your life with?"

Quinn's mouth fell open. It took several long sips of tea to recover. "I don't like the lying part."

"Kind of hard to build relationships based on lies, isn't it?"

She didn't answer.

"This is what I mean. There are a lot of things you are not considering, and it will affect your life. This is real."

She sat there in her chair, letting his words sink in before she answered. "Shouldn't it be my choice, either way?"

"Do the choices you make only affect you?"

"Of course not. Just like yours don't, William. You've been avoiding me all week hoping that it was going to result in me making a particular choice. Do you think that didn't affect anyone else? You could have been spending that time with your family who loves you and wanted to be celebrating and having fun with you. Instead, you were trying to force everyone into choosing what you thought was best. Did it work? Was it worth the cost?"

His mouth opened, and then closed again.

"You're free to make whatever choices you want. *I* would like it if we could be friends, regardless of what ends up happening. You could be the one person in Bristlecone I could talk to without lying, you know. And I could be someone you don't have to hide yourself from, if you just didn't waste all of this time trying to control things you can't."

"And then what? We go our separate ways in a few months when I graduate high school and pretend it never happened?"

"No, William. We don't ever pretend it never happened. I don't know what is going to happen in the future, nobody does. People go their separate ways all the time, but it doesn't mean that the friendship just never happened. It will never not mean something."

She swallowed hard. "My dad died when I was three. Just because I can't see him now, does that mean it never happened, or that I should pretend that it didn't? He loved me, and that still means something, it always will. It's never a waste of time to care about somebody."

William sighed, staring into his teacup. "So what do you propose, Quinn?"

"I say we should be friends. You stop avoiding me, and we talk to each other – no lying and no hiding. Whether I ever come back to Eirentheos, or I just see you in Bristlecone. We've already been through too much together to pretend that it doesn't matter. As far as the rest of it, whatever happens will happen."

He sighed again, and then nodded. "Okay."

"Okay what?"

"We'll be friends."

15

THE GATE

Quinn felt like her second trip to Eirentheos had been much shorter than her first. It seemed like she had only just arrived; it couldn't possibly already be time to leave, but it was. She spent the last day with the family in the sunshine, enjoying a picnic lunch and a friendly game of crumple. She was gaining some skill at the game, though Thomas had made a point of babying her injury – going so far as to make Linnea switch out with him to be on Quinn's team when he noticed Linnea using Quinn's bum arm to her advantage.

After several rounds of teary good-byes, she had mounted Dusk and followed Thomas and Storm onto the path. Her warm clothes and heavy winter coat were packed inside her backpack in one of the saddlebags. Already, she was dreading the return to freezing cold temperatures.

Dusk's other bag was loaded down with medical supplies and necessities. Once Quinn was back in Bristlecone, Thomas was going to spend the night in Mistle Valley before traveling to Cloud Valley in the morning to meet up with William. Usually, the brothers were inseparable when William was home; Thomas traveled everywhere with him. She knew that Thomas had stayed behind at the castle just for her, which made her feel a small twinge of guilt – her presence was depriving the brothers of valuable time they would have been spending together.

On horseback, the ride from the castle to the gate was short, they would have arrived at the bridge well before sunset even if they hadn't allowed the horses to run a couple of times, chasing one another and laughing.

Dismounting Dusk was hard. Quinn walked up by the mare's face and stroked her silky, gray neck, trying to swallow the lump in her throat.

"Did you enjoy yourself here?" Thomas smiled over at her, the late afternoon sunlight reflecting off his short, black curls.

"How could I not? Your family is so sweet and wonderful, I feel like I've been spoiled for ten days."

"Good. That was the idea." His gray eyes twinkled, as they usually did, though she had a sudden inkling that something wasn't quite right.

"Is everything okay?" She watched his face as she pulled her backpack out of Dusk's bag, relieving her horse of some weight.

"Sure – aside from the fact that you're leaving."

Quinn rolled her eyes, setting the backpack down at the base of the stone steps. He was grinning at her, but something was definitely amiss. "Did you ever figure out what Gavin was lying about, or what's going on with your cousin?"

Thomas' entire expression changed; she had hit on something. He stared at her, studying her face.

"What?" she asked. "What is it?"

After another long silence, Thomas reached into his pocket and slowly pulled out an object. It was a chain – no, a necklace of some sort, with a silver circle hanging from it …
She looked up at him, confused. "Your pendant?"

132

He shook his head. "Not mine," he said, pulling his own out from under his shirt to show her.

She didn't understand.

"It's my cousin's — it's Lily's. She's the one I was looking for at the wedding."

"Why do you have it?" This was the strangest conversation she had ever had with him. She had no idea where he was going with this.

"I found it."

"Where? At the wedding?"

"No. When we were in Bay Run on market day, one of the vendors was selling it from his jewelry stand — he disappeared as soon as he realized I knew what it was. I'm sure much of what he was selling was stolen items, or things he bought from disreputable sources."

Quinn frowned. "Wait. That doesn't make any sense. Didn't you say she lives in Philotheum?"

He nodded.

"Then how would it ... How do you know it's hers?"

Thomas held out the small pendant and set it gently in Quinn's hand. He pointed to the tiny words engraved near the bottom of the circle.

"I don't suppose there's another Lily Elise Rose somewhere?"

"Who's a fourth-born from the Eirenthean royal line? No."

Quinn looked closely at the silver design. Above Lily's name was an engraving of a flower she couldn't identify, though the same one appeared on William's pendant. She flipped it over and was surprised to find that the reverse side was blank. "Where's the design that's supposed to be on this side?"

Thomas reached for the pendant around his own neck and rubbed his thumb softly against the circular pattern. "The royal

133

seal only appears on your pendant if you are a direct child of the king, or his firstborn. My siblings and I all wear the seal, but only Simon's children will."

Quinn raised her eyebrows, "There are so many things I don't know about your world."

He shrugged, "I'll bet it pales in comparison to what I don't know about yours."

"Maybe ... so how are you thinking Lily's locket found its way to a market stall in Eirentheos?"

"I don't have any idea. At first, I thought it had to be something simple, like that they were in town for the wedding, and maybe ... I don't know. Theft is somewhat uncommon in our kingdom, but obviously it happens."

"But then she wasn't at the wedding," Quinn said, understanding.

"Right. She hasn't come back to Eirentheos at all in quite some time."

"Then how could the pendant possibly have gotten here by itself?"

"That's the problem I'm having."

Quinn frowned. "Maybe it's a fake?"

"No, that's next to impossible. Besides, I don't think I'd be any less concerned if that was the case."

She nodded, absently pulling her fingers through Dusk's mane, until the horse turned and nuzzled her hand, looking for a treat. Thomas pulled out an apple to toss to Quinn, but Dusk snagged it in mid-air, and then crunched it, looking pleased with herself. Thomas grinned.

"Maybe she lost it or it was stolen a long time ago when she lived in Eirentheos, and it's just now turned up?"

"I was going to go with an explanation like that, just hope that it was something simple – and maybe it is. Probably it is. Really, it was probably stolen in Philotheum and just somehow made its way here, although a common thief would be quite crazy to steal a royal pendant. There isn't much of a market for them, and they're so identifiable. But then …"

Her intuition flared – Thomas was right, there was something to this. "Then there was Gavin at the wedding."

"Exactly. I know he doesn't know what he's talking about – he never does – and I also know that he wasn't telling the truth, even about what he might know …"

"What did he mean, anyway, about 'accusations against healers in Philotheum,' or whatever?"

Thomas shrugged. "I really don't know. It could be all made up, but if I had to guess, I would imagine that there are rumors floating around after the whole shadeweed poisoning thing."

"What kind of rumors?"

"Well, my father took the whole situation very seriously, of course. They have been investigating the source of the poisonings and trying to figure out who was really behind it all. They know it wasn't just that one teacher. Anyway, healers are usually the most knowledgeable about poisons and things like that."

Quinn's eyes grew wide. "Do you think Lily might have been involved with that somehow?"

He looked aghast. "With poisoning children? Definitely not."

"I don't know these people, Thomas. I'm just trying to figure out what you're thinking."

Dusk and Storm had apparently grown tired of standing there as they talked; both of them walked down to the bank of the river for a drink.

"I know. I realize that you've never met Lily, but if you had, you would understand that asking if she was involved in something like that would be the same kind of thing as asking if William was."

Quinn nodded. "Okay, then." She frowned, trying to remember the conversation at the wedding. "So, Gavin said something like she wouldn't dare to come here. Do you think your father has accused her of being involved?"

"That's about as likely as my father accusing William of being involved."

"Okay, have you talked to your father about any of this?"

"I tried to." Thomas had always seemed so confident to her, now his eyes were on the ground as he spoke. "Yesterday morning, I went into his office to ask him about Lily. He said he didn't know why she and her family hadn't been at the wedding, but I could tell there was something about it he wasn't telling me. So, I told him about what Gavin had said."

"How did he respond?"

"He said that Gavin doesn't know what he's talking about – that yes, there is a lot of tension between Eirentheos and Philotheum right now, but that it wasn't something I needed to get involved in." He rolled his eyes.

"What did he say about the pendant?"

The tiniest hint of pink appeared on Thomas' cheeks. "I didn't tell him about the pendant."

Her eyes widened. "Why not?"

"I don't know. I was going to, but then I started getting annoyed that he was keeping something from me, and I left. Later, I almost went back to tell him. I was in the hallway, right near the door to his office when I just got this crazy feeling, like I *shouldn't* tell him, and then I just couldn't." He glanced up at Quinn sheepishly. "Have you ever felt like that?"

She swallowed hard. In fact, she had – exactly once. "Back before I came to Eirentheos the first time, the day I realized that William was the boy I'd almost run over in the street ... I saw him in the hallway, and I just knew it had been him. I turned to my friend Abigail, ready to tell her, and then something stopped me. It was like the words just stuck in my throat and refused to come out."

"Well, that's what it was like for me. So, my father doesn't know about the pendant."

The two of them were silent for a moment, both thinking, remembering. Below them, the river flowed lazily; a soft breeze made the leaves flutter in the trees. The light was starting to change; their shadows were growing longer. Soon, very soon, it would be time to walk back through the gate. She sighed, and started walking slowly toward the base of the bridge. Thomas followed her.

"Do you think there's a reason for it, Quinn? I mean, a reason you not telling your friend about William, and then you ending up coming here, still being able to keep it a secret?" They came to a stop, and Quinn climbed up the first step and leaned against one of the pillars.

"Like it was meant to happen that way or something?"

"Yeah."

"I think anything is possible, Thomas, but I don't really know." She looked at him carefully. There was still something he wasn't telling her. "Why, Thomas? What are you going to do?"

He was standing very close to her, there on the bottom of the bridge. Since she was standing up on the bottom step of the bridge, their heights were almost exactly equal, and his eyes were level with hers. "I'm going to go find her."

"Lily?"

"Yes. I need to see her, talk to her, make sure she's okay. There's something wrong, and I don't know what it is, and I just need to see her."

Quinn blinked, trying to understand. "You're going to go to Philotheum?"

He nodded.

"When?"

"Now."

"What? Tonight? By yourself? It's going to be dark."

"Well, tonight I am going to go to Mistle Village and stay with Jacob and Essie. I'll start traveling tomorrow."

"By yourself?" She asked again.

"Well, with Storm. I'll leave Dusk in Mistle Village."

A shiver ran down her spine. "This doesn't sound like a good idea to me, Thomas."

"I'll be fine. I'm sure Lily is fine, that everything is alright. I just need to see for myself."

"You can't wait for William to go with you? Or talk with your father and see what he thinks?"

"I'll be fine, Quinn." He looked into her eyes with an expression that disconcerted her, threw her off balance, and made her forget the next thing she had been going to say. Suddenly, though she could never figure out how it happened, he was kissing her.

As soon as his lips touched hers, she lost track of everything, she couldn't remember where she was. For a fraction of a second, she wasn't even sure *who* she was. The only sensations she understood were his arms around her, warm, comforting, gentle, his lips tender against hers. And then he stepped back, letting her go.

He reached down for her backpack, placing it on her shoulders while she stood there, half-stunned. "I will be fine, I promise," he said, kissing her again on the cheek. "It's time for you to go."

She stared after him as he walked away, back over to the horses. He mounted Dusk, knowing Storm would follow him anywhere. He didn't look back as he started down the road in the fading light.

As she watched him disappear, a slight wisp of cool air hit her neck, making her shiver. She straightened, realizing what that meant. She fished her heavy coat out of the backpack and put it on before closing her eyes and stepping toward the gate.

16

QUESTIONS WITH NO ANSWERS

The dream was so vivid. She was deep in a forest, surrounded by trees and plants she didn't recognize, and a few she did. Notably, the ground was covered in enormous yellow dandelions. Her hands trembled and her stomach shuddered as she ran. Something was lost, and she couldn't find it. She wasn't alone, but she wasn't sure who was with her, only catching the idea that she wasn't alone. Suddenly, a buzzing sound shook the ground beneath her feet, startling her. Where had it come from? Her heart rate was just beginning to settle when everything vibrated again.

She reached toward the source of the noise, and her hand touched a familiar object. Her cell phone?

"Okay, okay, I'm awake," she muttered, throwing back the covers and flipping open her phone. *Seven new messages?* She didn't usually sleep that soundly. How had she missed the phone buzzing that many times? She scrolled through the list. Four from Abigail and three from Zander. Both of them were apparently suffering from some serious impatience.

Not that she could blame them. Last night, when she had returned from Eirentheos, she had been too shell-shocked to

139

think. She had texted Abigail immediately, as she walked from the bridge back to Nathaniel and William's house to retrieve her car. Abigail deserved that much – to know that she had returned safely. But, of course, her friend had been dying for details, wanting to know where Quinn had been and what the big secret was.

Zander had called and texted several times last night as well, but she hadn't known what she was going to say to him. Finally, she'd sent a text saying that she was back, but that she wasn't feeling well and wanted to go home and rest. Her heart felt heavy telling him that – it felt like the only thing she had said lately that was actually true.

A ringing sound from downstairs startled her. It was a little early to be hearing the doorbell on a Sunday morning. She glanced down at the time display on her phone, and her jaw dropped. How could it be after nine? It had been many, many months since she had slept any later than seven.

There was a soft knock at her bedroom door, and the knob turned quietly. Owen's head appeared around the edge. "Quinn? Are you still sleeping?" his low voice probably wouldn't have wakened her if she had been.

"Yeah, buddy, I am. It's okay, you can come in."

The door swung open all the way. "Abigail is here."

Her eyes grew wide. "Um, okay. You can tell her to come here."

He nodded, studying her face with a serious expression, the kind that sometimes gave her the chills. How did such a young boy understand so much? "Are you okay, Quinn?"

"Yeah, I'm fine."

Owen disappeared into the hallway.

A few seconds later, Abigail came storming into the room, closing the door tightly. "Okay. Spill." She sat down in the middle of the bed, crossing her legs and making herself comfortable.

"I, uh …" Quinn opened her mouth and closed it several times, trying to figure out what she could possibly say. She felt like a fish. There had been one late night in Eirentheos, when she and Linnea had sat up giggling, in their pajamas on Quinn's bed, and the two of them had come up with dozens of possible explanations that she could give Abigail about where she had been. Right now, though, she could not remember a single one.

"Let's start with something simple. Where did you go?"

"I can't tell you that yet." *Or ever*, but maybe she could come up with a better explanation when she'd had time to think.

"Still keeping secrets? Since when have you kept secrets from me? What is going on with you?"

"If I could tell you, Abbie, I would." That was the truth. She felt a sting at the memory of William's words to her. Her lying, and her choice to go to Eirentheos was affecting people she knew and loved at home. She sighed. "It isn't anything bad, I promise. It's just … something I can't explain right now."

"You've got me worried here, Quinn. Especially when you tell me you're off with Dr. Rose and William. Dr. Rose was working at the hospital all weekend, you know. You weren't with him."

Her heart sank into her stomach. Abigail was checking up on her stories now?

The doorbell sounded again from downstairs. Both of their heads turned automatically at the sound.

"Quinn! Quinn!" Annie's excited voice moved quickly through the house. "It's Zander!"

Abigail raised her eyebrows, but Quinn could only shrug. A few seconds later, Zander appeared in the doorway.

"Oh, hey, Abigail. I didn't know you were going to be here." He looked a little startled.

"I just showed up a few minutes ago. Quinn, uh, forgot something at my house last night, and I thought I'd bring it to her while I was out." She stared pointedly at Quinn.

"Yeah. Um, thanks for bringing me my toothbrush. I was going to be missing it."

"Sure. I'll call you later when I get home from my grandma's house."

There was no mistaking the meaning of the glare in Abigail's eyes as she ducked through the doorway behind Zander. Quinn would be paying for this later. She was going to have to work on her story.

"What are you doing here?" she asked.

"I was worried about you. You didn't sound very good last night, and then you weren't answering my texts. I came over to see if there was anything I could do. Are you okay? You're never in bed this late." Zander shifted his weight, looking slightly uncomfortable standing there in the doorway.

Quinn shrugged. "I'm better now. I must have just been really exhausted."

"What did you and Abigail *do* yesterday?"

Did he notice how red her face was turning? "Nothing too crazy. I think it was just a really bad headache."

He frowned, sympathy in his chocolate-brown eyes. He took a step closer to the double bed. "I'm sorry. Is the headache all the way gone now?"

She nodded, pushing back the covers and standing up. Her arm was aching again and she glanced down, breathing a sigh of relief that she'd worn a long-sleeved pajama shirt to bed.

Zander stepped toward her and wrapped his arms around her neck, burying his nose in her hair and inhaling. "I missed you."

Quinn laid her head on his shoulder while a swirl of emotions twisted her insides. "I missed you, too."

He smiled, and kissed the top of her head. "Want to get dressed and I'll take you out for brunch, sleepyhead?"

"Sure."

Quinn nearly slept through her alarm on Monday morning. Somehow the dreams had taken on a whole new dimension. Instead of waking her, she felt locked in, unable even to escape by awakening. She was almost certain she'd seen Alvin in her dream last night, which left her with a shaky feeling as she got ready for school.

She hadn't decided whether she was looking forward to seeing William at school, or dreading it. Ever since their early-morning conversation in the common room, she had been missing his company. She felt like she was really beginning to understand him, and she wanted to see how their friendship was going to change.

On the other hand, she had no idea what Thomas had told him about what had happened at the gate. And what had Thomas even meant by kissing her? Trying to think about what had transpired left her feeling breathless, dizzy, and distracted as she walked out the door, pulled it shut, and turned to walk to her car.

She jumped, startled. Zander was coming toward her up the walkway. "Good morning." His smile was wide.

"Morning. Um, why are you here?"

His face fell slightly; there must have been something in her voice she hadn't meant to put there. "I thought I would surprise you and pick you up to give you a ride. Is that … okay?"

"Of course. Thanks." She stretched up to kiss him on the cheek, and he used his hand to gently guide her lips to his. The intensity of his kiss sent waves of heat running down to her toes.

"I'm supposed to pick up Annie tonight, though," she said, once they finally separated.

"You won't have to. I don't have to work tonight, so my mom's making dinner for everyone this evening. You and Annie can just hang out at our house after school. We'll do your trig."

They reached the school just in time for Quinn to be able to get her things together and make it to her first class on time. She didn't have a chance to look for William in the hallway. Her insides were tied up in knots, and she didn't know what to do. She slid in to her seat next to Abigail, who turned to her immediately, eyebrows raised.

"You never called me back yesterday," her friend accused.

"I know. I'm sorry. Zander hung out the whole day; he even stayed for dinner."

"So everything is all right between the two of you?"

"I told you it was, Abigail. Nothing bad is going on here, I promise."

"It's just so …"

The bell rang, cutting her off, leaving Quinn to wrestle with the conflicting thoughts in her head through the whole lesson.

It wasn't until after her third period class that she first saw William in the hallway. His back was turned, and he was walking quickly away from her. She hurried to catch up with him, glad that this was one time during the day that both Zander and Abigail had classes on the other side of the building.

"William!" she called when she got close.

His pace slowed, but he didn't stop, and he turned his head only barely. "Hey, Quinn. I don't have time to talk right now." He sped up again and disappeared into a classroom.

144

Quinn's heart took on an irregular beat. As distant as William could be sometimes, she had never known him to be so dismissive. She swallowed hard, confusion mixed with guilt chilling her veins. Maybe William had been right. Maybe it was a bad decision to even think about trying to balance friendships in two worlds. She was certainly making a mess of things.

For the rest of the day, she searched for an opportunity to speak to William. She needed to know what Thomas had said to him, if he knew what Thomas had been thinking, or if William was mad at her. She was having trouble concentrating on anything while these questions plagued her. But the chance never came. William seemed more elusive today than he ever had before. She caught only glimpses of him in the hallway between classes, always when she was with Abigail or Zander. He didn't eat lunch in the cafeteria.

By the time Zander drove her to his house that evening, she didn't know what to think. Abigail was still pressing her for answers about what had happened over the weekend. She wasn't going to accept Quinn just blowing it off, and Quinn had no answers for her.

Zander wasn't asking questions, but something had changed between them. He was around all the time. The whole day, he had met her outside of every class he could, carrying her books, and laying his arm protectively across her shoulders. Twice, she'd had to surreptitiously re-position herself to his other side so that he wouldn't rub against her injured arm as they walked.

Her arm was another issue. It was healing, but still sore. Some of the bruises were finally starting to fade from midnight black to a greenish purple, but it still wasn't anything she wanted anyone to see. She needed to talk to William to find out how long she was going to have to keep the stitches in. He had promised to give her some of the salve he'd used on her leg, too, that had prevented her from scarring badly. Even if he was mad because Thomas had kissed her, he was going to have to talk to her sometime.

Tuesday didn't turn out much better than Monday. Abigail had finally laid off on the constant interrogations, but now she was watching Quinn suspiciously, as if she were hiding something.

She still really wanted to talk to William; she was beginning to worry that he was really angry at her, or that he had decided he didn't want to be friends at all, and was just going to shut her out of his life completely. Again, she didn't see him much all day, and he didn't eat lunch in the cafeteria. She couldn't exactly go looking for him, either, with Zander hovering over her protectively and Abigail watching her like a hawk.

When she finished her shift at the library that night without once seeing William, a cold, sick feeling filled her stomach. Was this how it was going to end, then? Maybe Thomas' kiss had been one of good-bye. He had known that it was the last time Quinn would ever visit, ever be part of their lives. She wondered if, after she had talked to William that morning, he had gone and spoken to his brother, convincing him that their connection with Quinn really was a bad thing. Suddenly, her time with Thomas at the gate began to take on an entirely new meaning in her mind.

When she stepped outside and saw Zander's truck, waiting for her by the curb, she nearly burst into tears. She had lied to him, been hiding from him. From *Zander*, who was sweet and wonderful and caring. Who showed up late in the evening with a warm car, so she wouldn't have to drive home on the snow-packed streets. She didn't deserve him.

"What's wrong?" He asked, in a concerned voice when he pulled into Quinn's driveway. She had been quiet most of the way home.

"Nothing. I'm just tired," she looked up at him, trying to smile convincingly.

"Are you sure? You've seemed kind of … out of it, ever since the weekend. Did something happen between you and Abigail?"

This would have been easier if he had been one of those normal boyfriends who worried about sports and their hair. "No, everything was fine on Saturday. I think … I just haven't been sleeping well. I keep having these crazy nightmares." That part was at least true, and could explain some of her behavior this week.

"You didn't tell me that," he said, frowning and putting his arm around her. "What are you dreaming about?"

"It's the same kind of thing every night, but I can't remember very much once I wake up. I'm looking for something I can't find, and I'm lost, and there are trees … and flowers. And then I wake up."

He kissed the top of her head, and put his arm around her, pulling her closer. As he did so, his hand hit just the wrong way on the most sensitive of her healing cuts. She winced.

"What? What did I do?"

"Nothing, I'm okay. I just … I hurt my arm and there's a bruise."

His eyes were wide. "When did you hurt yourself? What happened?" He reached for the zipper of her jacket, putting his hand inside on her shoulder.

"It's nothing. I'm okay. I just fell and banged it up a little." She pulled away and yanked the zipper back up. "I'm freezing."

He looked a little stunned. "Okay. Let's get you inside, then."

He walked her inside, to the entryway, and she turned and stretched up to kiss him. The kiss turned intense more quickly than she was used to; he put his arms under hers and lifted her, deep into his chest. In the living room, Quinn's mom cleared her throat. Zander let her go.

"Um, thanks for the ride."

"You're welcome," he said, running his thumb from her temple to her chin. She shivered.

"Good night."

"Night." He kissed the top of her head.

"Good night, Zander," her mom called.

"Good night, Megan." Zander disappeared through the door while Quinn shrugged off her coat and hung it in the closet.

"How was work?"

"It was good. Not very busy, but there were quite a few new magazines to process, and lots of stuff to put away. It must have been busy earlier." Quinn sat down on the couch, across from her mom who was curled up in one of the big armchairs. A book lay open, upside down, on one of the arms.

"Did you have a good day at school?"

"Yeah, it was fine."

"Good." Her mom smiled. "I feel like I hardly ever see you these days. When you're not at school or at work, you're with Zander."

"You see me. We all just ate dinner together the other night."

"I know. But then everybody's there, and you and Zander are too busy making goo-goo eyes at each other to pay much attention to anybody else."

Quinn's cheeks turned pink. "We are not."

"So, things are going well between the two of you?"

She nodded.

"He always treats you as well as he does in front of me?"

She rolled her eyes. "Mom, it's Zander you're talking about."

"I know. It's so cute to watch the two of you finally getting together like this. He's been picking you up for school every day, hasn't he?"

"How do you even know that?" Her mom was the second grade teacher at Bristlecone Elementary. She left way before Quinn did in the mornings.

"I see him getting ready to come get you when I drop Annie off at Maggie's."

"Right. Yeah, he has been."

"How has everything else been? You're not neglecting your school work for him, are you?"

She shook her head. "School is fine."

"I was glad to see you go off with Abigail overnight last weekend. It wouldn't be good to get so wrapped up in Zander that you forget your other friends."

Quinn gulped. She hoped her face wasn't actually turning as red as it felt like it was. The weight of the lies she was telling everyone was settling like an enormous rock in her stomach. "I know," she said, in as normal a voice as she could manage.

By Thursday, she had made up her mind that William was right. It was entirely impossible to manage a life of lying and hiding things from everyone she knew. Abigail had texted her that morning, saying she was sick, so Quinn might actually have a few minutes to herself during the day. She was going to find William alone sometime, figure out when he could rip the stupid stitches out of her arm, and then she was going to be done with the whole mess. So what if Thomas had kissed her? It didn't mean anything. They didn't even live in the same *world*, for crying out loud. She had been crazy to think she could keep this up.

She was standing at her locker, getting ready for her first class when she saw him across the hall, walking toward her.

"William!" she called.

He didn't even look up. His eyes were on the floor, his lips in a tight line.

"William Rose!"

It was like he couldn't even hear her; he passed right by and disappeared into a classroom. Her stomach muscles clenched, and a swell of irritation rose into her chest. It was all she could do not to follow him and confront him right then, in the middle of his class.

Then, in World History, something happened that took her mind completely off William for a few hours. At the end of class, Mr. Black returned the essays they had turned in on Monday. He walked around the room, setting the papers upside down on the tops of the desk. Quinn flipped hers over and her heart nearly stopped. There, at the top of the paper, where there was almost always an A, with maybe the occasional B+, was a big, red D.

A "D". Never in her life had she received a D on anything. Her face turned shades of purple that she didn't even know it could. How could this have happened? The bell rang while she was still staring at the paper, stunned. Mechanically, she tucked it neatly inside her World History folder, and placed it in her backpack.

That afternoon, Zander drove her to his house, so they could hang out and do homework until it was time for her to go to work at the library. Her thoughts were a tangled mess. She was still stressed about the World History paper. She had been too ashamed to take the paper back out during school and examine it to find out what, exactly had been wrong with it. On top of that, she hadn't seen William again even once during the day.

She was starting to feel like she might explode.

"Is everything okay?" Zander asked. He was sitting next to her on the couch while she tried to read a book of essays for her English class. The words weren't making any sense, though, and she kept having to start over.

"Hmm?" she mumbled, not looking up.

"What's wrong?" His voice was serious now.

She closed the book and looked over at him. "I'm sorry. I've just been really distracted."

He crossed his arms over his chest, and sighed. "Quinn…"

At that moment, Maggie walked through the living room. "Hey guys, how's the homework going?"

"Good. Too much to do." Zander answered.

"That's senior year for you. How about you, Quinn? How is trig going?"

"It's been a lot better with Zander helping me."

Maggie smiled, and then stepped out of the way as Annie and Sophia came barreling down the hallway, giggling wildly. As soon as they saw Zander and Quinn sitting on the couch, they ran over and jumped on them.

"Ow!" Quinn yelled, sudden fire shooting up her arm when Annie accidentally kicked her as she splayed out in Zander's arms, trying to steal the pen he had been using. She realized her mistake immediately, and dropped the hand that had instinctively reached to protect her injury. "Be careful, Annie," she amended, as gently as she could while trying to discreetly rub her aching arm.

It was too late. He eyed her warily, staring at her arm.

They weren't alone again until an hour later, when Zander was driving her to work. He was silent during the ride, and the air felt unnaturally thick. Once the car had come to a stop in one of the parking spaces in the small lot, he looked over at her.

"Let me see your arm."

"Zander, I'm fine."

He raised his eyebrows, waiting.

She sighed, unbuckled the seatbelt, and shrugged out of her coat. Then she pulled up her long sleeve as far as she could. The thick, gauze pads that William had kept taped over her scabs and bruises had grown ratty by Monday. Quinn had just been replacing them with regular band-aids over the stitches themselves, to keep them from rubbing against her clothes.

Zander let out a low whistle. She knew her arm looked worse than it still felt. The deep, black bruises had now all faded to mottled purples and sickly-looking greens. A couple of the abrasions were still scabbed over, though other spots were a healing pink, and the black threads of her stitches were visible underneath one of the band-aids.

"What happened?" He asked through clenched teeth. A deep line had appeared between his eyebrows.

Her heart was racing, and beads of sweat were forming at her temples. "I told you, I fell and banged it up."

He reached over, and gently took her arm, just under the elbow, pulling it closer to him. With his other hand, he carefully lifted up the edge of one of the band-aids.

"When? When could you possibly have done this to yourself?" His voice was strained.

She looked down, stalling while she tried to figure out how many days her cuts had been healing. "About a week and a half ago."

"I'm not understanding this. Where were you? When did you do this? Why didn't you tell me? How? How could you have gone to the hospital and gotten stitches, and I don't even know? What in the hell is going on here?"

Her eyes popped open wide, tears forming in the corners, threatening to spill over. Zander had never talked to her like that before. Her hands were trembling and she was nauseous.

"Quinn!" The look in his eyes changed to one of concern. "Are you all right? You're scaring me here."

As hard as she was willing them to disappear, the tears betrayed her, drizzling down her cheeks in alarming numbers. She didn't know what to do or to say. She didn't have an answer for him.

He slouched in the driver's seat, looking crushed. "Help me out, Quinn. Please."

She tried to think, but she was only growing more nauseous. "I ... I'm sorry Zander. Can we talk about this later? Please? I have to get in to work."

His hands were tight on the steering wheel, she could see white near his knuckles. He didn't look up at her when he answered. "Whatever. I'll be here at nine to pick you up."

She climbed out of the car and closed the door, nearly falling against it as she gulped great breaths of the cold air. She still felt nauseous, but it was subsiding; she probably wasn't actually going to throw up.

It was still light, she noticed. All winter it had been dark or nearly so when she arrived at work. It was March now; the days were growing longer. Concentrating on the feeble light of the sunshine, instead of on the conversation she had just had, she wiped her face against her sleeve, trying to make the tears go away. It wasn't very effective on the waterproof coat, but it was better than nothing.

By the time she walked into the library, she was reasonably calm. After she clocked in, she looked around. There were a few patrons, but nobody needed help. There was a cart stuffed full of books near the desk, waiting for her to re-shelve them. Hoping that would keep her mind occupied for a while, she pushed the cart into the non-fiction section in the back.

She tried not to think about Zander -- every time her thoughts drifted in that direction, her heart rate accelerated – but it was impossible not to. When she heard the main door open only a few seconds after she'd started putting books away, she jumped and went to look, wondering if it was him, if he would be able to go all the way to the end of her shift without talking to her. Half of her hoped that there was no way, because she still didn't know what to say, but the other half just longed to be snuggled in his arms, feeling safe.

It wasn't him, though. The second time the door opened, her heart didn't respond quite so dramatically, but she still went to look. And her heart stopped completely.

It was William.

At the sight of him, several emotions slammed into her at once, with the force of a freight train, nearly knocking her over. She reached him before he was even halfway to his usual table.

"Look, William. It isn't my fault that Thomas kissed me. I have no idea what he was thinking. But you can't just be mad at me and ignore me forever. What in the world is going on with you that you can't even be bothered to say hi or have a friendly conversation with me in the hallway? I thought we were going to be friends. You agreed. You promised. And now, what? You're going to be mad at me forever for something that wasn't even my fault? You're not even going to give me a chance to explain? You're just going to punish me? Not even help me out and take care of my arm? What am I supposed to do?" Tears streamed down her face in earnest, dripping off her chin and landing on the front of her shirt. She couldn't be certain, but she thought her nose was running, too.

William stared at her, looking shocked. He didn't say anything for several minutes, he just stared.

Now that she was up close to him, she noticed for the first time that he didn't look right. His face was paler than she had ever seen it, and there were dark, nearly black circles under his eyes. His eyes themselves were bloodshot.

When he finally spoke, his words were not in response to anything she had said. "Thomas is missing."

The book she had been holding fell to the floor with a resounding thud. A cold chill ran up her spine, making the hair on the back of her neck stand up straight. "What?"

"Quinn? Is everything okay over there?" her boss called to her from across the room.

"Um, sort of. Is it okay if I go and talk to William outside for a minute? He's having an issue he needs some help with." Her voice shook, but a sudden calmness and clarity had overtaken her, and she knew they couldn't finish this conversation inside, where someone could hear.

"Is it anything I can help with?" Sylvia Williams was nothing if not kind and understanding.

"No, it's kind of … private." She didn't know what the older woman would think of that, but she would probably get away with it since the librarian adored both her and William.

"Okay, hon, whatever you need. Let me know if you need anything."

She almost ran to the door, expecting that he would follow. A few seconds later, they were on the front sidewalk.

"What about Thomas?" Was it possible for a brain to explode?

"I … we … don't know where he is. Or at least nobody did when I left Eirentheos on Sunday night."

"What do you mean?" She had never seen William like this, never heard him so upset he couldn't speak clearly.

"I mean … When he didn't come to meet me in Cloud Valley, I just figured that he'd had something else to do, or that he was still mad at me over the way I'd been treating you. Without the birds, there's really no way to send a message …" he paused, trying to catch his breath. Her heart sank into her stomach as she realized that there might be a completely different reason for his behavior this week.

"And then I got back, and everyone was asking me where he was, why he hadn't come back with me, and then we realized. Nobody had seen him or heard from him for eight days. Then Nathaniel went, and he came back here on Tuesday night. Thomas still had not returned. Nathaniel went back again, last night. I've been going out of my mind."

She did the math quickly in her head, her heart speeding in fear. "He still hasn't come back from Philotheum?"

"No, that's what I'm telling you … *wait*. What did you just say?" His face had gone from bone-white to dusky gray.

"Um," she tried to speak, her voice suddenly small, "Just before I left, literally right before I went through the gate, Thomas told me he was going to Philotheum to try and find your cousin Lily."

She really hoped he wasn't going to pass out, because if he did, she had no idea who was going to pick up either of them. Mrs. Williams was tiny.

"He went to Philotheum by himself without telling anybody?"

"He told me."

"And you didn't stop him?"

Her jaw dropped. "How was I supposed to stop him, William? What was I supposed to do? He waited to tell me until the gate was open, and then he kissed me and rode off into the sunset. Literally." Guilt tugged at her insides, though. She could feel panic setting in. She was suddenly overpowered by a familiar feeling – the exact same feeling she'd been having in her dreams every single night. Something was wrong. Very wrong.

"Why didn't you tell me?" He looked stricken.

"When was I supposed to? I've *been* trying to talk to you all week, but you keep blowing me off." The feeling was growing, like a large, heavy balloon slowly filling her chest, making it difficult to breathe.

"What are you talking about? I've barely seen you, and on the rare occasion I do, you're not alone. Or did you want me to let Zander Cunningham in on the secret?"

There wasn't time to argue about this now. Along with the heavy balloon was a sense of urgency. They had to leave *now*. They had to do something. She glanced up at the sky; it was nearly dusk. "Whatever, it doesn't matter right now. We need to go. Right now. We have time to make the gate if we run."

He didn't question her, just followed as she took off at a sprint, his pace matching hers. They wouldn't have to run far; the library was just off the main highway that ran parallel to the river. In a few hundred yards, they would be able to turn onto one of the many hiking trails that intersected each other, and follow one down to the riverbank.

She was so focused on where she was going, what she was doing, that she didn't even register the quick glimpse she caught of a black truck turning left into the parking lot as she and William ran out of it.

MISSING

Quinn and William were well into Eirentheos before the exercise had calmed either of them enough to realize what they had just done. William slowed first.

"What are we doing?"

She stopped, there on the path, and turned toward him. "We're walking to the castle."

"I gathered that part."

She paused, staring up at the nearly dark sky, at the blanket of twinkling stars that were beginning to look just as familiar as the ones at home. "I don't know. I just … We have to do this, we have to find him."

"You just walked out of your world, Quinn. Nobody knows where you are. You left work, right in the middle of a shift."

"I'm aware of that. I was right in the middle of a fight with Zander, too. I didn't even take my coat or my purse. I'm sure the police are there by now. But what, exactly, am I going to do about it right now?"

"Nothing."

"Right. I have ten days to worry about how I'm going to handle *that* situation. So, the only thing we need to think about right now is finding Thomas." She started walking again, quickly.

William kept up with her easily. The lights of the capital city were appearing on the horizon, the dark outline of the castle rising behind. It was a view that Quinn had come to love, peaceful and breathtaking at the same time. On her last trip here, she had stopped several times just to marvel at it. Tonight, she was focused on reaching her destination.

"So, let me get this straight. Thomas walked you to the gate, told you he was going to Philotheum to find Lily, and then he kissed you?"

"Yeah."

"Did he tell you that he hadn't told anyone where he was going?"

"Yes."

"Did you tell him that was a bad idea?"

"Yes, I did."

They walked in silence for several more minutes before William spoke again. "Quinn?"

"Yes?"

"I'm sorry for not talking to you at school, and not telling you what was going on. I was just so freaked out and upset; I don't think I could really concentrate on anything properly."

She stopped again. "I've been there. I'm sorry I didn't track you down, corner you, and make you listen to me, to tell you what I knew about Thomas. I just … I guess I just assumed that he had made it back safe, like he promised he would. And I thought you were acting that way because you were mad at me about Thomas kissing me."

The stress of the situation and the realization of the enormity of what she had just done were beginning to weigh on her. She glanced up into William's tired gray eyes, her bottom lip trembling. "And I thought you had decided we weren't going to be friends after all."

William didn't answer. He just put his arms around her and held her there, her head against his chest while silent tears ran down her face.

When she had finally run out of tears, William pulled his handkerchief out of his coat pocket and handed it to her, to wipe her eyes and blow her nose. "You even carry this when you're in Bristlecone?" she asked, when she was done.

He shrugged. "You never know when you're going to need to offer it to a crying girl."

This made her giggle as she tried to stuff the cloth into the pocket of her jeans.

"Give me that," he said, watching her struggle.

She looked up at him skeptically. "You don't want it."

He put his hand on her shoulder and squeezed it gently. "It's okay." Then he took the cloth and put it back in his pocket. "I have more if you need another one."

They followed the path all the way around the back of the castle, where they could enter the grounds through a small, private gatehouse, generally used only by the family and household servants. Quinn recognized Paul, the guard who was on duty.

"Master William! Miss Quinn! I wasn't told I would be expecting you this evening."

"I didn't tell anyone we would be coming. Has Thomas returned yet?"

Quinn knew, by the heavy expression in the man's eyes, what the answer would be. "No, Master William. We've not heard a word."

William nodded. "Thank you, Paul."

It was dinnertime; they could smell the aromas of the meal before they reached the dining room. Both of them paused outside the entrance, unsure how this was going to go.

"Let me go in first," William whispered.

She nodded. From where she stood she could hear the uproar when William entered the room. The younger children squealed in surprise and ran to surround him. Charlotte ran to her son and embraced him.

Suddenly, Quinn was aware of someone standing very close behind her, and she spun around rapidly, nearly falling over in the process.

Alvin caught her under the elbow and steadied her. "Careful there, Lady Quinn. It wouldn't do to have you injuring yourself at the beginning of your journey."

She looked up at him in surprise, not knowing how to respond. He still had a gentle hold on her arm.

"What are you waiting out here for? It smells like dinner has already been served." Without another word, Alvin guided her into the dining room.

Everyone in the room who had still been seated stood as Alvin and Quinn entered. Stephen and Charlotte looked up at them in surprise; William had not yet had the chance to tell them that Quinn had come with them. She noticed Nathaniel standing with them. Charlotte rushed over to her.

"Quinn! Sweetheart, what are you doing here?"

"I … I had to come."

"William and Quinn need to speak to you in private, Your Majesties," Alvin said, eyeing the throng of younger children surrounding them.

"Of course," Stephen nodded. "Maxwell and Linnea, please help the children finish dinner and then get them upstairs."

Linnea's eyes were wide; Quinn could see dark circles under them. It was clear she wanted to rush over to her and William to find out what was going on, but she obeyed her father and began to guide the younger children back to their seats.

"Let's go to my office," Stephen said, as he began walking out of the room. Charlotte, William, Quinn, Nathaniel, and Alvin followed him silently.

Quinn had never been in Stephen's office before. She was a little surprised by how ordinary it seemed, given that he was a king.

It was a beautiful room, as all of the rooms in the castle were. The floor was laid in a deep, reddish wood that matched the paneling and the big, polished desk. Enormous bookcases filled with books and papers lined two walls of the room, but the other two walls held vast numbers of painted family portraits. Quinn couldn't help smiling at one painting that caught her eye right away. It was of six very young children, recognizable at once. Thomas and Linnea were chubby-cheeked, smiling babies. William, a more serious-looking toddler, was holding his baby brother's hand protectively. Noticing this detail put a hot lump in her throat.

"All right," Stephen said, closing the door once everyone was inside. "What is going on? William, what are you doing here? And why did you bring Quinn?"

She swallowed back the lump, trying to keep herself composed. "He didn't bring me, Your Majesty, I just came."

"Why?" He turned his attention to her.

"She knows where Thomas went."

Every eye turned to her. Stephen's expression went from concerned to aghast. He took a deep breath, and Charlotte, standing by his side, gripped his hand tightly. "Tell us what you know."

Quinn relayed the story for them, just as she had for William, although she left out the part about Thomas kissing her.

Stephen's gray eyes looked almost black with his distress. Charlotte had to sit down. Nathaniel sat next to her, one hand on her shoulder.

163

"Why would he do such a thing?" Charlotte asked. "Why would he risk going into Philotheum now?"

"He doesn't even know how dangerous it is," Stephen said, his voice catching in his throat. "He came to me, just after the wedding, asking if I knew why Lily and Graeme hadn't been there."

"He said he felt like you were hiding something from him; it worried him more." Quinn felt like she might throw up just saying the words, but instinct told her that keeping back any information right now, regardless of how trivial, would not help Thomas.

"I was." Stephen sank into an armchair. He rested his head in his hands.

"Things have changed in Philotheum." Nathaniel spoke now. "Tolliver's father has turned over control of the Philothean army to him."

"So, what does that mean? What difference does that make?"

The king sighed. "Both Tolliver and his father have a very different idea of ruling a kingdom than what has been traditional in both Eirentheos and Philotheum for a long time. They believe we are weak when it comes to handling our people, that ordinary citizens have far too much power and decision-making in our policies. He can't change that in our kingdom, obviously, but he has begun to take more control over the people of Philotheum – or he's trying to, anyway." His voice grew dark at the last words.

"Trying to how?" Quinn asked.

"It's very complicated, there are many new laws, regulations, and taxes, but many of the towns and villages have begun to resist Tolliver's increasing intrusion into their lives. In an attempt to subdue them, Tolliver has greatly increased the size of his army, and many of the villages are living under the occupation of soldiers."

"Including the village where Lily and Graeme live." It wasn't a question; Quinn could see immediately where he was going with this.

"Harber Village, where they live, was one of the first," Nathaniel said quietly. "Graeme sits on the council, and with their connection to Eirentheos, and the fact that they have established a clinic there with our particular beliefs about healing … they were labeled as troublemakers immediately."

"So they didn't come to the wedding because …"

"Yes, because they are not allowed to leave their village, or at least it would be quite dangerous for them to try" Nathaniel answered her question before she could finish. "We haven't been able to get communication in or out of there in quite some time."

"Why didn't we know anything about this?" William sat down in a chair across from his father, eyeing him warily.

"We've been keeping the situation monitored and quiet as best we can," Stephen answered. He sat up straight now, making eye contact, and looking decisive, royal. "We have reason to believe that Tolliver has infiltrated Eirentheos and there are spies. The poisonings you discovered among the children, using the schoolbooks we provide to them, seem to have been a direct attack on our political structure, attempting to undermine the confidence of our people, to make them vulnerable, and cause them to distrust us."

"Tolliver was behind that?" Quinn felt sick.

"Yes. He has been quietly doing a number of things to undermine Eirentheos. Presumably, it has to do with our opposition to his legitimately taking the throne. He is attempting to put us in a position where we have no power to oppose him."

Quinn thought about that, turning all of the information over in her mind. "That seems rather extreme.

Why doesn't he just take the throne? Why does he care so much about Eirentheos?"

"Tolliver's father has always held beliefs which are … dissimilar to those we hold here, and, until now, have been held in Philotheum." He glanced over at Nathaniel, an odd expression in his eyes. "I'm told that Tolliver's father keeps an oracle as an advisor, a man who attempts to divine the future through riddles and so-called prophecies."

"And this great oracle is telling him to poison the children in Eirentheos?"

"We have no idea what the oracle is telling him, Quinn," said Nathaniel. "Other than some kind of nonsense to fuel his already over-inflated ego. We do know that, based on whatever he's been told, Tolliver and his father both believe that it's necessary for Tolliver to marry into the Eirenthean royal line."

Quinn was speechless, her eyes wide.

"He seems to be under rather a misapprehension that if he causes us enough trouble, then we'll hand over Linnea to keep the peace."

"Over my …" Charlotte didn't have the words to continue her sentence.

Stephen stood and walked over to sit down next to his wife, putting his arm around her shoulders. "Which, of course, is never going to happen."

Quinn thought she might be sick. "Have you told him no?"

"In no uncertain terms. Tolliver is many things, but he is not entirely stupid. At this point, I don't think he cares whether he bullies us into joining his version of a political alliance, or goads us into all-out war." Stephen's voice had grown heavy.

"Are you going to war?"

"The time is not yet right for decisions such as that, Lady Quinn." She turned around, a bit startled. She had forgotten

Alvin was in the room, standing behind her. "It is not yet time for Eirentheos to act."

"We need to go there. We need to rescue Thomas."

"We can send soldiers to find him," Charlotte said.

"No, love. Sending soldiers over the border would be construed as an act of war." Stephen stood again, and began pacing back and forth across the long end of the room.

"I will go." Nathaniel's voice was strong and determined; every eye in the room turned to him.

Stephen stared for a long moment, looking as if he were making a decision.

"I know your objections, Stephen. But it is time. This one is mine."

The king nodded.

"I'm going with you, Nathaniel." William stood, and walked over to his uncle.

"No!" Charlotte's eyes were wide. "We don't know how dangerous it's going to be … I can't have two of my sons gone."

Nathaniel, though, nodded at William and turned to face Charlotte and Stephen. "You have asked much of your son, and placed much trust in him, sending him to live in another world. Time and again, he has proven himself. Will you deny the need he has now to find his brother who is only in another kingdom?"

There was a long silence before the king finally spoke again. "We will spend tomorrow planning and preparing for your trip and you can leave the following day. We'll send the two of you with some trustworthy guards." He eyed his wife with this second sentence.

"The three of us," Quinn said, looking Stephen in the eye.

He looked distressed. "You don't know what could happen, Quinn. We don't have any idea how dangerous it might be …"

"I'm going. It's why I came here."

Stephen eyed her critically. "You cannot put yourself at risk over a sense of guilt. It isn't your fault Thomas decided to go."

She cleared her throat, and tried to steady her hands, which had begun trembling slightly. "I know. It isn't guilt. This is just something I have to do. I can't explain why, but I do."

"It is her decision, Stephen." Alvin's calm, quiet voice was suddenly right next to her.

The king closed his eyes, and took a deep breath. "I know it is." There was a long pause before he looked at her again. "Quinn, it is your choice to make. You should know, before you make it, that the journey to Harber Village is four days one way. It is certain that you will not make it back before the next time the gate opens, and it could be longer. You don't know what situations you will be facing."

This gave her pause. Disappearing from her world without notice for twenty-four hours was one thing. But longer? Her mother would be panicked. Her second thoughts were genuine, but another feeling pushed them away. She couldn't name it, and she didn't understand where it was coming from, but from somewhere deep inside of her rose a conviction that she *had* to go. It was as much a part of her as the fact that she *had* to breathe

She nodded. "I understand. But I'm going."

The expression in his eyes told her that he had known what her answer would be, though it didn't stop his last, almost desperate remark. "You still have tomorrow to consider your decision. There is nothing shameful about changing your mind."

"Thank you, Your Majesty." She felt as if she should bow, or shake his hand, or something, but the impulses disappeared when suddenly he embraced her, squeezing her tightly.

Charlotte was there the instant he released her, ready to wrap her own arms around Quinn. "You are as beloved a daughter of ours as those of our blood. Please return to us safely."

THE JOURNEY BEGINS

"Are you really sure about doing this?"

"Not you, too, Linnea. I already walked out of my world without telling anyone. I'm here. I'm not going to just sit around the castle and wait for news."

"Must be nice to have that choice," Linnea's voice was sulky. She had made several unsuccessful attempts to convince her parents that she should be allowed to go with William and Quinn on the trip.

After listening to the debacle for most of the day, though, Quinn was beginning to feel grateful that they weren't going to stop her and William from going. Truthfully, after listening to all of the points that Stephen and Charlotte made about the danger, she was beginning to wonder why they'd given in so easily about the two of them. Though she didn't at all understand why, she'd become convinced that it had to do with Alvin's presence at the meeting the night before.

"Sorry, Nay. I know it isn't going to be easy."

"What's not going to be easy?" William stepped into Quinn's room through the open doorway. She noticed he carried his medical bag.

"Staying here while you two run off to go find Thomas."

Quinn watched as conflicting emotions crossed William's face before he settled on sympathy. "Yeah, it's going to be hard on you, I know. I will send word as soon as we find out *anything*, I promise."

"You'd better. What are you doing in here, anyway?" Linnea asked, eyeing his medical bag.

"What? I'm not welcome to spend time with the two of you?" His expression was teasing, which surprised Quinn. He'd been so serious lately, and everyone's stress level was so high right now that she had figured she'd mostly be seeing his solemn, sulky side. Ever since they'd come through the gate together last night, though, he'd been downright friendly. She had always sort of thought that his serious side was his dominant one; now she wasn't so sure.

Quinn smiled, but Linnea glared at her brother. Her mood today had been unabashedly dark.

"Well, I did want to see what you were doing, and see if you needed anything else to prepare for the journey tomorrow, but mostly I thought it was time to get those stitches out."

She nodded and pulled up her sleeve.

The small group gathered near the stables in the pre-dawn light. Two of Stephen's most trusted castle guards, Marcus and Ben, had joined Nathaniel, William, and Quinn for the journey. Marcus was older, several years Nathaniel's senior, and the two of them seemed to know each other quite well. He had worked in the castle since he was a young man. His son, Ben, was around Simon's age.

Stephen was there to see the five of them off. All of their other good-byes had been said after dinner the evening before.

Everyone was dressed for travel in what might be challenging conditions. Their clothing choices were carefully nondescript so they wouldn't be easily recognizable. Rather than their usual finery and insignia, Marcus and Ben wore the same style of dark, woven pants and linen shirts as Nathaniel, William, and Quinn all wore.

The mood was somber as they finished packing the saddlebags and readying the horses. Aside from Mia, who had helped them put together the personal items and supplies they would need, no servants had been involved in their preparations. Stephen felt as though there were very few people he could fully trust after the poisonings had been traced to a teacher who clearly had been working for Tolliver, but had been living in Eirentheos.

Quinn looked on as Stephen hugged his son for a long time, a single tear running down the king's cheek. He then hugged Quinn tightly before helping her mount Dusk. "Be safe."

Nathaniel and Marcus led the way down a route Quinn had never taken before, northwest of the castle. The morning was warm and muggy, though the sun was not yet all the way up. It wasn't long before they'd ridden into a remote, wild area. For most of the journey, they would be taking back routes well off the main thoroughfares. She was glad of her experience with riding horses on mountain trails. Dusk had come to know Quinn well, and obeyed her lightest touches.

Every so often, there would be a rustling in the nearby trees, or a cawing sound overhead, and she would glance up to see Aidel, Nathaniel's seeker bird, keeping a close eye on the group. Each time she saw her, Quinn would feel another spurt of irritation, directed both at Thomas, for being stupid enough to venture off by himself without even Sirian, and with herself for not realizing this and stopping him.

William had told her yesterday that Aelwyn and Syrian's eggs had hatched, and it wouldn't be long before the baby birds were ready to start searching for food on their own. At that point, one of the parents would be willing to leave the nest for short stretches of time. Thomas could have waited for his companion, at least.

They rode in silence for most of the day, stopping only for a few minutes at a time to allow the horses to drink, and the humans to take care of necessities. They were entering a thickly forested part of the country, the trail winding through the trunks of giant, leafy trees. Quinn was fascinated at the scenery, so different from the evergreen forests of home. The soil here was rich and black, with a heady, musky scent, instead of the familiar crisp smell and the crunch of pine needles.

By the time they finally stopped, finding a clearing near a river in a thick part of the woods, the sun was low in the sky. It was so muggy here that there was a haze hanging in the air above her. She was hot, and her skin felt sticky. She was also starving; her fingers trembled as she worked the buckles to remove Dusk's harness.

"Let me get that." William appeared suddenly behind her as she was starting to pull the saddle from Dusk's back. He slipped his hands in front of hers and lifted the heavy saddle easily over their heads.

"Thanks," Quinn said, wiping sweat from her forehead with the back of her hand.

"Sure," he grinned at her, his eyes twinkling.

Nathaniel and Ben were a few feet away from them, searching for medium-sized rocks. They'd already formed a semi-circle with the rocks in an area where they'd cleared out the grass and roots.

"I think it might be a little too warm for a fire tonight," William called to them.

The two men stopped what they were doing and looked over at him. Nathaniel looked up at the sky; rays of evening sunlight shimmered through the heavy water vapor. He nodded.

The horses were clearly relieved at the break. Skittles headed straight for the water the instant William released her, and Dusk quickly followed.

"I need to walk around for a bit," William said, coming to stand beside Quinn. "Would you like to come?"

She nodded. "That would feel good."

"Anyone else?" he asked.

"No thanks," Nathaniel said. "Marcus and I are going to discuss some things, and Ben is going to do some scouting in the area."

William nodded, pulling some sandwiches and fruit out of one of the bags, and began walking downstream, following the narrow bank of the stream. She stayed right behind him. It felt wonderful to be on the ground, moving her legs, after the hours in the saddle.

When they were out of hearing range of the rest of the group, he turned to her. "I know I've asked before, and I'll stop after this, but are you still sure about your decision to do this?"

"I'm kind of in it now, don't you think?"

"Not necessarily. We have a seeker with us. One message and someone would come meet us, help you get back. Before we get too far, anyway."

"I'm sure."

His walking paused. They had come to a wider part of the stream; the water had spread out into a shallow pool. "Why are you doing this? It isn't your fault that Thomas did this, you know, regardless of what you think or how responsible you feel."

She looked up at him, staring into his eyes, trying to read what he was thinking. "I know it isn't my fault. I don't feel guilty; I know I couldn't really have stopped Thomas. I don't know exactly why. It just feels like it's something I have to do."

He frowned. "But you don't have to. It isn't your responsibility."

"I know I don't actually have to, William. Maybe 'have to' is the wrong phrase. It's more like I'm supposed to, like this is the right thing. I wouldn't have felt right if I hadn't."

He nodded, looking away from her, out over the clean, clear water. "What about your mom, the rest of your life?"

She shrugged. "I don't know. I can't think about that right now."

He didn't press the issue, which surprised her. Instead, he reached down to pick up a smooth, flat stone. He hurled it at the water, and they watched as it skipped four times before it plunked to the bottom.

Quinn stretched down, searching for her own rock. Her toss wasn't as impressive as his; she only managed to make it skip twice, but he smiled.

"I've been having dreams." She told him, as they looked for more stones.

"About what?"

"I can never be quite sure. I never remember them clearly when I wake up, although they're very vivid while I'm sleeping. But I know they're about your world. I think they have something to do with Thomas being missing."

He stood up straight, looking her in the eye. "Just the last two nights while you've been here or longer than that?"

"The whole time I was home. Nearly every night. One morning I woke up and found my little brother curled up beside me. He said I'd been talking in my sleep, that I had sounded scared."

174

"What did you say?"

"He didn't know. I guess I stopped talking once he opened my bedroom door and came in."

William threw another stone, this time making it skip an impressive five times. Quinn whistled, before she scooped up another rock. She tried to imitate his technique, and got three bounces.

"It has to be hard on you ... not even being able to tell your brother about any of this. I've always had Thomas."

She nodded. "Sometimes I think Owen knows me better than anyone else. He's mildly autistic, you know, but that doesn't stop him from anything. He's known that something is up with me ever since the first time I came back, sometimes he says things that make me feel like he must know my secret. He doesn't ask me about it, though, just comes to sit beside me or curls up under the covers with me."

"Sounds like a kid I would like to know."

"I'll introduce you."

They stood there for several more minutes, skipping rocks across the water, enjoying the slight breeze that blew across, giving them a reprieve from the oppressive heat of the evening. Afterwards, they sat down on the bank and ate their sandwiches, watching as the sun sank lower behind the trees.

"Do you think Thomas is all right?" she asked after awhile, although the question stuck in her throat.

"I'm sure he's fine. We'll probably reach Lily and Graeme's and they'll tell us he's left, gone back home on the main road, that we've gone to all this trouble for nothing." His voice was steady and calm, but Quinn could see a different feeling hiding in his eyes.

"Probably," she said. "We should get back and see if they need help setting up for the night."

175

The night didn't cool much at all. Quinn might not have slept at all if she hadn't been so exhausted from riding. She had been surprised when she and William had returned to the clearing, and Ben had already finished erecting dome tents, that looked like they'd been purchased at a sporting goods store in her world. William had shrugged when she raised her eyebrows, and she remembered another time, when he'd told her that he and Nathaniel took whatever small advantages from her world that they could – whatever items they could manage to carry with them through the gate.

Crawling into the smallest tent that evening felt weird. It was set a short distance from the two identical larger tents. She shone her flashlight around, intending to feel around on the floor to locate the softest spot on the ground to lay her sleeping bag over; the forest floor here was covered in rocks, fallen branches, and protruding roots. She'd spent enough nights in tents to know how quickly a night could be ruined by a stray rock under her sleeping spot. She was startled when she realized that her sleeping bag was already spread out, laid neatly on top of two saddle blankets for extra padding.

For several minutes, she ran her hand over the nylon floor without finding a single bump.

Climbing into her sleeping bag, she realized that she had never slept all by herself in a tent before, let alone in the middle of an unfamiliar forest in a strange world. Between the creepy feeling of being alone, wondering who had set up her bed so perfectly, and the general mood of stress in the group, she shouldn't have been surprised at the vivid, frightening dreams she had that night.

Well before dawn, she was startled awake by the sound of a zipper. She sat bolt upright, dripping sweat, her heart racing.

"Quinn! Are you okay?" Nathaniel's head appeared at the opening of the tent, suddenly reminding her where she was.

The moon was round and bright behind him; the light spilled into the tent and across her sleeping bag. She could make out William's silhouette next to Nathaniel.

"Uh, yeah. I'm fine. What's going on?" She crawled over to the door. It had been too hot to cover up, so she had been sleeping, still dressed, on top of the bag.

"You were yelling. It worried us. Are you sure everything is all right?" Nathaniel's eyes were full of concern.

"Were you dreaming again?" William asked, crouching down so they were all facing each other.

"Um," she shook her head, trying to think. "I must have been." She stood to climb out, needing to get out into the fresh air.

Nathaniel gently took hold of her elbow, helping her. His expression was worried. "You've been having bad dreams?"

"Sometimes they're bad, I guess. I usually can't remember the details once I wake up, just the feeling."

"She's been dreaming about Eirentheos," William told him.

Nathaniel raised his eyebrows. "For how long?"

She shrugged. "I think I've been having them for a long time."

"Since your first visit?" William asked, confused. "Or just since this last time?"

She swallowed, suddenly realizing a truth that had been hanging around in the back of her mind for a while now, a truth that startled and frightened her. "Longer than that. Since before I ever followed you through the gate."

William looked as shocked as she felt.

"What were you dreaming about tonight that made you yell?" Nathaniel asked.

"I think ... I think it was about this trip. We were here. Well, not exactly here, but in a forest similar to this one." She paused, searching inside her mind, trying to grasp on to the memory that kept slipping away, just out of reach. It refused to

177

come, but the feeling returned suddenly, slamming into her chest like a ton of bricks. Her eyes were wide. "Something is wrong. We have to find Thomas. We have to find him now."

"We're going to, Quinn. We're going to do everything we can." Nathaniel put his hand on her shoulder, squeezing it comfortingly.

By the time the first rays of sunlight reached them through the trees, they were already back on the trail. Nathaniel seemed to be taking her dreams more seriously than she had been, which made her feel odd.

Around mid-morning, they stopped in another clearing by the river. The water was higher here and flowed faster. All day they had been steadily climbing into territory that was hillier and rockier than Quinn was used to seeing in Eirentheos. Although these foothills were much smaller, and the forests still comprised of leafy, green, deciduous trees, the scenery vaguely reminded her of home.

"We're getting close to the Philothean border," Nathaniel told them as they walked the horses to the water. "We'll stop here for now. Quinn, William, and Ben, I want the three of you to rest the horses and yourselves. There is a town near here, Anwin. Marcus and I are going to go and talk to some people we know, try and get some information about what's going on."

"Is it safe?" Quinn asked.

Nathaniel and Marcus exchanged a look.

"It's safer than trying to continue without knowing what we're heading into." Marcus answered.

"We have friends in this village who will be able to help us. We'll be fine, but we don't want to risk going in a large group and drawing attention to ourselves." Nathaniel clarified.

The two men hiked into Anwin on foot, leaving William, Quinn, and Ben with the horses. The boys worked to unload weight from the horses so they could rest, while Quinn dug through the one of the food bags, pulling out a wrapped loaf of bread and the container of spread that was similar to peanut butter. They had eaten the same food since lunch yesterday, and when Ben saw it, he grimaced.

"We've got time," he said. "We should try catching a few fish."

William's eyes lit up, and he nodded, glancing disdainfully at the bread. "Definitely." He headed straight for one of the saddle bags on the ground, and dug out three small metal cases. "Do you know how to fish, Quinn?"

"Yeah, I do."

He looked at her skeptically. "*Fly*-fish?"

She raised her eyebrows at him. "*Yeah, I do.*" The quick change in expression amused her, and caused a flood of warmth to flow in her chest when she realized he looked … impressed.

"We'll clean them for you," Ben offered.

William chuckled at the dark look she shot him. "He's only trying to be chivalrous."

Her forehead smoothed. "In that case, you guys can cook them, too."

They both laughed.

"Agreed," William nodded.

Quinn and William followed Ben a short distance downriver from where the horses were drinking and cooling themselves in the water. Although it was slightly cooler here than it had been at the lower elevations, the heat of the day was still uncomfortable. This part of the river was ideal for fly-fishing. As soon as he found a good boulder to climb up on, William opened one of the cases and began assembling a complicated-looking pole.

She glanced over at Ben, who was already wading through the water, seeking out a fishing spot. He hadn't talked a lot so far on their journey, although she had a feeling he listened to everything, taking it in. She didn't know much about him, other than he and his father were both guards at the castle. Stephen and Nathaniel clearly trusted both of them implicitly. Still, she wondered what someone like Ben must think of all the fancy equipment Nathaniel and William carried – the tents and the fishing poles bought at a sporting goods store in her world. Were they in on the secret? She would have to remember to ask William later.

"Can I help you with those?" she asked, shimmying up the tall rock to sit beside William.

She saw his eyebrow begin to creep up for a fraction of a second before he thought better of it, shrugged, and handed her a case. "Sure, thanks."

As she carefully twisted the sections of the pole together, she watched Ben wade through the water, and listened to William working beside her. A hot lump rose in her throat. It should have been Thomas here with them, his booming laugh and teasing gestures lightening the mood. Tears stinging the corners of her eyes, she stole a glance over at William. She jumped, startled, when her eyes met his. He was staring at her intently, and she could see her own grief echoed in his expression.

They sat there on that rock, at the edge of the river, for a moment that was fleeting and eternal at the same time, each one's eyes locked on the other's, a snarl of inexplicable feelings hanging heavy in the summer air. He nodded, and she knew he understood, even before he squeezed her hand.

"It will be good to eat a hot meal," he said. "We're going to need the strength."

After less than an hour of fishing, they had caught eight fat ruskas. Quinn had snagged three of them.

Although he knew it was likely that she would be perfectly capable of helping him and Ben clean and cook the fish – the girl was full of surprises -- William thought she could do with a break. It couldn't be easy for a teenage girl to travel for this long in the wilderness with four men. The only privacy she had was inside the small, one-person tent they'd set up for her last night, and it wasn't even tall enough inside for her to stand upright.

As soon as they had enough fish to fill them, William told Quinn to take advantage of the calm break and the smaller group to bathe herself in the river and change. It also gave him a chance to spend some time with Ben.

Ben had been around for as long as William could remember, although he had never known him very well. Ben had always lived in the castle; his father Marcus had worked as a guard there before he'd ever married and had children. He was several cycles older than William, though – closer to Simon's age than his own, and so while they had always been friendly, they'd never been friends.

The two worked together amiably, Ben slicing and cleaning the fish with quick, sure strokes, finishing with six in the time it took for William to do two.

"Nice," William said.

Ben shrugged. "We should find something to season them with. There's miloseed growing everywhere around here."

"Sure." William jumped up and followed Ben into the forest, noticing that the older boy seemed sure about where he was going.

"You know this area?"

Ben raised his eyebrows slightly, giving William an impression that the question surprised him, as if he thought William knew the answer already. "Yes, good friends of both my father and Nathaniel live in Anwin. My family travels here

181

frequently to visit. I've been here many times with just my father and Nathaniel, as well."

Now it was William's turn to be surprised. He spent nearly all of his time when he was home traveling all over Eirentheos and Philotheum with Nathaniel, but they had never been to this area before, William was certain. He didn't know anything about the village of Anwin – he'd seen the name only on maps, and these hills were unfamiliar to him. He didn't know what to say, whether he should disclose this to Ben.

"Here we are." Ben saved him from responding, as he walked around a tree and into a patch of small miloseed plants. He bent down and began searching through them – the fully-grown plants with the largest leaves made the best seasoning for food. The seasoning would give the fish a savory, smoky flavor, with a hint of spice.

Before Quinn returned from the river, William and Ben had taken several of the small plants and crushed the red and green leaves into tiny flakes and then they sprinkled them generously on top of the meat in a little, square pan that could withstand the heat of the fire. William felt a sense of satisfaction over the impressed glance she threw at the simmering meal.

Nathaniel and Marcus returned just as William removed the pan from the fire. Quinn had retrieved the dishes from one of the bags, and Ben was filling a large water container from the stream.

Everyone was starving by the time they all sat down to eat, finding a spot in the shade as far as they could manage from the heat of the dying fire. The fish looked and smelled amazing, and the meal was doubly impressive when they added a few fresh vegetables that Nathaniel and Marcus had brought with them from Anwin.

"Thank you all. This will be a welcome change," Marcus said, surveying his small, metal plate.

Nathaniel's expression was somber. Quinn and William exchanged a wary look.

"What's the news?" William asked.

Nathaniel sighed. "Things appear to be getting very tense between Tolliver, his troops, and many of the people in Philotheum." He took a bite of his food and swallowed before continuing. "Of course, being Tolliver, not much of what he is doing is straightforward. Technically, the border is still open, and relations between our two kingdoms are friendly. There are many rumors floating around, however, and the people are becoming unsure of whom to trust."

"There have been disappearances," Marcus added. "In the village of Estora, just across the border, eight people are gone, including one family of five. Nobody knows where they are."

"Taken?" Ben asked, shock in his voice.

Nathaniel shrugged. "Perhaps some have been secretly arrested by Tolliver's troops. Others may be working as spies, or they have just decided to leave."

"Many believe that Eirentheos is behind their troubles, that Stephen is responsible for some of the disappearances."

William watched Quinn's eyes pop open as wide as his own. "That's impossible! Why would they think that?"

Nathaniel's eyes stayed on his plate as he spoke. "Tolliver and his father, the Prince Regent, have long undertaken a campaign to undermine the influence Eirentheos exerts over its people and political structure. They would like nothing more than to see a split between the two kingdoms, to have us out of their business, so to speak."

"So, while the border is open, and people are permitted to cross either way, many are afraid to, and we can assume that all border crossings are being carefully monitored and reported to Tolliver and his troops." Marcus set his empty plate on the ground in front of him.

"We're not going to just be able to ride across," Quinn said. William's heart sank. What did all of this mean for Thomas?

"No, we aren't." Nathaniel's expression was grave.

"Then what do we do?" Again, Quinn was jumping right into the fray. William didn't understand why she was so deeply involved with this, so willing to put herself in danger. He wondered if the kiss between her and Thomas had been more than his brother just trying to distract her, to get her through the gate before she could rat him out.

He had decided not to think about that, though, not to worry about it until after Thomas was safe. He had already hurt Quinn enough trying to push her away and keep her out of this. She had made her choice to come here for Thomas, and it couldn't be changed now. Continuing to alienate her wouldn't accomplish anything.

Besides, he had to admit that it was nice having her here. She often thought differently than anyone else, quickly seeing a solution that nobody else had come up with. And it was clear that she cared about Thomas, that she wanted him back as badly as he did. William was fairly certain that if it came down to it, if the group was forced to choose between the safety of all of them and a chance at finding Thomas, that Nathaniel, Marcus, and Ben would be practical. Quinn, though, would be with him.

"Well," Nathaniel answered, "Despite Tolliver's attempts to convince his people that Eirentheos is evil, his actions among his own people are stirring up resistance."

Marcus raised his eyebrows, "That's nothing new. There's been resistance to the regent and his son ever since..." He stopped suddenly when Nathaniel directed a look of warning toward him. "Ever since Prince Samuel died," he finished.

William understood, then, that there were several things he wasn't being told. Intuition told him that it probably wasn't just a coincidence that he had never been invited along on Nathaniel and Marcus' trips to Anwin. He saw a flash across Quinn's gray eyes, her reaction matching his.

"Anyway, our friends in Anwin, Charles and his wife, Thea, are heavily involved in the resistance. They are quite skilled at moving people across the border without being noticed. We will sleep here tonight. We can rest and regain our strength. In the meantime, Charles is going to contact some friends in Haedley, another town close to the other side of the Philothean border. They will come up with a plan."

"Did you tell them the situation? About Thomas?" William was growing more anxious with every word, an anxiety that grew as he watched Nathaniel glance over at Marcus before answering.

"They knew already. Members of the resistance – they call themselves Friends of Philip after the first king of Philotheum -- have been working desperately to figure out if he ever made it safely to Lily and Graeme's. We're afraid he may not have."

William swallowed back the bile that rose in his throat, his heart pounding in his chest. Fierce anger filled him too, next to the dark worry. His brother had always been carefree and reckless, but this …

He stood, the plate he'd forgotten was in his lap clattering noisily to the ground, though the sound was muffled by the blood rushing in his ears. He walked as quickly as he could, away from the people, from the discussion, from the situation which had suddenly become entirely too real.

He heard Quinn's voice behind him, and Nathaniel's response, but he couldn't understand them, his brain was past recognizing words. As soon as he hit the trees, his walk turned into a run. The forest flew past him in a blur of green, the rays of afternoon sun bouncing off his face as he ran. His pace grew faster and faster, as he tried to outrun the thoughts and

BREEANA PUTTROFF

emotions pounding against the inside of his head. He kept going until he could go no further, his legs giving way underneath him.

186

SAFE HOUSE

The angle of the sun had changed when William finally pulled himself up off the forest floor. It was late afternoon now, and the heat was stifling, even in the shade. The slight breeze that had felt so good earlier was gone now, and he was dripping with sweat. His mouth was parched and sour from vomiting earlier, a weakness he didn't like to admit, yet another reason behind his tendency to be as alone as he could when he got upset.

He stood still, listening carefully for the sound of the stream flowing nearby. The water was loud here, rushing over rocks, and he found the river easily. He wasn't worried about finding his way back. Even upset beyond all reason he wasn't stupid enough to wander far enough that he wouldn't be able to follow the river back to the campsite. He could never be as impulsive as his younger brother.

William cleaned himself up in the clear, clean water, and had a long drink before he began making his way back. He'd only gone a few hundred feet, though, when he heard a noise that made him freeze. He wasn't alone. The clip-clopping of horse's hooves and the snapping sounds of branches drew closer.

He knew it wouldn't be Nathaniel. His uncle had long ago learned to give William space when he needed it, to allow him to collect himself. He was pretty sure that Nathaniel would have made certain that the others in the group kept away. Thoughts of spies and Tolliver's troops patrolling the areas near the border twisted his stomach. Although he knew he was probably just being paranoid, he walked quickly to the nearest large tree, and stepped up onto the lowest branch, concealing himself in the leaves.

He watched the trail, listening as whoever it was came nearer. When Dusk's head finally appeared between two trees, he found himself irritated. Of course, *she* would come looking for him. Probably without Nathaniel's approval.

"What are you doing here, Quinn?" He called from the tree, taking small satisfaction from seeing her jump.

She looked all around, searching for him in the thick trees. Finally, she gave up, and just spoke to the empty air. "Looking for you."

"Why?"

Her eyes locked onto the tree where he was hiding. She was good; he would give her that. He could feel his irritation dissolving, and he climbed down, walking over to her. Dusk looked nearly as happy to see him as the girl did, and she nuzzled his hand as he stroked her head.

"*Why?* Has it occurred to you that right now might not be the best time or the best place to go running off on your own?"

William's face flushed red. He hadn't. Not until about a minute ago, anyway. "Is it the best time for you to come chasing after me on *your* own?"

She rolled her eyes, though he could tell that his retort had hit its mark. "Let's go," she said, hooking her thumb behind her, indicating that he should climb up. "Nathaniel's friend Thea has come to talk with us."

Climbing up onto Dusk behind Quinn was awkward; the saddle was really only meant for one person, and he didn't know where to put his hands. Not for the first time, he wished this sort of thing came as easily to him as it did to Thomas. He was sure that his brother would be laughing hysterically at him if he were here right now – if he wasn't already on the horse behind the girl, his arms wrapped securely around her waist. William blushed at the thought, but he supposed there wasn't any other way to do this. He scooted close behind Quinn, and, as casually as possible, put one hand lightly against her rib cage.

The girl stiffened slightly at his touch. He watched, amazed, as goose bumps appeared along her neck and down her arms. Instantly, his hand fell to his leg. Dusk jolted forward through the woods, and the motion nearly knocked him off. His hands automatically caught hold of Quinn's hips as he struggled to stay upright.

They rode all the way back to camp like this, Quinn straight-backed in front of him, William touching her as little as possible while still managing to keep himself on the horse. It wasn't a long ride, but his hands felt shaky and clammy by the time he dismounted Dusk at the campsite. The girl's cheeks were bright pink, almost distractingly so.

Nathaniel was the only one who glanced up when they came into the campsite, and he only did so briefly before turning his attention back to an intense conversation that he, Marcus, and Ben were having with a woman he had never seen before.

Quinn didn't hesitate before walking into the circle and sitting down on a log between Nathaniel and the guest. William followed, trying not to disturb the meeting as he sat down beside her. It didn't work, of course. As soon as he sat down, every eye turned to him. He suddenly regretted being stupid enough to take off like he had. This wasn't the time. Everyone was here, in the middle of the woods, possibly in danger, in order to find Thomas. This was hard on everyone, and he was the only one who had just thrown a fit like a spoiled child. He silently promised himself it would never happen again.

"William, this is Thea. She and her husband are working with the Philothean resistance." Nathaniel's tone held only the tiniest hint of reproof.

"It's nice to meet you, Thea." He extended his hand toward her, smiling in the friendliest way he could manage.

"It's very nice to meet you, too, Prince William."

"Please, it's just William."

She nodded. "That will be easier. I was just telling your uncle, Marcus, and Ben what we know about the situation in Philotheum. My husband, Charles, and another friend of ours have gone into Estora to see if there is any more news. They should return late tonight or early tomorrow. We will have a better idea how to proceed then."

"For tonight," Nathaniel broke in, "Thea has been kind enough to offer her home. We can rest there, and figure out what our next steps are going to be."

Quinn was surprised when the path Thea was leading them down opened into a small clearing. A rambling farmhouse and fenced pasture filled the open space. There had been no signs of the town of Anwin, where she had assumed they were going. Thea rode down a hill and followed a narrow, dirt path around the back of the house, pausing at a closed gate. Ben hopped down from his horse before Thea could, unlatching the gate for her. The tiny woman nodded in appreciation.

The inside of the house seemed larger than it had looked from the outside. The living room was huge, with large windows open to the surrounding fields and trees on both sides. A u-shaped arrangement of comfortable couches faced the massive stone fireplace. Thea led them all into the room.

"Please make yourselves comfortable."

She disappeared through an arched doorway at the far corner of the room. Quinn could see long counters and could smell a savory aroma drifting from there. Nathaniel, Marcus, and Ben looked surprisingly at ease with the new surroundings. Ben folded himself into a large, soft chair, and Nathaniel and Marcus took spots facing each other on the well-worn couches.

William still stood, shifting his weight from one foot to the other as he surveyed the room. Quinn was glad she wasn't the only one who felt somewhat out of place. She paced uncomfortably for a moment, and then ducked into the kitchen.

"Can I help you with anything?"

Thea turned from the giant pot she'd been tending, still holding a long, wooden ladle in her right hand. "It's Quinn, right?"

"Yes."

"You're a guest here, Quinn. I can imagine it's been a long, difficult few days for you. And the days in front of you are likely to be even harder. You should have a seat. Relax while you can."

Thea appeared to be about the same age as Quinn's mom, a thought which made a lump rise in her throat before she quickly pushed it away. The woman was small, with delicate features, and short, dark brown curls. Her eyes were a soft, summery blue. Quinn could tell she was stronger than she appeared, though. She watched in awe as the woman chopped vegetables with quick, sure strokes, even though Thea hadn't taken her eyes off Quinn.

"It doesn't feel right to make you do all of the work, after you were kind enough to invite us here."

"I'm not doing all of the work. I'm cooking a meal, providing shelter for the five of you, to support you in the work you're doing. We all have a role to play in this, and I think you're doing your part. Now go, sit. Take advantage of what comfort you can find. You never know when you'll need it to draw back on." She pointed toward the doorway with her knife, and Quinn didn't argue.

They slept that night on comfortable beds, in guest rooms off a long hallway behind the living room. Although Quinn was exhausted, and the bed felt incredible, after only a couple hours of sleep, insomnia crept up on her yet again. She couldn't remember the last time she had slept until morning. Tonight, she couldn't remember having dreamed at all – there wasn't even the faint disoriented feeling she often woke up to. She felt wide awake.

She lay there in bed, listening to the sounds of the night as she tried, ineffectively, to convince her body to go back to sleep. Gradually, she became aware of a sound she wasn't expecting. A murmur of low voices was coming from somewhere inside the house.

As far as she knew, everyone had gone to bed at the same time she had. Thea had led them to three separate guest bedrooms, William and Nathaniel had gone into one, Marcus and Ben another, and Quinn, as usual, had a space to herself. She hadn't yet decided if this was an advantage or a disadvantage to being the only girl. The privacy was nice, but when they were staying in such unfamiliar places, she thought company would have been good, too.

Either way, with her crazy sleeping habits, she was becoming accustomed to being awake and alone in the middle of the night. Nobody else seemed to have any trouble sleeping

– they were all too worn out after the long days of traveling. She wondered if she was misjudging the time, and it was closer to morning than she thought, but a peek out the window revealed the tiny sliver of a crescent moon, low and bright in the deep, black sky.

Perhaps someone else was having trouble sleeping, too? She carefully opened the door to her room and crept silently into the hallway. The voices grew louder as she approached the living room. Two voices, she could tell now, both of them male. She recognized Marcus' deep, resounding bass, but the second voice was unfamiliar.

"Who is the girl?" She was close enough now for the stranger's words to become clear.

Her heart stopped. She stepped a little closer.

"I don't know." It was Marcus' voice now. "She seems to just show up sometimes with William. Everyone is interested in her. Thomas appears quite taken."

"Why is she here?"

"From what I hear, she insisted upon coming."

"And Stephen just allowed that?"

"Alvin showed up with William and the girl. He said that the girl was to be allowed to come if she chose."

"But why? You don't think..."

A floorboard squeaked under Quinn's foot.

"Is someone else awake?" Marcus' voice interrupted his companion's.

"Hello?" the stranger called.

Quinn fled back to her room, closing the door behind her as silently as she could, throwing herself into the bed and feigning sleep. Over the pounding of her heart she listened for footsteps in the hallway, voices coming to check, but they never came.

When she woke the next morning, Quinn couldn't be sure if the conversation she had overheard in the night had been real or a dream. Marcus, Nathaniel, William, and Thea gathered with her at the breakfast table. There was nobody else. She surreptitiously glanced over at Marcus several times while Thea was serving the hot grain cereal and thick pancakes, but he seemed no different this morning than ever.

Once they were all seated, though, it was Marcus who spoke. His words seemed directed at William and Quinn – Nathaniel and Ben appeared to have already heard this.

"Today, we are going to cross the border over into Philotheum, into the village of Estora. There, more Friends of Philip will take us to a safe house, and we can decide what to do from there."

"Are we going to just walk across the border?" Quinn wondered.

"No. We cannot just all go together. We have no idea what movements are being tracked, nor what Tolliver's troops or his spies are reporting to him or to the regent." Nathaniel answered, glancing over at Marcus. "William, Marcus, and I are all too recognizable to go through a regular border crossing in any case. We will ride to a spot a couple hours north of here where the river is passable."

"Won't it be guarded?" Quinn asked.

"That's unlikely," Marcus said. "It's an extremely remote area on both sides. The greater danger will be trying to make it back to Estora in such a large group without attracting notice."

"Which is why, Quinn," Nathaniel said, "you and Ben are going to cross together on the bridge at the regular border crossing. The two of you are unknown, and will appear to be a young couple. You shouldn't run into any difficulty. We will meet up with you in Estora late this evening."

She nodded, glancing first at Ben, who was focused on eating his pancakes, and then at William, who was staring at her, a strange look in his eyes. Although he didn't say anything, she got the distinct impression that he didn't like the idea.

The idea of being separated from William and Nathaniel made her uncomfortable, but it made sense to her. She just hoped it wouldn't take too long.

Less than an hour after they'd finished breakfast, the horses were saddled and ready to go. Ben's and Quinn's horses were loaded down more heavily than usual; they had transferred as many supplies as they could, trying to lighten the load on the horses who would be fording the river later today. Thea had taken most of the bigger supplies, promising to have them delivered to the safe house in Estora.

Skittles was whinnying and snorting in expectation; she liked nothing better than a day of riding, even happier to be free of most of the weight in her packs. William wasn't feeling as excited.

Being separated from Quinn – even if it would be for less than a day – wasn't sitting well with him. He had considered arguing the point; it couldn't be that much more dangerous to travel in a group of five rather than three. He swallowed his objection, though, when he realized that no, it wouldn't be so much more dangerous for the group, but it would be riskier for *her*.

Quinn and Ben's ride into Estora would be quick and simple. In under an hour, they would be tucked away in a safe house. He liked the idea of that better than the thought of her traveling with them, through unfamiliar remote areas. He'd looked at the place they'd be crossing on Nathaniel's map. Calling it passable was optimistic. The wide Philotheos River ran the entire length of the border of the two kingdoms. Many bridges ran between them, but crossing was difficult most anywhere else. William glanced up at the brilliant blue sky, grateful that it hadn't rained in several weeks.

Nathaniel seemed to be having some difficulty parting with Quinn himself. He watched his uncle carefully check that all of Dusk's fastenings were secure before he helped the girl climb into the saddle. Once Nathaniel had finally walked away, William went over to her.

"Are you all ready?" He couldn't help tugging once more on the leather straps that held Dusk's saddle.

"Sure. It doesn't sound like it's that far of a ride."

He shook his head. "Yours isn't. We probably won't be meeting back up with you until dinnertime or later."

She glanced over at Ben, focused as always on what he was doing. He seemed reliable, and nice enough, but William had never seen him really even talk to Quinn. He wondered how she was feeling about spending time alone with him, but he couldn't think of a good way to ask.

"How far are we now from where Lily and Graeme live, from Harber Village?" She asked.

"I'm not sure. I've never come this way before; this area is all unfamiliar to me." He paused, contemplating his next words before he spoke them. "I'm not sure that's our destination anymore, anyway. It really sounds like Thomas may never have made it there."

Last night, once he and Nathaniel were in their room, he had pressed his uncle for more of the information Thea had been getting from other members of the Friends of Philip. There had been little contact with Lily and Graeme's village, and what news they could get didn't sound good. Nobody had seen or heard from either Lily or Graeme in weeks, and there was some fear that they had disappeared. Where that left Thomas was anyone's guess.

They were hopeful that some of their contacts in Estora knew more. It had been difficult to transmit any information at all across the border, so Thea's knowledge was limited. Her husband, Charles, hadn't come back yet with any news from his foray into Philotheum yesterday. It made William uneasy, too, that he didn't know the people Quinn would be meeting on the other side. This was certainly a lot to ask of her.

Although he hadn't admitted it to her – he wondered if he should – he was rather impressed by the girl's willingness to just jump into the fray. He really hoped that she wasn't just doing this out of misplaced guilt. None of this was her fault. The look she gave him now heightened those fears, as she processed what he had just told her.

"Where *is* Thomas, then, if he never made it?"

"That's what we're hoping someone can help us find out. So far, we don't know much."

"But what could have happened to him, William?" Her eyes were starting to take on a slightly panicked look. She didn't usually get like this. He mentally kicked himself for saying anything to her right now, just as she was about to go off into an unknown land with someone she didn't really know.

He looked directly into her eyes. "Right now, Quinn, we need to assume he's okay. He may have actually made it, or he may have been intercepted by other Friends of Philip, and he's somewhere safe. It's not like he can just call us up on his cell phone and tell us where he is. Communication is going to take time."

She nodded, calmer already. "You're right. Today we need to concentrate on getting across the border. With any luck, we'll know something more by tonight." She nodded again; he wasn't sure if this was directed at him. Then she looked back into his eyes. "Be safe. I need you back in one piece tonight."

He nodded back, patting her on the knee, and then walked over to Skittles, who looked as impatient as the other humans in the group who had been doing their best to ignore their little scene. He wondered where, exactly, the conversation had turned from him reassuring her, to her calming him.

PANICKING

The town she had been expecting appeared only about ten minutes after Quinn and Ben left Thea's farmhouse. They didn't ride through it, but every so often the trees would thin, or they would climb a hill, and she would see the houses and buildings spread out below them. It was larger than she had expected; she had been picturing a tiny village in her mind, much like Cloud Valley. The population of Anwin, though, might have been close to a thousand, with several shops and larger buildings.

The town reminded her of the capital city of Eirentheos, with its stone streets and well-built little houses. William had told her that he had never before been to Anwin, which surprised her. It seemed like a place he and Nathaniel would have traveled to many times to help with a clinic.

Ben stayed on the main thoroughfare as he led her past the town. He rarely spoke to her; she was unsure if he was shy or just naturally quiet. He was nice enough, looking over at her often, and adjusting his pace so they never became separated. Two times, other travelers passed them going the other direction, and

Ben would move a little closer to her, protectively, but the road was mostly empty and quiet. Soon, they sloped downhill, and Quinn could see the wide river spread out below them, the road leading to a large, wooden bridge.

Actually crossing the border had been the part of this that she was the most worried about. She had asked Nathaniel this morning if there was some kind of paperwork or identification she would need, but he had told her no, those things weren't necessary here the way they were in her world.

As they drew near to the bridge, Ben brought his horse, Scruffin, up beside Dusk as closely as he could. Quinn remembered that they were acting as a couple, and matched her pace to his. A few minutes later, they were on the other side.

"Welcome to Philotheum," Ben told her a little way up the road from the bridge.

She was stunned. That was all? Sure, they had passed by a few guards along the way. Two in purple on the road in front of the bridge, and three more dressed in green milling about on the Philothean side, but the guards had barely even acknowledged their crossing.

"That was easy," she said to him.

He shrugged. "We weren't expecting to be stopped or anything, at least not with just the two of us. The worry is more about what information the guards might be passing along without saying anything."

There was a village on this side, too, although it was much smaller. It looked more like a cluster of houses around the border crossing than anything. Very few people were out in the streets, which seemed odd to her.

Ben kept Scruffin right next to Dusk now that they were in Philotheum. He seemed to know exactly where they were going, following a trail that curved toward the southwest, away from the river.

The roads here were even more deserted than they had been in Eirentheos. In the twenty minutes they rode along the wide road up from the border, they passed only two wagons, and an older man walking up the road alone. But they also passed two different small groups of soldiers, dressed in green and gold uniforms, matching blankets draped over the backs of their horses. Although they appeared to be just casually running patrols, Quinn got a distinct impression that things were quite different in Philotheum than in Eirentheos. Ben didn't look at the soldiers, but he did match Scruffin's stride even more closely to Dusk's, and a few times he cast protective glances toward her.

When they turned off the wide, stone road onto a narrower, packed dirt one, she expected that they were heading into a sparse, rural area. So she was surprised when, after about ten minutes of riding, the heavy forest began thinning, and she could see signs of a populated area.

Small houses, made of stone and wood were nestled in clusters among the trees, blending in with the beautiful forest so well that they almost appeared as if they'd sprung spontaneously from the earth.

"We are nearing the village of Estora," Ben said. She jumped, startled; it was the first time he'd spoken since he had told her they were in Philotheum. "Is everything all right?" he asked, frowning.

She raised her eyebrows. "Yeah, everything's fine. You just surprised me when you spoke."

Now he looked surprised. "Why?"

"Um, because I think this might be the longest conversation you and I have had during the entire time I've known you, and it's only the second time you've spoken to me today."

"I'm sorry, have I offended you by not speaking enough?"

If Quinn had been driving a car instead of riding an intelligent, perfectly trained horse, she might have crashed, whipping her head around to scrutinize Ben's expression. He didn't look – or sound – like he was teasing. He looked … *worried.* "No, not at all. I just thought … I don't know, maybe you didn't really like me or something."

She was stunned as his expression changed from worried to outright terrified. "I have offended you, then. I'm so sorry."

"It isn't a big deal, Ben. You just surprised me, that's all. Besides, I'm sure it's just as much my fault, I haven't been terribly friendly to you, either." She realized now how true that was. Ben had just kind of been in the background for their whole trip, and she hadn't paid much attention to him. She had wondered once or twice if he didn't like her, or if he was just always quiet. She hadn't been offended. Now, though, he was kind of freaking her out.

"I'll try and remember to speak more," he said.

"Uh … okay. So, where are we going, anyway? I thought we were headed to Estora." While they had been having their odd conversation, they had passed what looked like the center of the village. There had been a large cluster of the stone houses, and several larger buildings of the same style. Now the pockets of homes were growing further apart, and the forest was closing around the road.

"We're not too far. You'll see." His voice was low, and his eyes searched the trees as he spoke, giving Quinn the impression that he was worried they'd be overheard. She started to study the trees and houses they passed more closely.

After about five more minutes of riding, Ben turned Scruffin down a much narrower path. It was definitely a path, not another road. She probably wouldn't have even noticed it on her own. It wasn't wide enough for them to ride side-by-side; Dusk had to follow single-file.

The trees were large and close together; making the sky seem further away. No houses or other buildings appeared between them.

"About five more minutes," Ben called back to her, loudly enough that Quinn guessed they were alone here.

"Where are we going?" she asked again.

"Another safe house. It belongs to some friends of my father and Nathaniel, Henry and Ellen. It isn't actually in Estora, but close enough."

"Are there a lot of these safe houses?"

Ben nodded, "A fair number. We're working on establishing more all of the time." A dark look crossed his eyes. "Things are only getting worse in Philotheum for those who oppose Tolliver – or support Eirentheos."

Quinn blinked, *"We're?* What do you have to do with the safe houses? Exactly how much do you know about what is going on here?" The questions were out before she could really stop to think about what she was doing. Everything he was saying – the way he was behaving – was contrary to how she had perceived him the whole time they'd been on this trip.

She realized she had assumed that Ben was here for the sole purpose of protecting her, Nathaniel, and William, a trusted castle guard who was just that – a guard. *Well, you know what happens when you assume*, she thought darkly, remembering a phrase her mother sometimes used.

Ben stopped riding and turned around to face her. His expression was confused, and slightly cautious. "I thought you knew," he said.

"Knew what?"

"My father and I are members of Friends of Philip – we're part of the resistance." He pulled the neck of his shirt far to the side, revealing a small tattoo over his heart. It looked like two conjoined circles, though she couldn't see the details from here.

"What? Why are castle guards from Eirentheos part of the Philothean resistance? Does Nathaniel know?"

"Of course he does. He's … I guess I assumed that you and William did as well."

"And Stephen?"

"Is very much in support of the Friends of Philip. Philotheum and Eirentheos have always been meant to be linked, two parts of a whole, not battling and mistrusting each other. Tolliver and his father are working hard to separate the kingdoms, but King Stephen and the Friends of Philip wish to restore things to how they should be."

"Are there a lot of people in Eirentheos who are Friends of Philip, too?"

"There are many who are willing to help."

She narrowed her eyes at his evasion of the question – what was he hiding? "But not full-on members, with the tattoo and everything?"

"There are some who are. All of my family are Friends of Philip."

"Why? How is it that you are so involved? It seems like you're avoiding my question."

His adam's apple bobbed downward for a second before he answered. "I don't know if I'm supposed to tell you this or not. I – I knew you didn't know everything, but you seem to know less than I expected. Maybe you should wait and ask my father or Nathaniel."

"How about you just tell me why you are so involved in this right now." The firm tone in her voice surprised her, but not as much as the fact that he looked up at her and did as she'd asked.

"I was born in Eirentheos, but my father is from here, from Philotheum. He was born in the castle, actually. His father was a castle guard there, as were his grandfather and great-grandfather. He grew up knowing that he, too, would be one of the guards who personally attended the family. He served King Jonathan himself, until the first prince was born. Then he guarded the children."

Ben paused, looking up at the clear blue sky. "When Jonathan died, everyone was devastated, my father especially so. He was off the day it happened, and he's always thought ..." he trailed off, seeming to search for what he'd been going to say.

"He thought what? How did King Jonathan die?"

"It was a horseback riding accident. He and Queen Sophia loved to take their horses out into the open country and race. That day ... somehow his saddle was improperly secured. One strap snapped, another was loose ... He hit his head just the wrong way on a rock."

Quinn had to remind herself to breathe.

"Their four children were very young when it happened. Shortly after the funeral, Sophia realized she was with child again. She was remarried to Hector, an ambassador from Dovelnia before Jonathan's last son was born."

"Not Tolliver," Quinn frowned.

"No. Tolliver was born two cycles later, and that is when things in the castle really changed. Everyone began to realize what Hector's true intentions in marrying Sophia by then. Everyone except Sophia; she seemed blind to what her new husband was doing."

Just then, there was a rustling sound in the trees, and they both froze. "Stay here," he said, under his breath, and he rode quietly toward the sound. Quinn trembled, sitting there waiting for him to come back. Dusk sensed her rider's tension and looked around, alert. When she didn't see any immediate danger, she snuffled in a calming way.

Although it felt like an hour, only a few minutes passed before Ben reappeared on the path. "It was a deer," he said. "But we'd best be getting to the house."

They hadn't traveled much further when a stone wall came into view. Mounted on Dusk, Quinn could see over it, but barely. The wall surrounded an enormous, lush, green yard, beyond which was a rambling house. The wood-and-stone construction was very similar to the houses she had seen along the road, but this home was much larger.

Ben led her around the wall until they came to a large, wrought-iron fence. Just inside the fence was a stone guard stand, occupied by a light-haired man she guessed to be in his thirties.

"Hello, Ryan!" Ben called to the man.

"Ben." The man nodded, coming out of the stand to unlock and open the gate. "We've been expecting you." He turned to look up at Quinn; his ice-blue eyes brimming with curiosity. "And this is the girl?"

"Yes, Ryan, this is Quinn. Quinn, Ryan is another Friend of Philip. He has worked for L… for Ellen and Henry for many years."

"Lovely to meet you, Lady Quinn."

"It's just Quinn, Ryan. I'm not anyone special."

He raised his eyebrows at her, and then glanced up at Ben before smiling back at her. "All right, then, Quinn. Let's get you down and inside. I'm sure you're tired after your ride."

She followed Ben down a path to a side entrance of the house. Ryan had told them he would have the horses taken care of. Dusk had whuffled a bit anxiously at the stranger – this place was new to her, too – but she'd gone after a few calming words from Quinn.

There was a little gate at the entrance to a covered vestibule; it moved easily at Ben's touch. She felt suddenly nervous as he clasped the giant, circular knocker on the wooden door.

It was opened almost immediately. "You're here!" The dark-haired woman who answered the door looked relieved to see them. "Come in, come in! How was your ride? Was there any trouble on the road?"

They'd walked into what appeared to be a comfortable sitting room. Light streamed in from giant windows on either side of the door, and along another wall. Soft couches and armchairs lined the walls. They weren't alone in the room. Another woman and two men occupied a couple of couches that faced each other over a low table. Quinn had the impression that their arrival had interrupted a serious conversation.

"Everything was fine. We weren't stopped even once," Ben answered. "Ellen, this is Quinn. Quinn, this is Ellen Fisher – over there is her husband, Henry." One of the men stood and walked over to them. "This is their home."

"It's nice to meet you, Ellen. Thank you for having us here."

"The pleasure is ours, Quinn," Henry answered, reaching for her hand.

"Please make yourself comfortable while you are here," Ellen added. Her eyes were a deep gray, and they shone with sincerity, in a way that seemed somehow familiar. Quinn liked her immediately. "You must be hungry after your trip. Would you like some bread and vegetable stew?"

"That sounds wonderful, thank you."

Ellen and Henry both smiled. "Come have a seat, both of you," Henry said. "Ellen will bring out the food."

They followed Henry over to the couches; Ben waited until Quinn was settled on one end of a couch adjacent to the couple before he seated himself on the other end. Henry returned to the seat he had been occupying before they'd come in.

"Quinn, Ben, this is Andrew Gramble and his wife, Natalie."

Quinn nodded. "It's nice to meet you." The man and his wife were very young; Andrew didn't appear to be much older than William. They both looked exhausted; Natalie leaned close up against her husband with her feet pulled up under her, a blanket over her lap. There were dark circles under her eyes, and she looked like she was having trouble keeping them open. Quinn knew the feeling.

"They're from Harber Village. They arrived here late last night with some news."

"What?" she asked anxiously. "Have you heard about Thomas?"

Andrew's expression was grim. "As far as we can tell, he never made it there. Or if he did, it wasn't for long"

For a moment, she wondered if her heart had actually stopped. "What do you mean, as far as you can tell? You must know Lily and Graeme. Did they ever see him?"

Andrew looked directly at her; his brown eyes intense and serious. "Lily and Graeme disappeared some time ago. Nobody knows where they are."

"How? How is that even possible? What is going on here?" She felt herself on the verge of a panic attack, and nobody here was familiar or comfortable at all. The edges of the room were getting blurry. She realized for the first time that she'd never actually done the math – although it hadn't been exceptionally long in her perspective since she had seen Thomas, it was beginning to dawn on her that he had been missing for a *long* time. This was not good. "We have to find him!"

"Yes, Quinn, we do." Ben's voice was steady; he was trying to calm her. "Everyone here wants to find Thomas now. Panicking is not going to help."

She nodded, trying to control her breathing. She'd never be able to think when she was like this.

"Marcus, Nathaniel, and William will be here in a few hours," Henry said. "We can discuss what we are going to do then. We have Friends in several towns in the same mountains as Harber Village who are trying to gather information about what may have happened to Lily and Graeme – and to Thomas. For right now, we need to regroup, and wait for more information."

Quinn took deep breaths, but it wasn't helping. She felt like they'd been doing nothing but *regrouping* for two days, always stopping, waiting for someone else, for information.

"Are you all right Quinn?" Ellen had returned and was standing in front of her. She carried a tray, which held two large white bowls and several thick slices of bread.

"Yes, I just ..." she couldn't, she wasn't. "Would it be okay if I went outside for a few minutes? I think I need some fresh air or something."

Ellen looked over at her husband, who nodded, and then back at Quinn. "Of course. Just ... it would be best if you stayed within the grounds."

"Would you like me to come with you, Quinn?" Ben asked.

"No thanks. I could use a few minutes to myself." *Or at least a few minutes not surrounded by complete strangers.*

Ellen led her to the door, and handed her the bowl of stew and a slice of bread. Quinn walked quickly away from the house, across the wide yard until she came to what looked like an orchard. She wished now that she had insisted on going with William and Nathaniel, it felt all wrong being separated from them, too.

Nothing had happened when she had crossed the border with Ben. They'd barely seen anyone. After that, she did not understand why they couldn't have all just come here together. She wondered if she was going crazy. It didn't *feel* like she was sleeping, but right now she was wondering if this was just another one of her crazy dreams.

Quinn spent the better part of the afternoon alone outside, trying to calm herself. She walked around the grounds several times, trying to clear her head and put all of the pieces together. Clearly, the political situation in Philotheum was much more complicated and dangerous than she had thought it was – much more so than Thomas had thought, too. She knew from her own experience what a miserable excuse for a human being Tolliver was; the thought of him ruling a kingdom made her shudder.

Once she had calmed down enough to actually be able to eat her soup – even cold, it was delicious – she was able to think a little more clearly. Of course, Nathaniel and Marcus had probably been right about separating. They had seen a number of soldiers along the road coming here. The fact that they hadn't stopped what would have appeared to be a young couple didn't mean they wouldn't have stopped a larger group.

Thomas was already missing – she couldn't assume that any of them were safe. Thinking that, though, made the panic rise up inside her chest again. None of them were safe, and William and Nathaniel were out there on the road somewhere, with the soldiers patrolling everywhere. What if something happened to them? What if William disappeared, too? She closed her eyes and took a breath, trying to push that thought out of her mind – she couldn't start thinking it. She decided, though, that this was the last time she would allow herself to be separated from him on this trip, regardless of what other circumstances they ran in to. She couldn't do this again.

After eating, she paced the perimeter of the orchard a few more times before her thoughts were finally a little more controlled. Waiting was going to be a part of this – she was just going to have to get used to that fact. She yawned – not sleeping much last night, and the long ride this morning were finally getting to her. Good. Taking a nap would make the wait for William and Nathaniel pass more quickly.

When Quinn woke up, it took her several minutes to remember where she was. The room was both unfamiliar and pitch black, which was disconcerting. It had taken her awhile to fall asleep in Henry and Ellen's guest room because it had been so bright in the late afternoon when she'd asked to go and lay down. She stumbled over to where she remembered the window being, and pulled back the thin curtain. It was completely dark; she could barely see the dark outlines of the trees on the other side of the yard. If there was any moon left tonight, she couldn't see it.

She fumbled along the walls, looking for a light switch, and then realized that she was never going to find one. Before she had gone to sleep, she'd noticed a small oil lamp sitting next to the bed, and a candlestick on a high shelf near the door. She reached up now toward the shelf, and felt around until she hit the hard, metal shape. Pulling it down, she reached up onto the shelf again, feeling for something to light it with. After several seconds, she touched a long, wooden match. She struck it against the heavy doorjamb. It snapped in half.

She swore under her breath, and felt for the doorknob. She would find her way out to everyone else in the dark if she had to. She needed to see William -- and Nathaniel. The door opened quietly, and she was relieved to find that the hallway was dimly lit with candles every few feet, sitting on the same kind of high shelves as the one beside her door. Walking quickly, she tried to reverse the way Ellen had brought her here earlier from the sitting room they had all been in.

She found it easily, impressed with her improving navigation in strange places. Through the open doorway, she could see Ellen and Henry on the couch. Henry was sitting up, leaning against a cushion, his head propped on his hand. Ellen's head was in his lap, her body curled up beside him. They were alone in the room.

Henry looked up at the sound of her footsteps. "You did wake up. We thought you might sleep all night; you must have been exhausted."

Ellen pulled herself up beside him. "We worried about you when you missed dinner. Are you okay?"

She nodded. "I was just tired, I think. Where is everyone else?" Had she slept long enough to have missed their arrival and they'd all gone to bed?

Ellen cast a wary glance at her husband. "Ben, Andrew, and Natalie have gone to bed. They were all tired after dinner as well."

Quinn's heart gave a jolt. "Where are Nathaniel, William, and Marcus?"

"They haven't arrived yet," Henry answered.

"What do you mean? What time is it? It was only supposed to take them a few hours."

Henry nodded solemnly. "They should have been here about four hours ago."

She started to hyperventilate. "Where are they? Has anyone gone to look for them?"

"Calm down, Quinn," Henry said, though the worry in his own voice made him unconvincing. "We cannot panic about it yet. There are many possible reasons for them being a few hours late."

"Four is more than a few."

"If they haven't arrived by morning, then we will begin to worry. At any rate, we cannot put anyone else at risk by going out to look for them in the dark. We will wait until first light. We know the route they were taking, and we can search it tomorrow if we need to."

"You should eat, Quinn," Ellen said. "You need to keep up your strength; this is a trying time. I saved you a plate from dinner, let's go to the kitchen."

Her heart was racing so quickly she was afraid it might burst. She was well past the ability to make any decisions on her own, so she nodded woodenly and allowed Ellen to lead her toward the kitchen.

At that moment, there was a knock on the door. Ellen rushed to open it.

"Nathaniel!" she cried, throwing her arms around him. "Are you all right? Is everyone all right?"

"Yes, we're fine," he said, turning her to the side to allow Marcus and William in.

Great, heaving sobs broke from Quinn's chest when she saw them. William nearly ran to her in alarm. "Quinn! What is it? What's wrong?"

The sobs caught in her throat. She couldn't answer; she could barely breathe. They just kept coming, tears streaming down her face, dripping off her chin, soaking the front of her shirt. William pulled her into his arms, cradling her head against his shoulder.

"She was getting quite worried," Henry said in a quiet voice behind them.

William nodded and pulled her tighter; she clutched the back of his shirt as her sobs grew louder, shaking both of them. "Hey, shh... shh... it's okay, Quinn. We're here now, we're here. We're all right. We're here." He held her like that for a long time, rubbing her back and swaying back and forth as he whispered reassurances into her ear. The wracking sobs subsided slowly, and though her tears still flowed, she felt him breathe a sigh of relief.

He reached into his pocket and retrieved his handkerchief. "Here, honey, shh ..." he gently wiped the drips from her cheeks and chin before handing it to her.

She felt another comforting hand on her shoulder, and looked up to see Nathaniel standing there, his eyes gentle and apologetic. "I'm so sorry we scared you. We never meant for that to happen. We're all here, and we're all okay."

She nodded, and Nathaniel hugged her tightly before giving her back to William.

He kept his arm around her shoulders as he gently led her over to one of the couches. She sat down, pulling her knees up to her chin, one hand still clutching the damp handkerchief.

"What happened? Why are you so late?" she demanded, when she finally trusted herself to speak. She saw a glance pass between William and his uncle. "Everything. Tell me everything. I'm tired of guessing about everything and never knowing as much as anyone else. How am I supposed to be helpful if I don't even know what's going on?"

"First," said William, his voice careful, "We had a little trouble at the river."

"The water level was higher than we had anticipated," Nathaniel said. "And crossing was very difficult. All of the supplies we were carrying were soaked, and some were ruined. We're fortunate that we left most of our necessities in Anwin, and we'll be able to retrieve them. We lost a considerable amount of time drying everything out enough that we wouldn't be noticed as we traveled."

"And then?" She demanded.

"We were stopped on the road by some patrolling guards," Marcus answered.

"What?" her heart raced again.

"Relax, Quinn," William said beside her. "We're here and we're okay, obviously nothing bad happened."

"So what did happen?"

"It was frightening for a few minutes," Nathaniel answered. "There were two guards, and one of them recognized us. They detained us, telling us we would have to be questioned."

She thought she might be sick.

"They took us back to one of their homes," Nathaniel continued.

"I've never been so freaked out in my life," William added. "But, obviously, we're okay," he told her again, this time squeezing her hand.

"When we got inside the house, both of them flashed us their tattoos," Nathaniel's voice was serious, but tinged with the relief he was obviously still feeling.

"We have Friends among the guard now?" Henry asked, amazed.

"We always have," Marcus answered, casting a look at Henry that held reproof and something else she couldn't decipher. "But it seems their numbers are growing. Clearly, Tolliver hasn't been able to offer enough incentive to all of his soldiers to keep them toeing his line."

"Not that any amount of incentive would ever have been enough for many," Nathaniel said, and after her conversation with Ben today, She understood the appreciative glance he directed at Marcus.

"We spent a few hours talking with them. They fed us dinner, and then accompanied us for a good part of our journey, though they didn't wish to come far enough to know exactly where we were coming." Relief was still evident on Marcus' face, though now that she was thinking more clearly again, She could also see a dark shadow underneath his eyes.

She looked over at Nathaniel, and then up at William, who was sitting so close to her on the couch that they were nearly touching. "What else happened?" she demanded.

Nathaniel sighed, his shadow growing darker, and a deep line appearing between his eyebrows. "The two guards – their names were Tobin and Derek – did share with us some news."

Quinn's stomach tightened ominously, and William placed his hand on her shoulder again.

"Lily, Graeme, and Thomas were all taken into the custody of Tolliver's personal guard some time ago."

The floor started to look uneven again; she felt William start to tremble next to her, though his expression was steady. "What? How? What? ..." She didn't know what question to ask ... or what she even wanted to know.

Nathaniel seemed to feel the same way. He stood and paced the floor, directly behind the couch where William and Quinn were sitting, as Marcus spoke.

"From what little information we have, it appears as though Thomas *did* make it to Harber Village, but he was followed there. Some guard recognized him at the border, and he was watched for the rest of his trip – he never knew. For two days, Philothean guards tracked his every move, reporting back directly to Tolliver."

William clutched her hand again – this was clearly no easier for him to hear a second time. Behind them, Nathaniel rested one hand on each of their shoulders. Quinn tried to concentrate on what Marcus was saying.

"Lily and Graeme have been targets for some time. Graeme is one of the leading members of the ruling council of Harber Village, and he has been outspoken against Tolliver's policies from the beginning. And then Lily – with her ties to Eirentheos, and her practice as a healer using the new methods ... Their prominence has caused no end of frustration to Tolliver, and those to whom he has promised positions of power in his 'new government.'"

"So where are they? Where has Tolliver taken them? To his castle?"

"Oh, definitely not. Many of Tolliver's current actions are in direct contradiction to what his father has ordered him to do. Hector is more patient than his son. He knows that directly provoking Eirentheos would not be a good plan. Our sources indicate that he doesn't know much about many of the soldiers' activities within the villages, either. The people are growing upset, and I don't think Tolliver begins to realize the consequences of that. Hector would."

"So where, then?"

"Derek and Tobin both seem to think that they would likely be held at one of the estates of one of Tolliver's head soldiers."

"But why? What would Tolliver *do* with Thomas? What good does it do him to hold him captive?"

William moved beside her. "Tolliver hates Thomas, for one thing. He's never much liked any of us ... but he now has a personal grudge against both Thomas and I for that incident at the naming ceremony. He's made no secret of that."

"So he's what? Holding Thomas as some kind of revenge for that?"

"No," Nathaniel answered. "I'm sure it's more than that. First of all, there's no way he could allow Thomas to reach Harber Village and interact with the people there. Right now, he and his supporters are spreading rumors there that Stephen has withdrawn his support of them, and that Lily and Graeme fled from them, effectively abandoning the village to Tolliver and his army. His soldiers have been terrorizing the village for over a cycle now."

"Terrorizing them how?"

"Tolliver has basically given them free rein to do as they please within the village. Essentially, they have occupied Harber Village – Tolliver's own people are under control of his army there. They've raided the shops, stolen things from people's homes ..." Marcus sighed. "Almost nobody in the entire village has any jewelry or silverware left. The soldiers just take what they like, and sell it wherever they can. Harber Village is very isolated – most of the population of Philotheum has no idea about what's going on there."

"So Lily's pendant ..."

"I'm sure was stolen some time ago, and found its way to that market in Eirentheos. The people In Harber Village are becoming more and more afraid of Tolliver and his guards. Some of them apparently have a habit of showing up, uninvited, in people's homes at mealtimes. Lily and Graeme were the most outspoken citizens against it. Stephen has been supporting them as much as he can, but it has been a desperate situation."

"So what do we do? How do we find them?" She was starting to get a little panicked again.

Behind her, Nathaniel rested both of his hands on her shoulders. "I know it's hard, Quinn," he said. "But we wait, we gather the information we need in order to proceed, and we do this the right way, without putting anyone else in danger."

"Or potentially creating *more* danger for Thomas," William added – she could tell that he'd felt her tense defiantly beside him.

"For tonight," Marcus said, "we go to sleep. It's late, and it's been a long day for everyone. I know I'm exhausted. I'll see you all in the morning." She watched as Marcus disappeared down the dark hallway toward the bedrooms.

"Are you going to be *able* to sleep again, Quinn?" Ellen asked. She looked over at Nathaniel. "She was so exhausted that she just slept for several hours."

She thought about it. She started to nod; her arms and legs felt unnaturally heavy, and she'd had to suppress several yawns during their conversation, but then an image of the dark, lonely room flooded her mind. William turned to her in alarm when she began trembling again – she couldn't help it. The panic she'd been holding back all day was still there, just under the surface. The idea of being alone again in a strange place, for hours on end brought it all crashing down on her again.

"What's wrong?" William asked.

Her hands were shaking, and she felt cold; all of her strength seemed to have drained away. She didn't know how to answer, so she just shook her head.

Nathaniel came around the couch and knelt down in front of her. "Quinn, what is it? Are you okay? What's going on?"

She swallowed and blinked furiously, trying to see through the strange tears that threatened to spill over. Nathaniel took her hands in his and looked up at William.

"Hey, come here," William said, adjusting her so that her head rested on his arm. Nathaniel sat down, close on her other side. She didn't speak, just stared ahead, still blinking against the tears.

William couldn't remember ever feeling so helpless before. He'd wondered when all of this was going to get to her, and now he felt like he should have seen it coming when he and Nathaniel had left her alone with people she didn't really know. It had bothered him, this morning, watching her ride off with Ben, all by herself.

Earlier tonight, when it had gotten dark and they still had a long distance to ride – he had known, then, that she would be worried. He'd had vivid flashes of what it would have been like if the situation were reversed, if she had been out on the road with Nathaniel and Marcus, and he'd been trapped somewhere, not knowing if they were safe – if she were safe.

He understood the panicked look in her eyes now, almost like a rabbit caught in a trap, and he was overcome by an urge to fix it for her – to take her into his arms and tell her that everything was going to be okay, that there was nothing to worry about, that he would take care of everything.

He couldn't do that, of course. For one thing, he didn't know if it was true. Right now, everything was such a mess; he needed someone to tell him it was going to be okay, because he really wasn't so sure.

So he did the only thing he could do – he sat there next to her, her head against him. After a few minutes, he took hold of her hand and squeezed it gently, without saying anything. He felt her nod slightly, and she raised her hand to her eyes briefly, wiping away a tear that must have slipped.

Ellen came into the room – he hadn't even noticed that she'd left – carrying a tray of sandwiches and mugs of steaming tea.

"Quinn never ate dinner," she said. "And I'm sure you might be hungry again by now. I meant to feed all of you before Marcus went to bed."

Nathaniel nodded. "Thank you so much, Ellen. We appreciate your hospitality more than you know."

William was suddenly embarrassed. "I'm so sorry; I've been so rude. You've been gracious enough to offer us your home, and I haven't even introduced myself."

Ellen chuckled. "I think we may be a little past all of the formalities, William, Prince of Eirentheos. We're all in this together. It's lovely to meet you, and please don't hesitate to make yourself at home here."

He nodded. "Thank you so much, for everything."

"The pleasure is ours," Henry said, standing and putting an arm around his wife's waist. "I only wish that we'd first been able to get to know one another in more pleasant circumstances. Please make yourselves at home here. Feel free to use anything you need, or ask if there's something you can't find."

"Thank you both," Nathaniel said, rising from the couch and walking over to them. Henry let go of Ellen long enough for Nathaniel to give her a long, fierce hug.

William was perplexed. Nathaniel was obviously quite close to Ellen and her husband, but today was the first time William had heard either of their names. After many years of living and traveling with his uncle in two worlds, he'd thought he knew everyone Nathaniel spent time with. This whole journey so far had been filled with surprises.

"Of course," Henry answered. "We're going to go to bed in a few minutes. There is plenty of food in the kitchen, if you need anything else."

Nathaniel nodded. He watched Ellen and Henry disappear down a long hallway, and then he turned back around and reached toward the tray Ellen had brought out. "Would you like a sandwich, William?"

"Sure. Quinn?" he asked, looking at the top of her head. Nathaniel, still standing over them, shook his head. "She's asleep."

"Oh," William mouthed silently. He frowned. What did he do now? He looked up to his uncle for help.

Nathaniel smiled, and then adjusted one of the cushions at the end of the long couch to act as a pillow. He helped William gently move the girl so that her head lay against it. Though her eyes never opened, she stirred slightly, her body grew stiff, and she mumbled, her voice so sad that he thought it might break his heart. "Not alone again … not alone."

William pulled her feet into his lap, reaching up to softly stroke the back of her hand. She seemed to relax, her head sinking into the cushion, and her arms curling into her chest.

When he looked up, he saw his uncle watching him, an intense look in his eyes that held meaning William couldn't decipher. Once William's eyes met his, Nathaniel shrugged, then handed him one of the sandwiches. He walked over to the hallway, and opened the door to a small closet there, which made William raise his eyebrows again. When he returned, he carried a pillow and two blankets, which he set next to William.

SHOCKING

Pale sunlight was streaming across her face when Quinn woke up. She remembered where she was, but she was confused about what she was doing on the couch in the sitting room. Just then, a motion on the couch across from her caught her eye. She sat up to investigate.

"You're really awake," William said. He was sitting there, leaning against a cushion on the end of the other couch.

"Yeah," she said, kicking off the blanket and pulling herself up so she could stretch. "Why am I out here?"

He shrugged. "You fell asleep out here. You were so tired … it didn't seem like a good idea to wake you."

"Oh … Did you sleep out here, too?" she asked, noticing the neatly folded blanket and the pillow on the other end of his couch.

"Yeah … Would you like some tea?" He nodded toward the low table between them; two steaming mugs sat in the middle.

"When did you make this?" She picked up the mug closest to her. It warmed her hands, and she sniffed at the steam, inhaling the scent of the tea she was starting to love. It had a taste that was somehow both sweet and a little spicy. She settled back against the cushions, pulling her knees up into her chest, and setting the cup on top of them.

"I just brought it in here a few minutes ago. You've been kind of stirring for awhile. Were you dreaming again?"

"Um ..." she closed her eyes, searching, and then shook her head. "If I was, I don't remember. Was I talking? Sometimes I talk when I have really vivid dreams."

"Not this morning, no."

His voice sounded a little too careful. Her cheeks flushed and she narrowed her eyes. "What did I say last night?"

He looked down, staring into his own mug of tea. "Nothing really ... just that ... you didn't want to be alone."

"Oh." Her face turned a furious shade of red now.

He looked up, watching her. "Hey, Quinn. It's okay – totally understandable, given the circumstances. We should have realized that would be hard for you."

"So you stayed out here with me?"

"Yeah."

Warmth filled her chest – and it wasn't from the hot beverage she was drinking. "Thank you."

They both sat there and sipped intently at their tea, neither really knowing what to say. She was relieved when Ellen came into the room.

"Good morning," she said. "Are you two hungry for breakfast?"

"Sure," she answered quickly. Her stomach rumbled – she realized she hadn't eaten since lunchtime yesterday. "Can we help you?"

She followed Ellen into the kitchen without waiting for a response; she needed something to do with her hands.

Quinn didn't know what the day was going to hold. After breakfast, Nathaniel, Henry, and Marcus announced that they were going to speak to some other Friends of Philip at another safe house on the other side of Estora. She was desperate to go, to be a part of things, get out and see for herself what was going on, but Nathaniel was adamant that she stay right where she was.

"There are things about this you don't understand, Quinn. We cannot risk having you out on the roads, among the people when we don't even know what's going on," he'd said.

"Then tell me! What don't I understand? How am I ever going to help here if you keep telling me that I don't understand? Make me understand."

Nathaniel's eyes had been set, more firmly that she had ever seen them before. "You're not going, and neither is William. We cannot risk another prince of Eirentheos when we have no idea what Tolliver is doing with Thomas. We simply do not know everything we need to know. I promise, Quinn, that I will tell you what I can – when I can."

The situation was starting to feel hopeless, an endless time of waiting, wondering, and not *doing* anything, which made her feel a little crazy. If she could be out, riding, heading somewhere, on their way to get Thomas, or find something, she would have felt better. Instead, they were stuck.

As she worked around Ellen and Henry's home that morning, she wished that something – anything -- would happen. Just before lunch, she regretted her wish.

She and William were in the kitchen, helping Ellen chop vegetables when there was a frantic knocking at the door. Ellen dropped the knife she had been holding and ran to pull it open, Quinn and William on her heels.

Ryan was standing there with Ben, who had gone outside to assist him with some things in the grounds. He looked panicked. "My Lady, it's Tolliver. He's just down the road, on his way here."

Quinn looked at William in shock. His terrified eyes matched hers.

Ellen's voice, however, was steady enough to surprise her. "How many guards has he brought with him, Ryan?"

"It appears to be only one, Lady."

She nodded, and then glanced over at Ben. "Have you ever met Tolliver?"

Ben shook his head, "I've seen him at a distance, but no."

"Good. Stay with Ryan. The two of you can take care of the horses and keep his … friend … entertained. When you have a chance to slip away, Ryan, you must go and find Henry, let him know what's going on, and get him back here, *without* Nathaniel and Marcus. You, and you," she turned her steel eyes on William and Quinn. Come with me. Now."

Shocked and frightened beyond speaking, they followed Ellen back through the kitchen, and into a large pantry behind it. The woman moved with quick, deliberate movements, though her manner remained calm. Once inside the pantry, she closed the door behind them. Quinn looked over at William, confused, then watched, amazed as Ellen reached into a concealed handle and pulled open a large section of the floor, revealing stairs.

"Wha…" she started to ask, but Ellen shot her a look that silenced her instantly. Ellen pointed down into the opening, and Quinn obeyed immediately, walking quickly down the stairs. William followed closely behind. As soon as his head dipped below the floor, the heavy door dropped silently closed. They heard the pantry door open and close again, and then the sound of Ellen's light footsteps crossing back across the kitchen floor.

Once the door had closed, the space they were in was completely black. Quinn had to edge her foot carefully forward to find the next step before she stepped down.

William caught up to her in the darkness, and, after a second, she felt his hand on her shoulder, steadying her.

Somehow, her panic grew stronger in this space. Her heart was hammering so loudly in her ears that she couldn't hear either of their footsteps as they cautiously made their way to the bottom of the staircase. The bottom was farther away than she imagined it possibly could be, but finally she felt the surface under her feet change from the wooden stairs that gave, and threatened to creak, with each step, to solid stone.

Still unable to see, she set both feet carefully on the floor and felt around, stretching one foot in every direction, trying to ensure there were no more hidden steps. William placed both his hands on her shoulders, moving with her, their motions in sync with one another.

"Are you okay?" William whispered, after several seconds.

She nodded, afraid to speak, but knowing that he would feel her gesture in the close proximity. Her heart was slowing enough for her to hear around her now, but there was nothing to hear, no sounds drifting down through the floor above them. The only thing she could hear was William breathing right next to her.

When several more minutes passed without a sound, some of her muscles relaxed. Both of them began slowly making their way across the floor. Whatever kind of room they were in felt long and wide. The floor was smooth and open under their feet. No light trickled in from anywhere. Even when plenty of time had passed for her eyes to have adjusted, she couldn't see anything. William stayed right beside her, at least one hand always on her shoulder or elbow.

After what seemed far too many tiny, shuffling steps for the enclosed space, William stopped. He lifted her hand so that she, too, could feel the stone wall with her hand. She was surprised at the relief she felt, touching the wall. The tangible boundary gave her a sense of place, and she was able to take a deep breath and calm herself a bit. He didn't drop his hand, still keeping it under her elbow as she slid carefully to the floor, leaning up against the wall. Then he sat down next to her, close enough that they stayed touching.

She wondered how long it had been. The dark, and the fear, were so oppressive around her that she had lost all perception of time. Their journey from the middle of the stairs to the wall where they now sat might have taken less than a minute, or more than half an hour. She had no way of knowing.

Suddenly, from right above them came the sound of heavy footsteps, moving across the ceiling. Then something being dragged across the wooden floor, just before the footsteps stopped.

"Have I interrupted you in the middle of preparing a meal?"

Quinn's stomach clenched – she would have recognized that voice anywhere; she often heard it in her nightmares. Beside her, William's body grew rigid.

"It is midday, Tolliver. Isn't this what people do?" Even through the floor, Ellen's voice still sounded calm, though with a slightly irritated edge.

"I wouldn't know, Sister. I've never felt the need to live away from the castle and from those whose job it is to worry about such mundane matters for those of royal blood."

Quinn's jaw slammed down so far toward her chest that she was a little surprised when it didn't break. She felt William's head snap around toward hers, and she had to work to keep her heart rate from distorting her hearing again.

"No, I suppose you wouldn't."

"Are you preparing all of this for yourself? Where's that husband of yours that likes to keep you out here in the weeds?"

Quinn sucked in a breath, thinking of the extra knives and things she and William had just left lying on the counter. It wouldn't look much like Ellen was alone up there.

"He's gone to visit with some friends in town. I do have servants, and they eat here, too. Much of this is for dinner – he will have returned by then."

"I trust you won't mind if your little brother joins you for that?"

"You're welcome to join us, Tolliver. You know there will always be room at my table for family."

Quinn took deep breaths; her attempts to calm her thudding heart were mostly unsuccessful. William took his hand in hers and squeezed it. Though his touch was gentle, she could feel his shock and stress radiating through the motion. She squeezed back, and then he allowed her hand to rest back on her lap, but his hand stayed where it was, intertwined with hers.

"So where are all of these illustrious servants of yours? I'm rather thirsty after my ride."

The sound was muffled by the floor between them, but the noise Ellen made next sounded to Quinn like something between a cough and a choke. Her stomach twisted, and William gave her hand another gentle squeeze.

"Tolliver, do you really think that after everything you've been doing lately that I would expose my servants to you? They're free to do as they feel they need to in my home, and if that includes making themselves scarce when someone they have reason to fear decides to just drop by, that option is available to them here."

"And what reason would they have to fear me?" Scorn was thick in Tolliver's voice. "Anyone privileged enough to have a place in a royal home in this country should be honored by a visit from the heir to the throne."

William's hand in hers was growing clammy and cold. This time it was Quinn who rubbed the back of his hand reassuringly.

"Don't start with me, Tolliver." The tone in Ellen's voice right then convinced Quinn that none of this was a charade – they had somehow found themselves in the home of Tolliver's older sister. "I've made my feelings on this situation clear enough. It's not up for discussion. You will keep your distance from anyone here in my home. Let me finish putting these vegetables in for broth, and we can go for a walk. How is Mother?"

The next moments – it felt like hours, but in reality was probably only ten minutes or so – were excruciating for Quinn. She could tell, by the short heavy breaths coming from next to her, and the sweat on the hand clutched in hers, that William was having just as difficult a time as she was, if not more so.

The conversation between Tolliver and Ellen that came through the floor became banal, his voice condescending, and hers clipped and serious. Quinn felt her empty hand clench into a fist over and over, while her foot tapped of its own accord. Every time one of them spoke, she wished that one of them would say something, *anything* that would be helpful, or useful, or give her an idea of what in the *hell* was going on here. Her fear of being discovered was dissolving as her irritation grew.

By the time they heard the footsteps crossing the floor again, followed by a door closing, and then silence, Quinn was holding herself back from flying up the stairs and confronting Tolliver herself.

"What *is* this?" She demanded as soon as they'd heard Tolliver and Ellen exit. She flew up from the floor, unable to sit still for even a second longer. Well past caution in the dark space, she paced back and forth, attempting to keep her head from exploding.

"Shh, Quinn. You don't know that it's safe."

She knew he was right, but she didn't care. "Ellen is Tolliver's *sister*? Did you know this?"

"No, I didn't." She hadn't heard him stand, but his voice came from somewhere beside her, not from the floor.

"Does Nathaniel? Marcus? Ben?"

"I don't know what anybody knows. Nathaniel has never brought me here before, ever. Although it seems like he's been here more than once." His voice was hard, strained.

"Why is Tolliver here? What is going on, William? Is this some kind of a trap? We're down in some dark dungeon and they've gone outside so they can set the place on fire?" She knew she was only getting louder, but she couldn't do anything about it.

"Hey, don't start thinking like that." His hand came out of the dark, tentatively feeling. He found the side of her upper arm first, right in the spot that was still a healing pink from her stitches. He paused, one finger gently tracing the new skin, and then lower, down past her elbow, all the way until his hand touched hers, and then he pulled her into his arms.

She stood there, still as a statue, consumed half by a paralyzing mixture of terror and anger, and the other half by another emotion entirely. Though she was rigid and unmoving, his arms still wound around her back, holding her tight. "We can't think like that, Quinn. We don't know what's going on; let's not make this worse by jumping to conclusions. Let's assume, for now, that we're okay. That she's hidden us only for our safety, and we'll find out what this is all about later."

She swallowed, trying to get past the fear and aggravation. Her fingers trembled. It wasn't working, trapped here in the dark and silence.

"It's going to be okay," he murmured against her hair.

She snapped. "Since when are you so Susie Sunshine about everything?"

He was absolutely still for just a second, before his entire body started shaking, in great, heaving motions coming from his chest. She was startled, confused, and then the silence was broken by his snorting, and the laughter overtook her, too.

Once she started laughing, she couldn't stop, and it was clear that neither could he. They both stood there shaking, trying to keep quiet, trying to stop, but every time one of them calmed down enough to take a breath, the other would snicker, and it would start all over again. Tears were rolling down her cheeks, her stomach was aching, and she could hardly breathe, but the laughter kept coming.

Finally, finally, she managed to pull in a breath at the same time he did. They clutched each other's arms tightly, trying to regain control. The hysterical giggles kept threatening to break through, but at last they were calm.

William softly cleared his throat. "Only one of us can freak out at a time."

She nodded. "Agreed."

And then, somehow, his lips were against hers. Softly, at first, his bottom lip grazed her top one. She knew, in the part of her brain that was still capable of rational thought, that she should have been surprised by this, but it wasn't thought that drove her now. Her mouth responded on its own, as did her hands, reaching around him, clutching the back of his thin shirt.

He pulled her body closer with one hand, the other finding the back of her neck, under her hair, his fingers gently caressing, twining in her hair ...

There was a loud thud directly overhead. They jerked apart, as if shocked by a jolt of electricity. After an eternity, his hand found hers again, squeezing it tight as they listened to the footsteps crossing the floor above.

COMPLICATIONS

The footsteps over their heads crossed the floor several times, going back and forth as William and Quinn stood frozen, holding hands while their hearts thudded in unison. After who knew how long, there was the sound of a door opening and closing, and then it was silent again.

Still barely able to move, or to think, Quinn reached out in desperation for the wall again, dragging him with her. As soon as she found it, she slumped down toward the floor, and he went with her.

They sat there as the sounds of their breathing returned to normal, William squeezing her hand while she curled into a ball.

"What *was* that?" she finally sputtered. She knew he would know that she hadn't meant the noise upstairs.

"I ... I don't know."

She nodded. "That makes two of us." Suddenly, she was grateful for the complete darkness, which hid her scarlet cheeks.

His deep sigh filled the silence.

Quinn felt like her entire world had suddenly shifted to the left, or flipped completely upside down. She had just *kissed*

William, or he had just kissed her, or … *no,* it had definitely been mutual.

Thomas had kissed *her;* she knew that for certain now. Even with Zander, aside from a few, shy, tentative attempts on Quinn's part, the actual kissing and other physical affection generally started and ended with him. She was always a willing participant, but … what had just happened with William was so entirely different that she couldn't wrap her head around it.

What stunned her even more was how they were both reacting now. They sat there, silent, right next to each other in the darkness, his hand wrapped around hers in a way that told her both that nothing had changed, and that everything had.

"Well," she whispered, after an eternity, "if we're going to be stuck here for awhile, we should see if there's anything else down here, or if it's just a crazy empty room."

"Okay." He moved beside her, getting onto his hands and knees.

She followed suit, crawling along the wall behind him, feeling around in every direction she could reach, but there was nothing. William finally reached the back wall, and there hadn't been anything but smooth floor and walls the entire way. It was a large, dark, empty prison. They stopped again, in that corner. No sounds came from anywhere.

Quinn curled her legs up under her, resting her head on her knees, trying to think. After a moment, her head snapped up. "The stairs, Will."

"What?"

"We never checked out the area by the stairs. If they keep anything down here, it's probably somewhere by the stairs."

He sighed. "If I had any idea where the stairs *are* now."

She chuckled, and then started crawling back along the wall. As she crawled the length of the floor, Quinn guessed that the space ran most of the length of the upstairs, at least the entire kitchen and sitting room they'd been spending their time in. She had no idea how wide it was, but the soft sounds they were making disappeared into the darkness, rather than echoing back.

When they reached the corner at the other end of the room, she turned and started edging toward where the stairs had to be, William stayed just barely behind her, breathing in quick gulps. Finally, she reached for the side of the wall, and her hand hit empty space. Stretching a little further, she felt the wood of the bottom step.

"Okay," she whispered, mostly to herself, though William's attention was on her absolutely. "A little further."

And then, just past the stairs, her hand reached into a wide, open space, then landed on the hard, unmistakable shape of a wooden box with a soft *clunk*. William was next to her instantly, sitting down with her as they worked to find the latch that would allow them to lift the lid.

The box creaked open, and William's arm appeared, blocking her way as she tried to reach in. She understood his protective sentiment, and in a different situation, she might have appreciated it, but her reaction now was to knock it out of the way.

He chuckled softly in the darkness, and then shifted his body so that she could feel inside the box, too. It was heavy and full. The top of the box was filled with folds of heavy cloth in different textures; she couldn't make sense of what it might be. But as she and William dug further, reaching under the material, she heard a muted metallic clunk. She reached toward the sound, but before she found the source, her fingers closed around something softer – something waxy.

"I think I found a candle," she whispered, pulling it out.

William reached for her hand, feeling the object, then plunged back into the box. Quinn set the candle down next to

235

her, freeing both hands to help dig. The two of them lifted the heavy cloths out, tossing them aside. The bottom of the box was filled with different types of things, most of which she couldn't identify by touch. She pulled out several more candles, laying them in a neat pile beside her next to the first one she had found.

"Yes!" William whispered triumphantly. A second later, she heard a scraping sound against the stone floor, and then a tiny flame flickered to life.

As small as it was, after being in complete darkness for so long, the light nearly blinded her as she fumbled for a candle from the stack beside her. Shielding her eyes with one hand, she stretched the candle toward William with the other, and a new point of light pierced the heavy black that surrounded them.

Quinn blinked furiously as she watched William lean over the box with the candle. The dark forms and shapes started to make sense as she wiped the dripping water from her eyes, and she lifted out a metal candlestick. Wiping her sleeve across her eyes one more time, she reached and took the candle from William. His own eyelashes fluttered so rapidly she doubted he could see as well as she could. She set the candle carefully in the candlestick, and then moved the small light away from them, until their eyes could adjust.

William nodded, rubbing his eyes as he blew out the match.

After several minutes, when they were finally comfortable, William reached into the box for another candlestick. He lit another candle with the flame from the first one, and then handed the holder to her.

The soft, orange glow from the flames transformed the space. She could see her own shape, stretched out in a shimmering dark shadow along the wall of the alcove under the stairs, William's form next to hers. Her eyes grew wide. The small storage area was filled to overflowing with crates and wooden boxes like the one they had just opened. The pile of heavy fabric they had set to the side now revealed itself as several thick blankets.

The bottom of the box they had opened was lined with more candles, candlesticks, and a number of small wooden boxes filled with long matches. There were several other small, metal objects in the box, but in the dim light she couldn't tell what they were.

Quinn and William worked together silently over the supplies. He lit several more candles while she folded the blankets neatly and laid them further to the side, creating more space to work.

The next box they opened contained jars and jars of food. She raised her eyebrows, a creepy feeling in her stomach all over again, as she wondered exactly what this place was, and for how long people were intended to stay here.

A nearby crate held several heavy, down pillows, and another box was filled with more thick blankets. After they opened a box that was completely filled with more of the white, waxy candles, they stopped digging; it appeared that they would keep finding more of the same kinds of supplies.

She grabbed one of the lit candleholders from the floor, and started walking away from the stairs, back into the long room. William stood, and grabbed his own candle to follow her.

In the dim light, the room was much the same as she'd suspected, bare stone walls and a smooth, stone floor. It wasn't quite as big as it had felt in the complete darkness, but it wasn't small. Aside from the high shelves every few feet along the walls, it was completely empty.

She was reaching up to set the candlestick she was holding in one of the sconces, when they suddenly heard a light patter of footsteps across the kitchen floor upstairs. They both froze, listening.

The steps kept crossing, moving toward the back of the kitchen; when she strained to listen, she could hear separate patterns, one heavier than the other.

"Two?" she mouthed to William.

He nodded.

As soon as the footsteps crossed back into where she was sure the pantry must be, she extinguished her candle. They flew around the room blowing out the candles they'd lit, and ran for the alcove under the stairs, their motions perfectly in sync, though they didn't speak. William, holding a single candle, climbed over boxes until he reached one large enough to conceal them both. Quinn slid in next to them just as they heard the quiet *whoosh* of the trapdoor opening. William licked his thumb and forefinger, and pinched the tiny flame.

Neither one of them breathed as the footsteps moved down the wooden steps. Though she didn't dare to look up and over the wooden box that sheltered them, peering barely around the side of the box, she could see a feeble, flickering circle of light dissipating the shadows near the bottom of the stairs.

The footsteps came to rest on the stone floor, and she was able to make out a shadow – no, two shadows, and two small flames. Needing to know, she stretched just a bit further around the box, and then William caught the back of her shirt and pulled her toward him.

"Lady Quinn?" It was a woman's voice, but Quinn couldn't place the soft, almost whispering, tone. The small circles of light moved cautiously around the room. "Prince William?"

"Where are you?" The second voice was male, and though he, too, spoke just barely above a whisper, it sounded more familiar to her. "It's Andrew and Natalie. It's all right. You're safe."

"Who?" Quinn jumped at the sudden feeling of William's breath, directly in her ear.

She felt for his shoulder, to squeeze it gently. "I think it's okay," she whispered back.

"We're here," she called quietly. "What are you doing here?"

She had completely forgotten about the young couple she had met when she'd arrived here yesterday. She wondered what they had been doing all day today – she hadn't seen either of them since she'd gone into the sitting room yesterday and announced that she needed to rest.

Natalie had nodded reassuringly at her, and said something about seeing her at dinner, but Quinn had slept right through that.

"We're looking for you," Andrew answered.

William stood up, positioning himself in front of Quinn. "Who are you?"

"My name is Andrew Gramble. This is my wife, Natalie. We are Friends of Philip." He stretched the candle he was holding toward William, and used his free hand to pull the collar of his shirt to the side, revealing the small tattoo.

William's tension tangibly eased, and he started climbing back over the boxes to reach Andrew and Natalie. He held one hand up behind him, as if he were cautioning Quinn to stay back, but she ignored him and went around the box the other way.

"What are you doing here? How did you find us?" William asked.

"We've been here …" Andrew started.

"I met them," Quinn interrupted. "But I haven't seen them since mid-afternoon yesterday. I had completely forgotten they were here." She turned back to the couple. "Where have you been?"

"My wife hasn't been … feeling so well," Andrew answered, putting his arms around Natalie protectively. Quinn looked over at her and saw how pale her face was in the dim candlelight. As she started to turn her attention back to William, she caught a glimpse of the young woman's shadow, and was startled as she noticed the round bulge under her dress. "I've been staying with her in our room, hoping she can get some rest."

William nodded; she could tell that he'd noticed Natalie's condition before she had. "How did you find us?" he asked again.

"Once we saw that Tolliver was here, we were certain that Ellen would have shown you how to get down here. We hid in our room until we saw through the window that Tolliver and Ellen had left to go riding, and then we came."

"What is Tolliver doing here?" Quinn asked.

Andrew shrugged. "I'm sure we will have a chance to hear about it later. He drops by to visit Ellen on occasion, I know. He still thinks he has some kind of influence over her."

"Doesn't he? Did you know that Ellen is Tolliver's sister?" William's voice was rough.

A deep crease appeared in Andrew's forehead. "Yes, of course. Half-sister, anyway. Ellen is the daughter of Queen Sophia and King Jonathan. Did you not know?"

William shook his head. "No. We had no idea. Why have we been brought to the home of Tolliver's half-sister?"

"There aren't many safer safe houses than this one. There isn't much I would put past Tolliver, but he won't interfere with Ellen."

The frustration was building inside her. "If this house is so safe, then why are we locked in a dark basement with no information?"

Not for the first time, Andrew's expression was completely confused. He turned to look at his wife, mouthing something at her that she didn't catch. Natalie shrugged her shoulders, her confusion matching his.

William's voice changed from confused to shocked. "Are you saying that Tolliver's own sister is part of the resistance against him?"

"Of course. Jonathan's children wish to see the crown of Philotheum restored to where it belongs more than anything."

Quinn considered this.

"Are you all right?" William's concerned voice interrupted her thoughts. She followed his gaze, and saw immediately who he meant. Natalie, who had been standing there silently throughout the exchange, had grown pale white. Beads of sweat formed on her forehead.

William didn't wait for her to answer; he pulled one of the crates from the alcove over to Natalie. "I'm all right … just tired," she said, as William and Andrew both helped lower her down onto it.

"How long before the baby is due?" William asked, his eyes darting between Natalie and her husband.

"Another week or so," Andrew told him.

William raised his eyebrows, as did Quinn. "In other words," he said, "any time now?"

Natalie nodded. "I don't think it's time yet, though. It's just been a very difficult few days for us."

"Is this your first baby?"

"Yes, but my aunt is the midwife in Harber Village. I've seen plenty of babies born. There aren't any signs that this little one is ready to come today."

"You're sure?"

She nodded. "I'm okay. It's just a backache."

Just then, there was another sound upstairs. A soft thud, perhaps a door closing, was followed by two sets of footsteps, one heavy and one that was lighter. Quinn's heart began racing again.

"Sounds as though Tolliver has returned," Andrew whispered.

The four of them grew silent, each straining to listen to the muffled conversation that drifted through the floorboards.

"When should we expect Henry to decide to join us?" Quinn could almost *see* the condescending sneer on Tolliver's face.

241

"He'll be here when he gets here. You're the one who showed up unannounced, remember?"

"Fine. Then I guess we can begin our discussion without him."

"Ah… I rather wondered when you would drop the charade of just coming by to visit with your sister."

"Speaking of that, darling *sister*, I'm thinking that it's high time you began meeting your familial obligations and supporting your brother."

"Excuse me?"

"Let's not pretend you don't know what I mean. I'm going to need your undivided support once I become king."

Quinn's stomach turned furiously, and William moved closer beside her.

"Whatever makes you think I would give it to you, Tolliver?"

"Do you not value your property here, this home, this life of luxury you lead?"

"Don't make me laugh, little brother. Does your father even know you're here? Does *Mother?*"

William raised his eyebrows. Quinn glanced over at Natalie and Andrew. They were listening to the conversation overhead, but they didn't seem particularly surprised.

"Look, Ellen. I need your help with something. And you are going to give it to me."

"Does this have anything to do with your ridiculous scheme of holding captive a prince of Eirentheos?"

William reached out towards Quinn, and she took his hand, squeezing it tightly.

"What? How do you know about that?"

"Keep trying me, Tolliver. You'll find out what I know, and it won't be to your benefit. So what is this asinine plan of yours with that boy? What do you possibly hope to accomplish by taking one of Stephen's sons?"

"I'm not going to keep him. It's not one of his *sons* that I'm after. And this is where your help comes in. I need someone with your … *diplomacy* skills to help me make the exchange."

Ellen's laughter shook the floor.

"I don't know why you're laughing, Ellen. You owe this to me, to your future king."

"I think you have me confused with someone else, Tolliver. Are you still obsessed with the stupid stories from that fortune-teller of your father's? You really believe you can become the "true heir of Philotheum" by forcing one of Stephen's daughters into a marriage nobody wants?"

"The prophecy is very clear about the thrones being united, sister."

"Uh-huh … this is the same guy that threatened grave risk to Samuel's child, right? Too bad he didn't see Samuel dying before he was even of age. How your father's little oracle didn't see the death of the stepson your father was supposed to be protecting is beyond me, especially when it was a death they were plotting together."

"Oh, stop. My father had nothing to do with that idiot falling into a river and going over a waterfall."

"Yeah … a skilled outdoorsman like Samuel just 'fell into a river' and drowned, never to be seen again."

"However skilled you may have perceived your big brother to be, Ellen, he's dead, and he's not our concern anymore."

"*Our* oldest brother being dead does not make you heir to the throne, Tolliver. And even marrying a princess of Eirentheos wouldn't change that."

"I don't see anyone else standing in line, Ellen, do you?"

"The last time I checked, Charles was alive and well."

"And just what do you plan to do with him? He's not even in the country – unless you're hiding him, too. Besides which, he's a third-born. Even with your ridiculous traditions, he's not the rightful heir to the throne."

"A third-born prince is better than a *sixth*-born nobody, Tolliver. Besides, he has an heir. And in the absence of an heir from Samuel – or from me, the crown rightfully belongs to Charles' child."

"The child can't possibly be of age."

"Do you think that matters to the people of Philotheum? Or Eirentheos, for that matter? And have you even considered what will happen if you do something to their prince?"

"I had heard rumors that Charles' first-born was only a girl – no threat to me."

"For a person who has no regard for our history and traditions, you seem to rely awfully heavily on inconsequential details to protect you."

"What do you mean?"

"The fact that thus far, all of our kings have managed to produce sons as their first-borns doesn't mean anything. There is no rule against a girl taking the throne."

The silence was palpable. Having had her own experience seeing the amount of regard Tolliver had for women, she had no trouble imagining the look on his face now.

"And surely, dear little brother, it hasn't escaped your notice that Stephen has much more to offer in the way of eligible sons than he does daughters."

"You can't be suggesting …"

"I'm not *suggesting* anything, Tolliver. You are not prepared for war against your own people and Eirentheos. I'm willing to bet that your father doesn't know the half of what you are doing, and that Mother knows nothing. And who do you think would stand behind you if a royal firstborn of Philotheum *were* to marry into the Eirenthean line? Whatever support you think you have would disappear overnight.

"Furthermore, I've met Stephen. If you allowed something to happen to his son ... the Maker help you. Don't force his hand – or mine. Return the boy. And do it *now*."

Quinn's hand was sweaty as she clutched William's for dear life. Both of them struggled to remember to breathe.

"Do you really know where Charles' heir is?"

"Do you want to find that out?"

"If I return Thomas, how do I know that you won't just turn around and produce Charles and his heir?"

"You don't."

The silence in the air was thick, on both sides of the wooden floor. Quinn was starting to feel dizzy from straining to listen over the train-like pounding of her heart.

Andrew was kneeling beside his wife, his arms around her, his head pressed against her round belly. Quinn was amazed she could have missed it the day before. Natalie didn't look very well.

Suddenly, Tolliver laughed. The sound turned Quinn's stomach. "I think I'll go out to your stables and check on my horse. Let me know when dinner is ready, will you?"

No one even breathed as Tolliver walked across the floor, and then the sound of his footsteps disappeared with the sound of a slamming door. Quinn felt like she might fall over, though William was standing so closely behind her shoulder that he would have caught her if she had.

Natalie let out a low groan, and William's entire demeanor shifted instantly. He squeezed Quinn's shoulder and then somehow, in the next second he was kneeling in front of Natalie; Andrew moved to her side to watch.

It was difficult to see anything in the pale light of the candles that Natalie and Andrew had brought with them from upstairs. Quinn moved automatically to retrieve the ones she and William had been using from underneath the stairs.

Relighting them, she carried both of them over near the chair and set them on the floor.

William nodded at her as he carefully touched the young woman's stomach. "That was definitely a contraction," he said. "I think you're in labor, Natalie."

"Already?" Andrew asked, panic in his near-whisper.

"Yeah ... You can't hide this forever Natalie," William murmured. "How long has this been going on?"

She shrugged. "Most of the day. I thought ... I just wanted this to happen when we weren't hiding out."

"We were going to try and travel, to make it to the town where her sister is living before the baby came." Andrew said.

William squeezed Natalie's hand. "None of that will matter once the baby is here, I promise."

She nodded.

"Can we help get you lying down, so I can get a better idea of what's going on?"

Quinn took the few short steps to Andrew's side, and bent down next to him. "Come on, there are lots of blankets and pillows in the area under the stairs."

Andrew stood to follow her. "There are plenty of medical supplies and lots of water in the crates as well," he said quietly to William, who looked up at him in surprise.

"Medical supplies?"

"Yes, these rooms below the safe houses are well-stocked for nearly anything. Twenty people could survive down here for weeks."

Quinn raised her eyebrows, but nobody said anything as she and Andrew carried blankets and pillows over to William, and then walked around the basement, lighting candles and setting them on the high shelves. She wondered how many safe houses there were, complete with these underground rooms filled with supplies – and how many people were inside them right now.

She was reaching above her head to set a candle on one of the small sconces when there were suddenly three loud stomps on the floor directly above her. Startled, she dropped the candle, and the candlestick clattered noisily against the stone floor. The fall through the air extinguished the flame, but droplets of hot wax splattered on her neck, shoulder, and down her arm. She bit her tongue to stop herself from crying out, terrified that whoever was above her would already have been alerted by the noise.

Panicked, her eyes instantly searched for William. His expression matched hers.

"It's all right. That's Ellen." Andrew's voice was calm as he came to stand beside Natalie, and loud too, or at least it felt that way. He was speaking in a normal voice, rather than the soft whispers they'd been using the entire time they were down here. "She's letting us know there's nobody in the house besides her, that we don't have to be so careful."

While William went to dig through the storage alcove to find the crates that held medical supplies, Quinn and Andrew folded and piled several blankets on the floor to create a soft bed for Natalie. Andrew helped his wife get settled and comfortable just as William returned.

"Can you come and help me for a second, Quinn?" he asked.

She nodded, and followed him over to the alcove. There was a strange expression on his face as he pointed down into an open crate.

"What?" she mouthed.

In response, he reached into the crate, and lifted out a stethoscope. Underneath it were piles of cloth-wrapped packages. The open one on top revealed several different sizes of gauze bandages. Next to it lay what looked like several feet of plastic tubing rolled into a circle. A stack of metal boxes lined the edge of the crate. It took her a minute to realize what was upsetting him. She looked up at him in surprise.

"From Earth?" she whispered, so low that she almost couldn't hear herself.

He nodded.

"How? What?"

He shrugged, his expression as confused – and wary – as hers.

STILL TRAPPED

William could not understand what was going on – how all of the medical supplies, so clearly from Earth, had found their way into the basement of a safe house in Philotheum. Of course, there was only one person who could have brought them here, and that fact was the source of his frustration.

He had realized last night that Nathaniel had been here before, that he was familiar not only with the house, but also with Ellen and Henry. Did Nathaniel know that Ellen was Tolliver's *sister*, as well? None of this made sense to him anymore.

All of these things were running through the back of his mind as he tended to the young woman. Her labor was advanced – if nothing changed, if they weren't rescued soon from this basement, he would be delivering this baby by himself. This thought terrified him. He knew what to do – in theory. He had read about it in medical textbooks, and even been in attendance at four births with Nathaniel, but even his uncle delivered babies only rarely. On Earth, he wasn't an obstetrician, and here, in their own world, mothers were almost always attended by experienced and skilled midwives, not healers.

As if the fact that he was going to be delivering his first baby in a dark basement while hiding from *Tolliver* wasn't enough, his thoughts were in a muddle over what had just happened with Quinn. He didn't understand it at all. One minute they'd been laughing and the next ... he hadn't seen that coming, at all.

He had often wondered, during this trip, how it could come so easily to his younger brother, how Thomas could just up and kiss the girl, not even considering the consequences. He'd never pictured himself doing something like that.

Guilt churned in his stomach when he thought about Thomas. He wondered, yet again, why his brother had kissed Quinn. Did he really have feelings for her? He must, on some level. Although interacting with girls was a natural skill for Thomas – and certainly he'd kissed more girls than William had – he would never have done something like that if he didn't really care for Quinn.

Did he actually intend to pursue a relationship with her, though? William had no idea, other than he couldn't imagine Thomas not making his intentions clear to Quinn if that were the case.

He shook his head, trying to shake the convoluted thoughts loose. He couldn't worry about it right now. Not about how Thomas felt, or how Quinn did, or even how he, himself did. They were where they were, and there were things to do. First and foremost, there was a baby to deliver.

William held up his stethoscope for Natalie and Andrew to see. "This instrument will let me hear the baby's heartbeat, so I can check on him – or her." He placed the drum on Natalie's stomach, searching for the baby's heart. He smiled when he found it, right where it should be, thrumming vigorously.

"It sounds perfect," he said. "Would you like to listen?" Once Natalie had finished marveling over the sound, he helped Andrew fit the stethoscope over his ears. He couldn't help smiling when he saw the young man's eyes light up with amazement and pride.

A surprising sense of jealousy hit him as he watched the scene. Andrew was only a cycle or two older than William. An unanticipated drawback to his life of traveling between the two worlds, and spending his energy and efforts on building up the clinics here, had been the lack of time – and the opportunity – to meet and court any young ladies in his world. Being alone, and not starting a family, was the price Nathaniel had been paying for his choice for many cycles – would that happen to him, too?

Time stretched interminably in the dark basement. There was no way for Quinn to know how much time had passed. William, Andrew, and Quinn all tended Natalie as best they could. Andrew had located a large storage container filled with water, and they'd used it to drink, and to wet several small cloths that they wiped across Natalie's sweaty forehead to keep her comfortable, whenever she was sitting or lying down.

Most of the time, she paced the room, leaning on her husband as he supported her. Quinn stayed near William, alternately walking around and sitting down on some of the crates they'd dragged close to the makeshift pallet they had created for Natalie on the floor. They couldn't see much in the pale, flickering candlelight, and they kept as silent as they could, whispering to one another only when it was absolutely necessary, even though it had been quite a while since any sound other than Ellen's light footsteps had come through the ceiling above them.

She could tell that William was nervous, and she did what she could to reassure him – which wasn't much since this whole thing kind of freaked her out, too. But time kept passing, and nothing really changed.

Despite the stress of the situation, for the first time in as long as she could remember, she was beginning to feel bored.

And then, everything changed at once. Natalie had let out small groaning noises several times before, but the sound that came from her now was different, louder, and more urgent. William stood and flew across the room to her.

At the same time, there were new sounds upstairs. A loud bang shook the floor – the front door hitting the wall as someone threw it open, followed by several pairs of heavy footsteps.

Tolliver's voice resonated through the basement ceiling; he was laughing – a sound that turned Quinn's blood to ice in her veins. There was another man's voice, one that she didn't recognize. He was chuckling, too.

"So, what about it, Ellen?" Tolliver called loudly. "Have you finished slaving over dinner yet? Your husband has finally decided to grace us with his presence; he's just coming up the road now."

Tolliver's voice was different, less polished than usual – *slurred?* She wasn't sure what to make of it. She looked over to William, to see if she could decipher his thoughts on it, but his attention was on something else entirely.

Andrew and William both had their arms around Natalie, gently guiding her down onto the blankets. Her breathing was heavy and rough. Her eyes widened with every sound that drifted through the floor, and Quinn could tell that she was having great difficulty remaining silent.

Quinn knelt down quickly, arranging pillows behind Natalie, trying to help make her as comfortable as she could.

William looked up at her, his eyes round with alarm. "The baby is coming, any minute now," he whispered, almost inaudibly, his voice cracking.

Panic twisted her insides. What were they going to do? They couldn't let Tolliver hear them, and at the same time, they needed to hear *him*, to know what he was saying. She stood and walked away from them, over to the spot directly underneath where she could hear the voices coming through the floor.

"Dinner is nearly ready, Tolliver. Perhaps you and your guest – I'm sorry, I didn't catch your name, sir – would like to have a seat in the dining room? I can bring out some wine, Tolliver. It's not necessary to sneak sips from a flask in your pants like a peasant."

A chill ran down Quinn's spine. What was Ellen thinking, antagonizing Tolliver? And offering to let him get drunk? Either Ellen really knew what she was doing, or she couldn't be trusted the way Andrew – and Nathaniel – seemed to think she could be. It didn't matter much, she supposed. Tolliver was definitely dangerous, and Ellen already knew where they were.

"At least you've preserved some of your skills as a hostess, sister." Tolliver was snickering as his voice drifted away, into some part of the house that was not above the basement.

Quinn listened intently, until she could be certain that three sets of footsteps had exited the kitchen – Tolliver's, his guard's, and Ellen's. She squinted through the dim candlelight to William. He was crouched down in front of Natalie. Andrew sat directly behind her; her head was in his lap, her hands clutched tightly to his.

Any minute, the baby would be here. Quinn dashed for the stairs, climbing them quickly, as darkness closed in around her. At the top, she pushed gently on the ceiling. The trap door moved easily at her touch, but no light trickled through the small crack she opened. She pushed harder, opening it all the way, and climbing out into the pantry before setting it back down silently. A thin ribbon of light shone beneath the door, but no sounds came from the kitchen.

Her heart thudded violently in her chest as she stood there, trying to decide what to do next. Before she'd decided anything, she heard the swish of one of the kitchen doors opening, and then the sound of someone – one person – walking into the kitchen. She crouched down on the wooden pantry floor and craned her neck until she could see out through the crack under the door.

She held her breath, straining to catch a glimpse of whoever had entered the kitchen. After a moment, familiar-looking leather sandals under the hem of a long, cotton skirt came into view.

An unexpected wave of calm washed over her. She stood, and opened the pantry door just wide enough to poke her head out.

"Ellen," she whispered.

Ellen's face turned white with surprise, and she crossed the room quickly, stepping into the pantry in a way that forced Quinn to back up to the far wall.

"What are you doing?" she hissed. "Do you not realize how dangerous it is for you to have come up here?"

Quinn's eyes met the older woman's straight on. "Andrew and Natalie are down there with us."

Ellen nodded. "Good. I was hoping they would realize that I'd gotten Tolliver out of the house for a bit and go down there *to safety*." Her tone was sharp, reprimanding. As she spoke, she was reaching down toward the floor.

"The baby is coming. Right now," Quinn said.

Ellen had already begun to pull up the trapdoor, and right at that moment, a low moan came through the opening. The door fell shut with a muted *thud*, and she turned steely eyes on Quinn.

"I'll do what I can to keep Tolliver away from this side of the house," she said. She turned and exited the pantry quickly. Her demeanor suggested that she was in charge and had everything under control, but in the second that the pantry was flooded with light before the door closed behind her, Quinn could see that her hands were shaking.

She nodded to herself, and reached again for the hidden handle of the trapdoor. Before she had it all the way open, though, there was the sound of another door in the kitchen, and more footsteps going in, rather than the sound of Ellen going *out*. She carefully eased the door back down, and then crouched, hiding as best she could, in the corner of the black pantry.

"I came as quickly as I could. What is Tolliver doing here?"

Quinn breathed a silent sigh of relief. It was Henry.

"Why do you think he's here? He wants my support in trying to trade Thomas for Linnea."

"Of course he does. And now we have to feed him?"

"I was just about to take in some glasses of wine." Her voice dropped even lower, "Natalie is about to have her baby."

"Did they make it safely ... *down?*" Quinn had to strain to hear Henry's words.

"Yes. And the others are with them."

For a moment, Quinn thought that they had stopped talking, but then Henry made a noise that sounded like a gasp. Disregarding the possible consequences, she stood and pushed the pantry door open just far enough to be able to look out. Henry's arms were wrapped around Ellen's waist, and she was stretched up, whispering in his ear. Her eyes were on the pantry, and Quinn watched them narrow at the movement of the door.

Her heart sank.

Ellen whispered something else to her husband, and he, too, turned to face the pantry.

For what felt like many minutes, they both stared, unmoving, and she looked back at them.

Finally, Henry lifted two heavy, crystal goblets from the countertop. "I'll take these to the dining room," he said, and disappeared through the door.

Ellen crossed the room to the pantry so quickly that Quinn had to blink. She threw open the door and stepped in, backing Quinn up into the far wall.

"You need to get downstairs, *now*." Her whisper was the most commanding sentence Quinn had ever heard, but she wasn't as intimidated by it as she knew she should be.

"What are you hiding from me?"

Ellen's pause was so minute that at any other time, Quinn would have missed it entirely. Then she rolled her eyes. "You're not entitled to know as much as you think you are, *Lady* Quinn. If Tolliver discovers you here, you have no idea the damage that will cause. *Please*, for the love of the Maker, go back down and *stay there*."

Ellen turned and walked out of the pantry. As the door swung back and forth on its hinges, Quinn could see her pick up a large ceramic bowl and carry it through a doorway into another part of the house.

For a moment, long enough to surprise herself, she considered *not* going back down into the basement. She didn't know what Ellen and Henry were hiding, and the whispering conversation she had just witnessed reminded her a little too strongly of the stranger's voice two nights before at Thea's house.

The longer she was on this journey, the less she trusted anybody.

It was a difficult decision. Though Tolliver scared her more than anyone else ever had, he was *here*, in the same house, and he knew where Thomas was. If he would just let one thing slip …

Regardless of her suspicions about Ellen, though, Quinn knew she was right about one thing. If Tolliver were to discover that she and William were here ... her last two encounters with him left her with no doubt about what would happen if he ever got his hands on her. And if he was bold enough to kidnap and hold one prince of Eirentheos – as soon as an image of William being held by Tolliver flitted across her mind, she lifted the trapdoor.

The heavy wood had barely fallen closed when there was a muffled moan from somewhere below her, and then the distinct, quiet cry of an infant. Quinn ran down the stairs as quickly as she could, carefully keeping her hand to the stone wall in the blackness, as she didn't have a candle.

By the time she stepped into the pale, flickering light of the basement room, it was silent again, except for the labored breathing of those who had been working to deliver the baby, and the even softer sounds of the little person lying in Natalie's arms, suckling for the first time.

Although Quinn tried not to make any noise, William's head still snapped around in her direction as soon as she stepped off the stairs.

"What's going on?" he whispered. "Where did you go?"

She crossed the floor and knelt down beside Natalie, who looked sweaty and exhausted, but stared, enraptured at the tiny face nestled against her chest. Andrew looked nearly as tired, but he, too, was fascinated by the baby, a little girl, still naked and streaked with blood. William unfolded a large, heavy, quilt and laid it over mother and baby. Quinn helped tuck the edges around them.

"I told Ellen what was going on," she said. "She's going to do what she can to keep Tolliver away from where he'll easily hear us."

William nodded, relief evident on his face.

"Of course, that means we won't be able to hear him, either."

Andrew looked over at her, scrutinizing her face. "We can trust Ellen to tell us what we need to know. I know you're not convinced of that, but she wants Prince Thomas back safe, too."

Quinn wasn't convinced, but she gave him a half-smile anyway. Then she and William turned their attention to silently cleaning up the mess and getting the new family comfortably settled.

When, at last, they'd done as much as they could with their limited resources in the dim space, and Natalie and the baby both slept, wrapped in Andrew's arms, Quinn and William retreated to the opposite wall of the basement. They laid out several blankets and pillows to distance themselves from the cold, hard floor, and then simultaneously collapsed.

"Thank you," William whispered, after several minutes.

She lifted her head from the pillow she had buried it in, and looked up at him. A question about why he was thanking her rested on the tip of her tongue, but when she saw the sincerity in his eyes, she bit it back, and nodded instead.

Warmth ran through her when he stretched his hand toward hers, and she grabbed onto it. She didn't know what it meant, or even how things would be between the two of them tomorrow, but for that moment, she didn't care. Tolliver was upstairs, and Thomas was still missing. Her mother was surely in a panic, and Zander was probably never going to talk to her again. The only thing in her world that felt right just then was her hand in William's.

THE FRIENDS OF PHILIP

"Quinn!"

The frightened whisper roused her instantly from sleep, although she could tell she'd been deeply under. She blinked several times, trying to focus on William's face in the candlelight, trying to shake off the vivid dream she'd been having and decide if this was real or yet another vision.

"What's going on?" she whispered back. William didn't look fully awake, either. She wondered what time it was.

He didn't answer, but a second later she didn't need him to. The sound of heavy footsteps on the wooden floor above them reverberated through her body, speeding her pulse. There were no voices, but at least three different people were walking across the kitchen. Her breath caught when all three reached the back of the kitchen, paused, and then the steps moved inside the pantry.

It wasn't a conscious decision – by the time the first foot touched the top wooden step, all but one of the candles had been extinguished, and William and Quinn were crouched on either side of Andrew and Natalie, both of them awake and

259

wide-eyed in the faint glow from the single flame that William held close to his face, one hand cupped around the light, ready to extinguish it instantly. The tiny girl in her mother's arms let out a quiet grunt as she shifted in her sleep.

The footsteps slowed and softened as they came down the stairs; the sound was almost cautious. Only one person was actually coming down. Quinn frowned at William, and he nodded. Her breathing calmed.

"Hello?" the soft, familiar voice called from the bottom step.

William held the candle out in front of him, casting a small circle of light over their huddled group. "We're over here, Nathaniel."

"Is everyone all right?" Nathaniel asked, his eyes surveying the disarray.

William stood. "Yes, everyone's fine," he whispered.

"Tolliver is gone now," Nathaniel said, speaking in a low, but normal voice. "Ben and Marcus followed him for quite a while. He isn't coming back, at least not tonight."

Quinn hadn't realized just how tight the muscles in her chest had been until they suddenly released the tension they'd held the whole time she'd been down in the basement.

"Did he … do we know where Thomas is?" she asked.

Nathaniel shook his head, his eyes on the floor. "Marcus and I were able to come up with a few leads today, but we don't have anything solid yet."

"What kind of leads?" Quinn pressed, a growing sense of urgency rising within her as images from the dream she'd been having assaulted her.

"We …" Nathaniel looked around, studying the little family on the floor, the massive pile of dirty linens. "It looks like it's been a long night for everyone. It's very late, or rather, it's very early. We can talk about this in the morning, upstairs in the light, when we've all had some rest."

"Thomas is hurt."

The lines around Nathaniel's eyes grew tighter, but he didn't look surprised. "That's possible."

"We need to find him. *Now.*"

"Yes, Quinn, we do. But not in the middle of the night with Tolliver still out and about not far from here."

She jumped when William's hand found her shoulder. He was trembling, but his squeeze was reassuring. "Tomorrow. We'll find out where he is tomorrow, no matter what we have to do." His voice was determined, fiercer than she'd ever heard him, and his words were just enough to get her through the next half hour as they worked to get everyone upstairs and settled.

There was no discussion of William or Quinn heading for their separate rooms this evening. William pulled blankets and pillows from the linen closet, and they lay down on couches opposite each other in the sitting room. Nathaniel told William that he would take over the nighttime care of Natalie and the new baby, after congratulating him on a job well done.

Quiet voices and low clinking sounds coming from the kitchen woke William from his light sleep. He glanced over at the windows – only the barest hint of light came through the cracks in the curtains. It was still before dawn.

He looked over at Quinn, asleep on the couch across from him. She appeared to be soundly asleep, which relieved him. Her dreams during the night had been vivid, making her restless. He worried that she wasn't getting enough sleep, and even more he worried about how much more often her dreams had been coming, and the way she often woke disoriented and frightened.

He was afraid that their increasing intensity didn't bode well for any of them, Thomas in particular.

He made his way into the kitchen, and was surprised to find Ellen, Henry, Marcus and Ben gathered around the table, fully dressed and awake, finishing breakfast. Nathaniel sat by himself at the long counter, bleary-eyed over a large mug of tea.

"What's going on?" he asked.

Ellen stood, and began carrying dishes to the sink. William walked over to the table and started gathering up the serving dishes.

"We're getting ready to leave," Marcus said, his deep voice still thick with exhaustion. "We're going to try to get in touch with some contacts who might have an idea of where Thomas is being held."

"We're?" William raised an eyebrow.

"Yes," Ellen interrupted. "The four of us. You, Nathaniel, and Quinn are going to stay here with the Grambles."

"What? No! I want to go – Quinn will want to go."

"What you *want* is not the issue here," Ellen said, meeting his gaze squarely. "Nor is what Quinn wants. It is too dangerous. You're a prince of Eirentheos, William. We can't risk having you out on the roads, or in the villages, exposed. Putting you, or Quinn, or even Nathaniel at any more risk of being discovered here could jeopardize *everything*, and none of it will bring Thomas home safely."

"But …"

"It doesn't matter. The decision has been made. Nathaniel wasn't happy, but he has agreed. The dreams that Quinn has been having – we will find your brother William, and we will do it today. But you must stay here. My home is the safest in Philotheum, and it's close enough to the border to get you all out quickly. I know you don't trust me, I can see it in your eyes, but for right now, it's a chance you need to take."

He sucked in a breath, and looked over at his uncle. Nathaniel stared back, a pleading expression on his face, and finally, William nodded.

Quinn awoke just after everyone had departed. He had been sitting on the couch across from her, watching and waiting.

"Where is everyone?" she asked, sitting up and rubbing her eyes. Strands of her auburn hair had come loose from her braid while she slept. The sight of her caused a strange, warm feeling in William's chest.

"Nathaniel is back with Natalie. Everyone else left."

"What? Where did they go?" In an instant, she looked wide awake.

"Ellen said they are going to try and find some contacts that might help them find out where Thomas is being held. I got the feeling they weren't all going to the same place.

"And what are we supposed to do? Just sit around and wait all day here again?"

William shrugged.

"That's all we really can do right this second." Nathaniel said, as he appeared at the end of the hallway. "It's safest for the three of us to be here, rather than out where we might be seen, or worse."

William's irritation with Nathaniel came flooding back.

"What exactly are we doing *here?* Why didn't I know any of this, Nathaniel? How could you have brought us to the home of Tolliver's half-sister without telling us? Does my father know?"

Nathaniel was silent for a long time as he studied William's and Quinn's faces. William was beginning to grow impatient when he finally began speaking. "I'm very sorry for not telling you about this, I really am. I've never made a habit of keeping things from you, William. It's been my privilege and joy to watch you grow and help raise you, and to share with you the things that I know. Keeping these secrets has been very difficult for me."

263

"Then why, Nathaniel?" Quinn asked. "Why bring us all the way here without telling us?"

"There are reasons. Maintaining the privacy and anonymity of the Friends of Philip is of utmost importance. Before we arrived, and I was able to communicate with Ellen, I wasn't sure what I was going to be able to share with the two of you. And yes, William, your father knows. He knows everything."

"Is Ellen someone we can trust?" Again, Quinn beat him to the question he'd been about to ask.

"I would trust Ellen with my very life. Her goals are the same as ours, I promise."

"Ours? William and I are here for one reason Nathaniel. To bring Thomas safely home. What are *your* goals?"

Quinn's question startled William, but he realized that he wondered the same thing. He scrutinized Nathaniel's face as he answered the question, but his uncle met Quinn's gaze flatly, his tone steady.

"My number one priority is the safety of Thomas – as well as protecting William, and you, Quinn. There is nothing more important to me than returning the three of you safely back to Eirentheos – and returning you home to your mother. Nothing takes precedence over that – *nothing.*"

William could see in Nathaniel's eyes that he was telling the truth. He hadn't realized how rigidly he'd been standing until that realization relaxed him a little. He glanced over at Quinn; her tight fists and shallow breathing told him that she wasn't as convinced.

"You are right, though, Quinn, that I have other goals." He reached up to the collar of his shirt and pulled it aside. William gasped when he saw the joined circles – the symbol of Eirentheos melded with the circle that represented Philotheum, inked in an odd shade of blue.

264

"I don't think I understand. Why are you ... How long have you been in the Friends of Philip?" Though William had no experience with these things, nothing about the tattoo looked new.

"From the beginning of the movement, or at least from very early on. I have always been involved in the effort to oust Hector – and now Tolliver, and restore the crown to its rightful place – to restore the full connection between Eirentheos and Philotheum."

"Restore it to whom?" Quinn asked. "Who should actually be the king of Philotheum?"

"When the rightful heir to the throne dies – in this case, King Jonathan's firstborn son, it passes to the heir's firstborn, naturally. In the absence of the heir's firstborn, it passes directly to the next firstborn in line. For example, if something happened to Simon before he produced an heir, the crown would pass naturally to Maxwell's first child, or then to Rebecca's, if Maxwell didn't have a child either. Jonathan fathered five children before he died. With no heir from Samuel, the crown should belong to the child of Ellen, who is the second-born. As she has no children, the next heir in line is Charles' first-born daughter, Gianna."

"Can a girl really have the crown?" Quinn asked.

Nathaniel shrugged. "There is nothing in our history, in the original edict from the prophet of the Maker that prohibits it. In fact, the only stipulation is that the heir must be the first-born; there's no mention of gender. Through whatever accident of nature is at work, the first-borns of first-borns in both Philotheum and Eirentheos have been born male going back many generations. We've never had to deal with the question until now."

"So where is Charles' heir – Gianna, now?" Quinn spouted forth her questions without hesitation – all of the things William wanted to know, as well, but he couldn't seem to make his mind work fast enough to form the questions. He felt another wave of gratefulness for the girl's presence.

Without her, he'd probably have made it all the way back to Eirentheos not understanding half of this.

"Gianna – and all of Charles and Thea's children," these words sent an electric shock through William, "reside most of the time in an undisclosed location with relatives in Eirentheos. For their safety – and the protection of the Friends of Philip – their identities are kept secret. Gianna is only ten cycles of age."

William swallowed hard. "So what is your plan? A child can't take the throne."

"Our hope was to stave off Tolliver's actually assuming the throne for as long as possible, while we worked on those challenges. We hoped to avoid war. Nobody in the Friends of Philip – or in your country, William, wishes to fight. Even one casualty would be too much. Now, though, with Tolliver's increasing impatience, and with what Thomas has done..."

William nodded.

"So it sounds like we need to just get Thomas, *right now*, and worry about this other stuff once he's safe." Quinn said.

He could see, in the change of the girl's posture, and the look in her eyes, that her concern had shifted. The anxious tapping of her foot, the twisting and untwisting of her sleeve – these were over Thomas. A different expression had appeared in her eyes, though, a new question. Something Nathaniel had said had put a new question in her mind. Perhaps it was the same thing that had put a new, niggling worry in William's thoughts, though he wasn't sure exactly what it had been.

The rest of the day, alone in the house with little to do, the three of them were at loose ends. Quinn felt the nerve-wracking anxiety starting to take over again. The small Gramble family stayed secluded in the back bedroom, sleeping and caring for the new baby. Nathaniel had gone in a few times, Quinn and William only once.

Out in the sitting room, every second dragged by. William's face was ashen, and the dark circles under his eyes seemed darker every time Quinn looked over at him. Nathaniel didn't look much better. Every time there was the slightest noise outside, one of them would jump.

She could tell that she was on the verge of losing her composure again, but she was determined not to this time, so when Nathaniel, after the fifth time he'd paced back to the guest bedrooms, returned with a deck of strange-looking cards, she agreed that having a distraction seemed like a good idea.

"How do you play?" she asked.

William and Nathaniel spend the next hour teaching her how to play choice. The cards were surprisingly similar to the kind of playing cards she was used to at home, except that there were five suits, and the only cards besides the thirteen numbers were the "choice" cards – on the deck they used these were marked with the seal of Eirentheos, though William told her that different decks might have different designs.

The game wasn't overly complicated – after an hour she won her first hand – but it was enough to keep her mind occupied. Playing seemed to help William and Nathaniel as well. Early in the afternoon, they stopped for long enough to prepare lunch and check in again with Natalie and Andrew, and then they settled down for another round in the sitting room. They were just beginning a new game when there was a sudden, frantic pounding at the door.

Cards flew everywhere as Nathaniel and William raced to the door, Quinn right behind them. Her heart jumped into her throat when they pulled it open to reveal, not Henry, Ellen, Marcus, or

Ben, but two men she'd never seen before, both dressed in the full green-and-gold regalia of the Philothean guard.

Her heart pounded a thousand beats per minute as the two men stepped through the door and into the sitting room. William moved instantly into a defensive position in front of her as the guards walked around, noting the playing cards all over the table and floors. The guards looked very similar, especially in the matching uniforms they wore, except that one of them was taller, and clearly much older.

"Is anyone else here?" the taller of the two men asked.

Nathaniel began to shake his head, but at that moment, there was a loud cry from the back hallway, as the tiny, newborn girl made her presence known. "Yes," he said instead. "A young couple and their newborn baby are here as well."

The guard paused, appearing to consider his next words carefully. "Are they Friends of Philip, as well?"

Quinn thought her heart might have stopped beating altogether. She glanced cautiously at William. Sweat dotted his hairline.

Nathaniel seemed stunned into silence. Everything was in slow motion as Nathaniel swallowed hard, his eyes darting between William and Quinn, and the guards. The baby's cries continued in the back room.

Nathaniel took a deep breath, and closed his eyes for a long moment before he answered. "Yes."

The younger man nodded, and then looked over at his companion, communicating something with his eyes. Quinn could see now just how much younger he was. Up close, she wasn't sure he was older than William. After a long pause, both men turned to face Nathaniel. Simultaneously, they drew back their collars, revealing tattoos.

William had to put out his hand to steady Quinn, to keep her from keeling over backward into one of the low tables.

"Who are you?" Nathaniel asked.

The older man answered. "My name is Dorian Blackwelder, and this is my son, James."

"What are you doing here?" Nathaniel's voice was still suspicious, and William kept edging closer to Quinn.

"Where is Lady Ellen?" Dorian asked.

"She has gone on … an errand." Nathaniel answered.

"When will she return?"

"Soon, we hope. Along with her husband and two trained guards from Eirentheos." Nathaniel's voice shook only a little.

Dorian paused, and studied each of them in turn. His eyes stopped when they reached William's face, widening in recognition. "Prince William!"

Now she knew her heart had stopped; she tried to breathe, but the air refused to come.

"Why? What's wrong? Where is Thomas?" Nathaniel's voice cracked on the name.

"The prince is … He has been injured."

"Where *is* he?" Quinn demanded.

"Follow us."

Nathaniel's eyes narrowed. "Let me see those tattoos again."

Quinn's heart thumped wildly as Dorian and James pulled their collars back again. She scrutinized Dorian's face, and as she did so, a sudden, overwhelming sense of recognition nearly knocked her over. He'd been in her dream last night.

"Let's go with him, *now*. We can trust them."

William and Nathaniel both stared at her in surprise, but she shook her head at them. "We don't have any time to waste."

Moments later, the three of them were following Dorian and James across Ellen's wide lawn and through the gate. For a brief second she wondered where Ryan, the gatekeeper, was but right now it didn't matter.

A short distance up the dirt road from the house, Dorian led them through a break in the trees and into a small clearing. In the clearing was a small wagon hitched to two weary-looking horses.

Over the side of the wagon, Quinn could see two people, a man with tousled brown hair, and a woman whose long, disheveled locks were nearly black, just like William's and Thomas'. As they walked toward them, the woman turned her head, revealing eyes that were a familiar shade of gray with dark, heavy circles underneath them.

"Lily!" Nathaniel's voice came out in a choking gasp. And he and William broke into a run.

For a few dizzying seconds, Quinn had no idea what was happening. She stood there frozen, watching everyone around her as if it were a movie, rather than something actually happening in front of her. She hadn't expected to be led to a wagon carrying Lily and the man, who must be Graeme. Why were they here? Where was …

"Thomas!" William yelled, jumping over the gate at the end of the wagon so quickly that she might have imagined the movement. Nathaniel fumbled with the latches, but had difficulty lowering the wooden plank until Graeme reached over to help him.

Once the gate was down, Nathaniel's face turned a ghastly shade of white before a fierce red flowed from his neck up to his hairline. It was the look on his face, somehow simultaneously anguished and furious that made Quinn start moving again, and she ran down the slight hill to the wagon.

"What's going on?" Panic rose in her voice as she reached the end of the wagon. William's and Nathaniel's bodies blocked her view. They were crouched over the still form of someone lying on the wooden floor. "Is that Thomas? Is he …"

It was Lily who heard her terrified voice and turned to face her, her gray eyes sunken deep behind cheekbones that were too prominent in her pale face. "He's alive," she said. "He'll wish he wasn't when the valoris seed wears off again, but he's alive."

Nathaniel's head snapped up at Lily's words. "Valoris seed, but ..."

"I know you're worried about the Roses reacting to it, Nathaniel. And it does affect him strongly, makes him unconscious, but his pulse and breathing are strong ... trust me, it's the best we've had to offer him right now."

Nathaniel's mouth opened, but then closed again, and he nodded. "What happened to him?"

"We don't ... know all of the details," Graeme answered. "He was kept separate from us most of the time. Once Tolliver knew we were all together, I don't think he much liked the idea of us being able to talk with Thomas.

"I believe the official story is that he fell down some stairs." Sarcasm was thick in Lily's voice. "Although how someone could fall down a flight of stairs hard enough to shatter an arm and a leg without also injuring his face, I'm not certain."

Quinn tasted bile in the back of her throat. *Shattered? Thomas' arm and leg shattered?*

"Is it safe to take him back to Ellen's house?" Dorian asked. He and James had finally joined them and now stood near the wheels of the wagon. "We heard rumors that Tolliver was in the area yesterday."

"Yes, he's gone, headed north late last night. Ellen's gatekeeper, Ryan, followed after him. He sent a message this morning that he didn't think he'd be headed back this way anytime soon, but he's been staying in Merinth to keep an ear out, just in case."

Quinn raised her eyebrows – she hadn't known any of that.

"Then we need to get him back there, and quickly," Lily said. "We were only barely able to get his leg stabilized for the journey – his femur is in bad shape."

She didn't know what they were talking about, but it didn't sound good. She started to climb up on to the wagon's gate, wanting to see Thomas for herself. Graeme held up his arm, blocking her as he looked over at Nathaniel and William.

"It's all right, Graeme. Let her up," Nathaniel said softly.

Graeme frowned. "Who is she?"

"This is Quinn. She's a … friend of William and Thomas."

Graeme moved his arm and allowed her on to the wagon, but Lily shot Nathaniel a look that was accusing and wary. "What is she doing here?" she hissed. "Bringing her into Philotheum? Into *this*?"

The expression on Nathaniel's face as he looked back at Lily surprised Quinn. There was something behind it that was clearly serious, but she had no idea what it was. "Leave it be, Lily," he said, his voice cold and commanding.

The short ride from the clearing back to Ellen's home was excruciating. When she'd finally gotten close enough to Thomas to get a good look at him, nausea had twisted her stomach again.

There were no visible injuries on his face, but it was far too thin, as was the rest of him. His eyes were sunk far back into their sockets and there were dark circles underneath them. Several scrapes and bruises dotted his right arm; both his left arm and left leg were splinted and wrapped too completely to see at all. Wide, white bandages tightly circled his torso. Although he never fully woke, there were several times that a jolt of the wagon tightened the muscles in his face.

When she could no longer stand to watch him in such pain, Quinn turned her attention to the newcomers, Lily and Graeme. They, too, were sallow and thin, and both of them looked like they might fall over at any moment. They were uninjured, except for a fading bruise over Graeme's right eyebrow.

At one point, on the road just outside of Ellen's gate, she noticed a glint of sunlight off the chain around Lily's neck. A hot lump formed in Quinn's throat. Thomas had gotten Lily's pendant back to her.

William followed her gaze, and his eyes met hers, her own emotions were mirrored in his expression. He reached for her hand and squeezed it tightly. She squeezed back.

Once Dorian and James had brought the wagon to a stop right in front of the door, they came around and lowered the wagon gate.

"Where should we take him?" Dorian asked.

Nathaniel looked at Lily, anguish and helplessness in his expression. "We have to get this leg stabilized."

She nodded. "His fractures have started to heal badly — some of them need to be re-broken to be set properly."

All of the color drained from Nathaniel's face. Despite the hot day, Quinn felt cold. William's hand in hers grew suddenly clammy.

"The sooner we do it, the better," Lily said. "But we're going to have to open his leg to reduce the fracture in his femur — and he's already lost so much blood."

Nathaniel sighed; moisture was building in the corners of his eyes.

"We're going to have to do what we can. His femur … we have to save his leg." He looked up at Dorian. "The dining room table would be best. We'll need a firm surface."

Terror churned in Quinn's stomach as Dorian and James carefully lifted Thomas from the wagon. He let out a cry when the movement jostled his leg.

"William, go down into the basement and go through the crates," Nathaniel said in a strained voice. "Bring up everything you think we might need for surgery. He's definitely going to need something stronger than valoris seed. There's probably not much, but hopefully there will be something. We're going to need whatever blood we can get our hands on, too, so bring up supplies for that."

William darted into the house ahead of the two guards carrying Thomas. Quinn followed him, grabbing a candle from a counter in the pantry, and lighting it as they made their way down the dark stairs.

In the basement again, she used the candle to light several more, so that William could find what he was looking for in the alcove.

They opened crate after crate. William would dig through one, pull out what he thought he needed, and then shove the crate out of the way, across the open floor. Both of them were past words, needing this task to keep them from falling apart completely.

Quinn took a crate that held only blankets, and pulled them all out, stacking them neatly along the wall, and then started packing the pile of supplies that William was building inside of it. His shoulders shook as he worked. Once she'd gotten everything he'd laid out so far inside the crate, she walked over to him. She laid her hand gently on his shoulder and he turned to face her, silent tears streaming down his face.

"He's here," she said. "And he's *going* to be okay."

He nodded, and she pulled him into her arms, embracing him tightly until his shaking subsided.

"We're going to get through this," she said. "Let's get this stuff upstairs. We can always come back down for more if we need it."

Upstairs, the dining room table had been covered with several white sheets. Thomas lay on top of it, thankfully back asleep, while Nathaniel and Lily worked busily around him. Nathaniel looked up as William set the large crate down near the table.

"Thank you," he said. "Did you find any morphine?"

Quinn held up the small glass vials she'd carried up in her hands.

"Thank you," Lily said, taking it from her.

"We're going to need some blood on hand before we begin," Nathaniel said, looking at William. "Hopefully what you and I can give will be enough – Lily and Graeme are so weak already ... and I don't know if anyone else is a match."

"What about me?" Quinn asked. "I don't know if I'm a match, either. But if there's a way to check ..."

Nathaniel looked at her, deep emotion in his gray eyes. "You're a match, Quinn. You're underage ..."

"What difference does that make right now?" Her voice was harsher than she'd intended it to be.

"You're right. It doesn't make any difference right now," he acquiesced.

"Are you sure you want to do this?" William asked, as he helped her get settled on a couch, propping pillows behind her back.

"I'm sure," she said. "Thomas needs it."

"And you don't want to wait for Nathaniel to do it?"

"No, it's okay. He's busy finding out if anyone else is a match, and we need to do this as quickly as possible. You've stuck me with needles plenty of times already. You're not getting scared to do it now, are you?"

William rolled his eyes.

"Good, because if *you* were scared, then I might really get freaked out." She smiled.

"Are you scared?" As he spoke, he was wrapping a rubber tourniquet tightly around her upper arm.

"Um," she took a deep breath. "You have seen me around needles before, right?"

He chuckled. "You're no worse than me."

"I've heard that, but I think I'd have to see it to believe it." She swallowed. "Is it going to hurt?"

"No," he said, rubbing the inside of her forearm softly with his thumb. "One little pinch, that's all."

She nodded, and tried to relax while he cleaned the spot on the inside of her elbow.

Just then, Nathaniel came down the hallway. "It looks like it's just us," he said." Nobody else is a match."

"Will that be enough?" she asked, looking up at his worried eyes.

"It will have to be. We'll do what we can. We need to do the surgery as soon as possible, before his bone sets any further that way. We can't wait for anyone else to return."

Her hands were starting to get sweaty, and she could feel her pulse behind her ears. "Okay, William, just do it already!" she snapped.

To her surprise, he laughed.

"What's so funny?"

"I told you it wasn't going to hurt."

"What?"

She glanced down at her arm, but he had just finished covering it with a small, white towel.

"It's better if you can't accidentally look at it," he said. "Trust me."

"Drink your juice, though," Nathaniel said, handing her a tall glass from a nearby table that William had poured in the kitchen. "It takes a little while, and sometimes it makes people lightheaded."

She sipped obediently at the sweet liquid, amazed again at William's skill, a feeling that hit her often.

"Okay, Will, your turn," Nathaniel said. "Might as well get it done now."

She knew that if Thomas were out here, he would be laughing at how quickly the color drained from William's face. Quinn just wanted to hug him. She stretched her free hand toward him as far as she could. "It's not going to hurt," she said.

"He knows." Nathaniel chuckled. "I think it's the *idea* of needles for him more than anything."

William shrugged, grinning sheepishly at her, though he was paler than she'd ever seen him.

In the end, Quinn actually did better with the blood donation than William did. He survived the needle perfectly, but while she was completely fine afterward, he had to lie on the couch for quite a while, waiting for the color to return to his face. Lily had to come and collect the blood from Nathaniel while Graeme watched Thomas.

Aside from not feeling well, William was upset. Nathaniel, and Lily had refused to allow him to be part of Thomas' surgery, which they were in the back of the house preparing for now.

Nathaniel had been apologetic, telling William that he knew how hard it would be, but that it would be even harder if he was in the room. Thomas' operation was not going to be easy. While the supplies they had included several kinds of strong painkillers, there was nothing in the stash that would put Thomas completely under. He would be medicated and groggy, but not all the way asleep while they re-broke his femur and two bones in his left arm.

Lily had been definitive, telling William that she would prefer if he wasn't in the house at all while it happened, but if he insisted, then he had best stay far away from the back of the house. She didn't care how well-trained he was; he was still underage, and anyway, it was inappropriate for him to participate in his own brother's surgery. The two guards had been given explicit directions about keeping him from even approaching the hallway.

So Quinn sat with him, trying to keep him calm. She, herself, was terrified, but she was determined to keep her end of the bargain – if William was going to freak out, she would not. If she needed to, she would just sit here in silence, next to him on the couch all night.

She curled up on the end of the couch and leaned against the cushions, glass of juice in her hand. William's glass sat on the table, barely touched, while he leaned forward with his head in his hands, but she was done suggesting that he might feel better if he sat back and actually drank it.

She thought about how much their relationship had changed in just a few short days. Was it really just over a week ago that she'd flown into a rage when he'd come into the library? In some ways it felt like that was another lifetime. This trip had changed her perspective on everything.

Although there was a part of her, in the back of her mind that obsessed constantly over what was going to happen when she got back home -- that wondered exactly how much trouble she was going to be in, there another part with a different worry that was growing every day she spent here. How was she just going to go back to her life after this? After everything that had happened?

And now … there was this whole thing with William. She still had no idea what to think about the kiss they had shared yesterday in the basement – had it only been yesterday? They hadn't discussed it at all, but it was there, hanging over them, the fact that it had happened. She had been a little afraid, that once they'd gotten out of the basement things would be strained between them -- that he would pull away from her, and into himself, as he'd done so often before. But it hadn't happened. If anything, she felt closer to him than ever.

It pained her now, watching him suffer over his brother. She knew that William was closer to his younger brother than he was to anyone, even more than Nathaniel, who he lived with almost all the time.

And, of course, she had kissed Thomas, too. Or he had kissed her, if there was a difference. It wasn't like she had pushed him away. What had he meant by that kiss? And what had she? Thomas had won her over from the first minute she'd known him; she'd been enchanted immediately by his warm, loving personality. She knew, now, that she loved him, but she wasn't sure in what way, wasn't sure at all what she *wanted* that kiss to mean.

She wasn't sure about anything.

Down the long hallway, there was a sudden, heart-rending scream. She looked over at William, and saw him staring back at her, terror and pain in both of their eyes. Thomas' surgery had begun.

STEPHEN AND CHARLOTTE

Sometime well before dawn, Quinn stirred, waking them both up. It took William a minute to orient himself, though once he had, he wished he hadn't. Memories of the awful events of the night before came flooding back to him. He didn't remember falling asleep here on the couch next to Quinn; he only remembered her sitting close beside him, their hands clenched tightly together, as they waited for the terrible thing to be over.

It hadn't lasted so long; probably less than twenty minutes passed before the anguished noises from the back room had quieted, but the sounds – and the things they imagined going along with them -- had left both of them breathless and sweating, hanging on to one another for dear life, praying for it to be over.

He glanced at the girl next to him now. Her gray eyes were wide open, bright points in the dim room – she was as fully awake as he was, and she looked as surprised to have woken up this way as he was.

A subtle motion from across the room caught his eye, and he looked over to see Nathaniel, watching them with interest, though his eyes were more exhausted than William had ever seen them before. He looked as if he were having trouble keeping his head from falling over onto his chest.

Fear broiled in William's stomach. "Thomas?" he choked out.

"He's okay." Nathaniel's voice was barely more than a whisper. "Ellen and Henry returned late, and they are tending him now. Lily and Graeme had to go and sleep – this is all very difficult for them, too, and it was a long night. Thomas is resting, mostly. I could do with a few hours' sleep as well. I imagine Ellen and Henry could, too."

William nodded. The words his uncle didn't say were communicated plainly enough with his eyes – he was going to be allowed this time with his brother.

"I'll go and tell Ellen and Henry now, that we should go to bed while we have the chance."

When Nathaniel had disappeared down the hallway, William turned to face Quinn. Her expression told him that she'd understood everything, which didn't surprise him.

"Do you want me to give you some time alone with him?" she asked softly.

He paused for a moment, thinking about this. A week ago, there would have been no question about how he felt in a situation like this. He'd often found himself resenting her intruding in on things, on her insistence on being places she shouldn't technically have been a part of. Now … the thought of her going into that room with him didn't bother him at all. In fact, the idea of her being there was comforting somehow. She would understand.

And besides, he knew what it would do to her to be left out here alone, when waiting even five more minutes would feel like years to her, the way it would have to him. Yes, she understood.

"It's okay," he said. "I think I'd like to have you with me. And I know Thomas would, too."

Nathaniel came to the end of the hallway again and nodded at them. "You can wake me if you need anything," he said. "But everything we have is in that room. It's not enough; we're going to have to try and get more supplies today, somehow. There's a good record of what we've given him."

"All right."

He stood and walked over to his uncle, looking into his drawn, exhausted face. "Thank you, Nathaniel."

Nathaniel nodded, and William reached out for him, wrapping his arms around his chest, suddenly remembering why he had always trusted him. If Nathaniel was keeping information from him, there had to be a reason, didn't there? Thomas hadn't trusted the information their father had held back, and look at what happened to him. He hugged Nathaniel tightly, truly grateful.

Once Nathaniel had gone back down the hall, William turned to Quinn. "Are you ready?"

She nodded, taking a deep breath as she came to stand beside him.

Inside the bedroom, Thomas lay on the narrow bed, which had been moved to the center of the room, giving those caring for him room to walk around and work. William was grateful that there had been enough in the supplies downstairs to place a single IV port in Thomas' left hand. There wasn't a drip, of course, aside from the blood, and he was sure there wasn't much in the way of strong meds, but it was better than nothing. He knew enough about making solutions from scratch to at least keep his brother hydrated – and if they were lucky, comfortable.

Quinn stayed by the door, giving him space as he approached the bed. Thomas was asleep, though his eyelids fluttered every few seconds, and his breathing was shallow. He picked up the notebook beside the bed and ran his finger down the list of medications, and then, because he couldn't resist, flipped back a page and scanned the notes from the surgery.

He swallowed hard, reading about the makeshift way they'd had to repair Thomas' broken femur. He didn't often wish that he practiced medicine on Earth. He loved his own world. And he loved using the scientific methods and technologies he had learned in his Earth studies along with the long history of traditions, and healing practices from here. But today, he wished for a fully-equipped hospital with a general anesthesiologist and some metal pins and screws.

On Earth, Thomas would probably have full use of this leg back in six months. Here… well, William wasn't going to worry about it now. They would do what they could do, and he would pray about the rest.

He motioned to Quinn, who still stood by the door, letting her know it was okay if she came over; he pulled a chair right up next to the bed for her, so she could watch Thomas while he slept. Neither one of them spoke, though Quinn watched him carefully – he could tell that she had seen the change in his expression as he'd read over the notes. William squeezed her shoulder gently, and she reached her hand up to his as they looked at Thomas' pale face.

He was so thin. Much thinner than the last time he'd seen him. Lily and Graeme both looked the same way – their skin too white, almost translucent, and bones prominent in places they shouldn't be. His stomach turned as he tried not to think about what the three of them had gone through during their captivity in Norland. He'd been raised not to hate anyone, but the thick feeling that rose in his chest now refused to be subdued.

"If I ever get my hands on the guy who did this to him …" he whispered.

Quinn squeezed his hand and nodded.

Thomas blinked, struggling to open his eyes. "Not if I get to him first," he mumbled, so quietly that until Quinn chuckled, he wasn't sure he'd hear him correctly.

"Hey buddy, how are you doing?" he asked, kneeling down next to him.

Thomas was silent for several seconds before he strained to whisper an answer. "Been better."

Ever so carefully, William took his brother's one uninjured hand in his own, not wanting to move him at all. "I'm sure. I'm so sorry ... If I had known ..."

"It's not your fault ... Ow."

"Where does it hurt?"

"Everywhere." He tried to force a half-grin, but he didn't quite make it.

Then his eyes landed on Quinn, and they widened. "Hey beautiful," he whispered. "What are you doing here?"

She paused. "What? Like I wasn't going to come back and look for you after what you did?" He could tell she was working to keep her tone light. A new kind of ache filled his chest at the way Thomas smiled at her as she leaned in closer to him, and he succeeded in the half-smile he'd been working so hard to accomplish a moment ago.

Thomas fell back asleep within minutes after William gave him another dose of morphine, a larger dose, probably, than was wise to do without a heart monitor and a pulse oximeter, but he didn't care. He wasn't going anywhere; he would stay right next to Thomas and watch him.

For a day where every minute felt like an hour, Quinn was stunned at how quickly the sun seemed to move across the sky outside the window of the room where she and William tended to Thomas, who drifted in and out of consciousness, depending on how medicated William was able to keep him.

She couldn't believe that half the day had already gone by when Ellen poked her head into the room and asked if they wanted her to bring them something for lunch. William had nodded, though neither of them felt very hungry. He also asked if Ellen could possibly make up some broth – he wanted to try to get something into Thomas, if at all possible.

When the door opened again a few minutes later, Quinn didn't even look up, until she heard a voice that she didn't expect to hear – one that she would know anywhere.

"William! Quinn!"

"Mother!" William flew across the room, straight into the arms of Queen Charlotte. "What are you doing here?"

"We came as soon as we heard what happened." King Stephen stood in the doorway, just behind his wife, his face as panic-stricken as hers as they gazed at Thomas' sleeping form on the bed. "How is he?

"I'm okay," Thomas called weakly from the bed, although he sounded anything but, and Charlotte and Stephen both nearly ran to his side, kneeling down together next to the bed.

"Come on," William whispered to Quinn, placing his hand gently between her shoulder blades as he led her out of the room.

When they reached the living room where they had slept the night before, she was surprised by the number of people in there. Marcus and Ben had returned, from wherever they'd been – she figured they must have had something to do with Charlotte and Stephen's arrival, along with another guard from the castle in Eirentheos, Jeremiah, she thought his name was. The two Philothean guards were there, and so were Ellen and Henry. Lily and Graeme sat close together in the middle of one of the couches, holding two small children.

In Grame's lap was a tiny, dark-haired girl, maybe around two cycles old. A little boy of about four was wrapped around Lily's neck, looking like he might never let her go again.

Quinn vaguely remembered hearing that Lily and Graeme had children. She wondered where they had been when their parents were taken hostage. She was surprised, for a moment that Charlotte and Stephen would risk bringing them here, but then she realized that regardless of how upset Tolliver might be, or what happened later, nobody was going to be foolish enough to tamper with the king and queen of Eirentheos while they were here.

She shuddered, though, when she contemplated what this turn of events was going to do to the already-strained relations between the two kingdoms, and she was suddenly very anxious to get out of Philotheum.

Everyone in the room was wrapped up in their own conversations. She glanced over at William and noticed that he looked as tired and speechless as she felt. They continued past the busy living room and into the kitchen. On the counter, two large bowls sat on a wooden tray, forgotten, most likely, in the activity that had just ensued. William carried the tray over to the table, and he and Quinn both sat down, although actually eating seemed too complicated a task just then.

Both of their bowls were still mostly full when King Stephen came into the kitchen and sat down at the table with them. He looked tired, too, and the skin underneath his eyes was puffy and red. He immediately put one arm around William and pulled him tight to his chest, kissing his son on the temple before he released him.

"Are you all right?" he asked.

William nodded. "How did you know where we were?"

"Aidel brought us a few messages from Nathaniel. As soon as we heard that Thomas had been captured by Tolliver, we left the castle. We've been staying just outside the border, trying to keep updated on the situation, and figure out the safest way to approach.

"Tolliver's soldiers wouldn't bother your mother and me of course, if we revealed who we were, but we were worried about compromising the safety of the Friends of Philip."

"So you knew about all of this?"

Stephen nodded. "Of course I did, son. But most of this is not information we want falling into the wrong hands, even accidentally."

"And you didn't think you should tell us, even knowing we were coming here?"

The king looked down at his hands, folded in front of him on the table, then looked up, making eye contact with each of them before he spoke. "That was a mistake. I realize that now. But we were still foolishly hopeful that nothing was really wrong – that Thomas had merely been waylaid for longer than he expected." His voice was heavy, tinged with sadness and apology.

"How did Lily and Graeme's children get here?" Quinn asked, deftly changing the subject.

"Marcus was able to make some contacts and found out that Lily and Graeme's children had been staying with Graeme's older sister, since about a week before Lily and Graeme were taken. They had been worried about something like that happening.

Marcus and Ben went to get them yesterday – your mother was insistent on bringing them, of course, knowing what it would be doing to them to be separated. We didn't know he'd been rescued and brought here by James and Dorian yesterday – we would have come last night."

William sighed, the shadows under his eyes growing perceptibly darker.

Stephen paled, and grabbed William's hand. "I'm so sorry son – I can't imagine what that must have been like for you."

William just nodded, squeezing his father's hand in return.

288

Then the king turned his kind, gray eyes over to her. "And how are you doing, Quinn? I'm sure this has been a very difficult few days."

"It has. I've definitely been better. But I'm okay now that we've found Thomas."

26 ASTOUNDING

There was a soft knock on the door of her bedroom before it opened just enough for Queen Charlotte's voice to reach her. "Quinn, can I come in?"

She set the book she'd been reading down next to her on the couch. "Of course."

"How are you doing?" Charlotte asked, sitting down in one of the soft armchairs across from the couch.

Quinn shrugged. "I'm okay. How is Thomas this morning?" She'd gone to his room a little while ago, but stopped outside the door when she heard him in there chatting with William and Charlotte.

Charlotte smiled. "You know Thomas, always making the best of everything, although I think he's getting a little frustrated with being stuck in bed."

Quinn nodded. Although Nathaniel and William both said he was recovering better than anyone could expect, the surgery that they had been able to do in Philotheum was just not enough to restore any kind of strength to Thomas' leg. His arm was healing nicely, but he still couldn't move around on his own, at all. He had been just barely stable enough to be brought back to the castle in Eirentheos in a wagon eight days ago.

"Nathaniel has finally made the decision that we must send Thomas to your world for a different surgery," Charlotte said.

"And you and Stephen have agreed?" Quinn asked. William and Nathaniel had been talking about the possibility for a couple of days, trying to sort out how that would work.

"Yes. It will be difficult to be away from him again, to know that he would be alone much of the time … but it is what he needs. Nathaniel will make all of the arrangements after he goes back through the gate tomorrow with you, and then we will meet him the next time the gate opens with Thomas."

"It's hard to believe I'll actually be going back tomorrow. I'm starting to get a little worried about what will be going on in Bristlecone when I get back there."

Charlotte nodded. "I can't imagine what the last two days have been like for your mother."

"I'm sure she's in a panic."

"Go easy on her when you get there, Quinn – you don't know what it's like to worry about one of your children." There was a look in the queen's eyes that made Quinn feel like there was an extra meaning in her request.

"I will. I'm just hoping I don't walk through the gate tomorrow and find police officers searching the river."

Charlotte reached across and squeezed Quinn's hand. "I'm sure everything will work out in the end."

"I hope so." Seeing the concerned, motherly look on Charlotte's face only heightened her anxiety. She had been so preoccupied with the rescue for the first part of her journey, and then assisting with Thomas and his recovery after his surgery, that she hadn't thought much about actually going back home. Yesterday evening, though, it had hit her that it was actually going to be happening.

"Are you still having bad dreams at night?" Charlotte asked.

Quinn nodded. "It hasn't gotten any better." During the nights she had been sleeping at Ellen's house, right at the time of Thomas' surgery, she hadn't dreamed at all. She'd hoped, foolishly, she supposed, that knowing that Thomas was safe would stop the crazy dreams permanently.

Looking back, she realized that probably the only reason she hadn't dreamed on those nights was that she'd barely slept. She and William would crash out together on the couches, exhausted, for a few hours each night before getting up to do it all over again.

The dreams had returned with a vengeance the night they were traveling, as she slept in the tent, Queen Charlotte in a sleeping bag next to her, so she wouldn't be alone. Her yelling had woken up everyone.

"And you still haven't remembered anything about them?"

"No ... I mean, sometimes I wake up, and it's like I can still *feel* the dream. I'm still scared, or worried, or it feels like there's something I have to *do* when I wake up, but I don't know what."

It seemed like, if she could at least *remember* what happened in them, it would solve something. It was like missing the last piece to a thousand-piece puzzle, or the topic sentence to a five-page essay.

Charlotte just listened to Quinn speak, sympathy in her eyes.

"Does any of that make any sense? Have you ever had a dream that you couldn't quite remember, but you knew it was important? It just seems so weird."

The queen shook her head. "*I* haven't, but I don't think it's strange. In our world, it is quite common for some people to have dreams that give them insight to something they don't understand, or that help lead them a certain way. He doesn't tell me anything now, but when Simon was younger, he used to have vivid dreams whenever he had to make a choice about something – sometimes even something as simple as which subject he was going to study next."

"Really? Simon?" Quinn's eyes were wide.

"Yes. And, he never said anything, but right before he met Evelyn, he had just begun to court another young lady. The feelings he had immediately for Evelyn were obvious to everyone, but he didn't pursue her at first – the other girl was quite lovely and sweet, and he did care for her. He didn't want to hurt her, and I don't think he knew what the right thing to do was.

But one morning, he woke up, and his decision was just … *made*. He rode off to the other girl's home straight after breakfast, and that evening, brought Evelyn to dinner at the castle. A short time later, they announced their betrothal."

"So you think that my dreams mean something?"

"I don't know, but I do believe that sometimes dreams do have meanings or that they carry some kind of message."

"How am I supposed to understand a message from a dream I can't remember?"

Charlotte chuckled. "I don't know, dear one. Maybe you can't remember because you're not quite ready for it. Perhaps there is something else you need to understand, or another choice you need to make first." They both turned as the bedroom door creaked open again.

"Thomas is asking for you, Quinn," Linnea said, as she came into the room, bouncing baby Hannah gently on her hip. "And this one is asking for you, Mother."

Charlotte smiled, and looked at Quinn. "Go to him." She stood and placed her hand on Quinn's shoulder, squeezing it gently, before she went to take the infant from Linnea.

"Hey, beautiful," Thomas said as Quinn entered his bedroom. He was alone, which was unusual, sitting up in his large, four-poster bed, and leaning against a stack of pillows.

"Hi," she answered.

He grinned widely. "Did you hear the news? I get to visit you in your world again soon."

She smiled. "I did hear. I just wish that it was for a different reason."

He shrugged. "I'll be all right. Will says that hospital rooms in your world have televisions."

"I think they do." She laughed. Even after everything he had been through, Thomas was still himself, and she loved him for it.

"So, I haven't really gotten a chance to talk to you – to tell you how sorry I am." The sudden change in Thomas' voice startled her.

"What? For getting yourself captured and almost killed? As long as you don't ever pull something like that again …"

"Well, I am sorry about that … but what I'm really sorry for is putting you in the position I did, kissing you like that right before you went through the gate."

Her cheeks turned bright pink, though she tried to shrug it off. In all the days she had been spending with Thomas and William, keeping him company as he'd recovered, this was a subject that had never come up – or, more to the point, they'd avoided. "Yeah, what were you thinking with that, anyway?"

Thomas grew quiet, and stared at her with an intense look. A bubbling feeling started to rise in the pit of her stomach – she wasn't sure she was ready for whatever he was going to say.

"Quinn, you know I love you. The moment I met you, I knew that you were someone I want to know forever."

She swallowed hard, afraid of where he was taking this.

"But it was horribly unfair of me to do something like I did, to confuse you like that, and mess with your heart. I never meant to put you in a position like that."

The bubbling feeling in her stomach started to feel a lot more like nausea. She looked down at the floor.

"It's not that I didn't mean it, Quinn. Because, I did. In another time, in different circumstances …"

She looked up at him, stunned.

It took her a minute to process what Thomas was saying, but as soon as she did, she knew he was right. She blinked, not knowing what to say.

"If you're mad, I understand."

She shook her head. "I'm not mad." She forced herself to look him in the eyes, to let him see the truth.

He smiled, kindness and warmth in his expression, before his eyes became serious. "You have big choices to make, Quinn."

"Wh…" she started, but he put his finger up, silencing her.

"I know you think you don't have a lot of choices -- that all of this is just some accident you stumbled into, and that soon you're going to leave and go back to your 'real life.' You and William are the same in your feelings about that – believing that the most difficult choice is the wrong one to make. But it's not true. It's always easier to leave a weed alone in the garden than fight to remove it, but if you leave it there, soon it starts to make all of the rest of the decisions about the garden for you."

"But, I …"

"Shh, sweetheart. Don't answer. Just know that whatever you decide, I'm here for you always. And … despite the fact that you often see evidence to the contrary … I'm not the only one."

She only partially understood what he meant, but she nodded.

"Are you ready, Quinn?"

"No. But I don't think that really matters, does it?"

William chuckled. "No, not really."

"Do you want one of us to go through first?" Nathaniel asked.

"Are you going to go and find my mom and give her some perfectly logical explanation about where I've been for the past two days, and then come back and get me?"

Nathaniel burst out laughing. "No, I think you're going to have to handle this one on your own."

She nodded, taking a deep breath as she put her foot on the bottom step of the stone bridge. "I was afraid of that."

"I'll walk you home, if that will help," William said.

"Really? You're going to involve yourself in this?"

"I probably can't avoid it completely," he said. "Mrs. Williams did see us leaving the library together."

"Right." She hadn't even thought of that. "I wonder if I'm even still going to have a job."

"We've discussed this, Quinn," Nathaniel said. "We're just going to have to assess the situation when you get there. All of this worrying about it isn't going to do you any good. It might be pretty rough when you first get back, but you'll be okay. You're going to make it worse, though, if you don't get going." He pointed up to the darkening sky.

"Okay." She climbed the rest of the steps, and then closed her eyes and took the next step forward.

In an instant, the warm, humid air was replaced by a frigid breeze. The sound of a truck zooming by on the highway above her was disorienting. She paused, steadying herself, and took a deep breath before she opened her eyes.

Well, she thought, *there are no flashing lights or police officers, anyway.* She glanced around at the riverbank, deserted except for some birds squabbling over something at the edge of the water.

Suddenly, she caught a motion out of the corner of her eye, a splash of red that shouldn't have been there. Her heart almost stopped. "Mom?"

Her mother stood up from the boulder she'd been sitting on, nearly motionless as she stared at the broken bridge.

There was a new movement behind her, the air stirred as Nathaniel appeared on the steps behind her.

"Hello, Nathaniel," her mother said, with an astounding lack of surprise in her voice.

"Megan." Nathaniel nodded.

Quinn's mother turned to her, ice in her eyes, her expression harder than Quinn had ever imagined it could be. "Go get in the car, Quinn. Now."

**The story continues in Thorns of Decision,
Available now in paperback, Kindle, and Nook editions.**

ACKNOWLEDGEMENTS

The creation of the Dusk Gate Chronicles has been an incredibly exciting journey, and there are so many people without whom it would not be possible.

If you are reading this book, and you've enjoyed it, count yourself on this list.

In my wildest dreams, I never imagined how wonderful it would be to share a story like this, and to have people respond, and come along on the journey into Eirentheos with me.

The following people have been an enormous source of inspiration and love to me during this time, and I appreciate and love you all.

(And believe me, this in no particular order!)

Michelle Patrick

Tonya Christensen

Alisha Andersen

Maureen Schilling

Jill Fout

Noel Elhardt

Kacie Worth

Peggy Bradow

Kristy K. James

Tonya Cannariato

Jen Kush

Krysta Hunt

Sara Henry

Nic Benner

Jeannie Bugg

and

Callie Bradow

(the author of the first-ever school book report on Seeds of Discovery)

ABOUT THE AUTHOR

To learn more about Breeana Puttroff,
please visit http://www.breeanaputtroff.wordpress.com

FIND ME ON FACEBOOK.
You'll find exclusive content, and sneak previews just for
my Facebook fans!
http://www.facebook.com/duskgate

Follow me on Twitter! @bputtroff

Or, find me on Goodreads, where I host special contests,
giveaways, and discussions.

CPSIA information can be obtained at www.ICGtesting.com
Printed in the USA
LVOW06s1918161213

365566LV00002B/519/P